The Fitzgerald
Ruse

Books by Mark de Castrique

The Buryin' Barry Series
Dangerous Undertaking
Grave Undertaking
Foolish Undertaking
Final Undertaking

The Sam Blackman Series
Blackman's Coffin
The Fitzgerald Ruse

The Fitzgerald Ruse

Mark de Castrique

Poisoned Pen Press

Copyright © 2009 by Mark de Castrique

First Edition 2009

10 9 8 7 6 5 4 3 2 1

Library of Congress Catalog Card Number: 2008937751

ISBN: 978-1-59058-629-7 Hardcover

Poisoned Pen Press
6962 E. First Ave., Ste. 103
Scottsdale, AZ 85251
www.poisonedpenpress.com
info@poisonedpenpress.com

Printed in the United States of America

For Linda

Chapter One

The night sky around Asheville can play tricks on the eye. Points of light might be stars, or they might be the sparkling illuminated windows of hundreds of houses dotting the ridge tops around the city.

Making the distinction between the two isn't so difficult, except for those evenings when valley mist hovers like a sheer veil between earth and heaven. Or when an extra glass of wine creates a misty veil in the brain, blurring not only the horizon but also objects closer at hand.

I focused on the sidewalk in front of me, taking each step with painstaking determination. Thunder sounded in the distance, signaling that the clear night sky would soon be changing. As the mountaineers say, "If you don't like the weather, wait fifteen minutes."

Few people shared my walk, an activity I'd undertaken to clear my head. That had been a mistake. Walking on an artificial leg was difficult enough without carrying the effects of three-quarters of a bottle of pinot noir.

My slight inebriation wasn't my fault. My business partner and girlfriend, Nakayla Robertson, hadn't held up her end of the festivities. We'd agreed to split everything fifty-fifty, but she claimed her single glass from the bottle had been enough. I, however, am not one to leave a task undone, polishing off both of our dinners and the wine.

And so I found myself struggling along Patton Avenue, headed toward our office on Pack Square with two goals in mind: first, not to stumble and look like a drunken derelict; and second, to pick up the lockbox in our office that we were holding for a client. Not just any client. Our first and only client and the reason for tonight's celebration.

I'm Sam Blackman, former Chief Warrant Officer, U.S. Army, and present and forever amputee. I'd lost a leg in Iraq, but found a life in the western North Carolina mountains. Now I'd planted both feet, although one was artificial, in my adopted community, and as a taxpaying business owner, I was on the way to becoming a model citizen.

"Good evening, Sam. How are you doing tonight?"

I looked diagonally across the intersection of Patton and Biltmore Avenue where a uniformed officer emerged from the shadows.

He gave a slight wave, and though I didn't recognize him, I wasn't surprised that he knew my name. I was a familiar face around the Asheville Police Department—as a colleague, not as an inmate. I straightened and concentrated on maintaining flawless balance as I crossed to the corner opposite him.

"Can't complain. Wouldn't do any good if I did."

He laughed. "I hear you. Well, take it easy." He turned away, heading down the block to the department.

Take it easy. Lugging the lockbox from the office to the parking deck would be anything but easy. I regretted telling Nakayla not to come with me. She'd parked her car near Tupelo Honey Café where we'd eaten, and when I'd declined a ride, she should have headed home. But Nakayla knew me too well, and there was a good chance she'd be waiting at the office. I'd be grateful to see her, even if it meant hearing her say "I told you so."

I slid my shiny new key into the dead bolt of the building's main entrance and was surprised to find it unlocked. Nakayla probably had come back to help me.

The security guard locked up every weeknight at seven and began rounds, which meant the tenants had to meet clients at the door for after-hours appointments. I expected that would happen frequently to Nakayla and me. Private investigators don't work bankers' hours, and clients often prefer to come under the cover of darkness.

I left the door as I'd found it, figuring we'd lock up on our way out. The hardwood floor creaked as I stepped along the hall to the elevator. The old structure had character, something you don't find in the cubicle and drop-ceiling world of office parks and glass skyscrapers.

I pushed the up button and the elevator opened. Nakayla was teasing me. She'd sent it back down, and I was surprised she wasn't inside poised to punch three.

Nearing our office, I saw the frosted glass of our door's window. No light shown through it. A dark crack marked the gap where the door stood ajar. I gently pushed it open in case Nakayla crouched behind, ready to leap out and scare me.

"Honey, I'm home!" I shouted.

Silence.

"Nakayla?" I stepped into the darkness. My prosthetic left foot caught on something soft and I tumbled forward. Flinging my arms out to break my fall, I collided with an end table and twisted onto my back. My head cracked against the floor, but instead of dazing me, the jolt drove the wine-induced haze out of my brain. I scrambled around, fear numbing my pain, and reached out for the obstacle that had tripped me.

My fingers grabbed locks of hair. In the dim glow, I could barely make out the body of a woman.

Chapter Two

A little more than twenty-four hours earlier, I'd been sipping champagne and christening the new business.

"To Blackman and Robertson." Nathan Armitage had raised his glass and smiled. "Or is it Robertson and Blackman?"

I shook my head. "Don't go there. I told her ladies first but she wouldn't listen." I tilted my glass of bubbly to Nakayla Robertson sitting on the sofa. She'd slipped off her shoes and tucked her slender feet against the brown leather cushion. A tag with the red word SALE dangled from the armrest under her elbow.

"Here's to a prosperous partnership of investigations," I said. "And to not being investigated ourselves."

"I'll drink to that." Nakayla took a sip and then tipped her glass toward Nathan. "So, have you got any hot referrals for us?"

The older man sat in one of two matching armchairs with his back to the wide window. He was in his mid-forties, about twelve or thirteen years older than me. Silver had begun to creep up the temples of his jet-black hair.

Behind him, Pack Square lay three stories below. Our new offices looked out over the core of Asheville's past and the hub of its present. The stone monolith commemorating Civil War governor Zebulon Vance dominated the historic square and the wall of Blue Ridge Mountains provided the city's backdrop beneath the pink clouds of an early September evening. Although the rent was more than our potential income could justify, the location in the renovated Adler Court Offices offered proximity to the Asheville Police Department and Buncombe County Courthouse, two necessities for any respectable private eye.

"Sorry," Nathan said with exaggerated smugness. "Armitage Security Services only works with licensed investigators."

"You think we invited you up here for champagne because Sam and I bought some furniture?" Nakayla turned to me. "No wonder the man's company doesn't do detective work."

"You got them?" Nathan's voice rose with excitement.

"Special delivery from Raleigh this morning." I held up two manila envelopes. "Both of us. They gave Nakayla full credit for her three years of insurance fraud investigative work."

"Terrific," Nathan said. "Chief Buchanan must have helped fast-track you through."

The Asheville Police Chief had written a strong recommendation to the Private Protective Services Board of North Carolina. Nathan, Nakayla, and I had solved the murder of one of Buchanan's detectives, and he and his entire force had been profuse in expressing their gratitude. Nathan Armitage had taken a pistol shot to the chest in the final confrontation and had been released from the hospital less than a month ago. This visit to our new office was one of his first ventures out on his own.

"And a little bird told me you dropped a letter to the governor," I said.

"About time I got something for my campaign contributions. What about counter-intelligence?"

"That license too. For me."

"Everybody knows I'll be the intelligence behind our business," Nakayla said, "so Sam would have to be counter-intelligence."

We took a collective sip of champagne.

Counter-intelligence meant I could sweep for bugs and other surveillance devices. Within the confines of the law, I could now also utilize them. As a former Chief Warrant Officer in the Criminal Investigation Detachment of the U.S. military, I satisfied the Board's requirement for three years of experience in investigative work three times over, but the three years of counterintelligence needed for that license wasn't as clearly documented. Evidently support from the Asheville law enforcement community had trumped any objections.

Nathan set his half-empty glass on the new oak coffee table. "That's enough alcohol. Doc Warner still has me on a restrictive diet." He looked around the room. "So, how are you going to set things up? Will you have a receptionist?"

"No," Nakayla said. "We've hired an answering service. Phones are installed tomorrow. We don't want anyone in the business but us."

Nathan nodded. He understood. This wasn't meant to be a moneymaking operation. Last month I'd received nearly three million dollars for my parents' wrongful death settlement, and I could live comfortably on the interest. The case that put Nathan in the hospital had also left Nakayla with a considerable fortune, one that hadn't been reported to the authorities but was rightfully hers. Part of my fortune would be used to launder hers. Offshore accounts and trades in untraceable gold and gems would be the means for converting her assets into legitimate holdings. The Blackman and Robertson Detective Agency provided an explanation for how a disabled Iraqi vet and an African-American woman of modest means managed to support themselves.

I stretched out my prosthetic leg to ease the tingle in my stump. Sitting too long in one position often caused the sensation. "We'll use this central room as a combination reception and conference area. Nakayla will have the office on the right and I'll be on the left."

Nathan looked at the dark wood paneling, the overstuffed chairs and sofa, heavy end tables, and the Oriental rug centered on the hardwood floor. "Looks more like a sleepy British gentlemen's club than the image of a high-tech, hard-driving investigative team."

"Yes," Nakayla said. "Because we have no intention of being what we seem. To be underestimated is to hold the advantage."

Nathan reached for his glass. "To hell with Doc Warner. That philosophy deserves a drink." He took a deep swallow and then grinned. "You might make this detective agency a success in spite of yourselves."

A knock sounded from the door behind me. "Come in," I said.

A uniformed security guard entered. She appeared to be a few years younger than me—late twenties, closer to Nakayla's age. Her curly black hair was clipped short in military fashion and her sharp features exaggerated the scowl on her face. "Are you authorized to be here?" she snapped.

Her eyes moved from me to Nakayla to Nathan. Then they widened as her mouth dropped open. "Mr. Armitage," she sputtered.

I noticed the patch on her chest pocket, a Roman warrior holding a shield over a woman and child and the banner above them reading Armitage. The logo of Nathan's company. He'd once told me he'd been tempted to use the acronym of Armitage Security Services instead, but his wife had objected.

"That's all right," Nathan told the young guard. "Forgive me. You are?"

"Amanda Whitfield, sir. My duty sheet said the tenants weren't moving in until later this week. And since it's after hours –"

"You did the right thing," Nathan assured her.

I twisted in the chair and gripped the back to help me to my feet. "I'm Sam Blackman. This is my partner, Nakayla Robertson." I offered my hand and she shook it.

"A pleasure to meet you. I've read all about you." She looked to Nakayla. "Both of you."

"Reporters like to exaggerate," I said.

Nathan cleared his throat. "Except for the part about them saving my life. Keep a good watch over their office, Amanda."

She straightened at the order. "I will, sir."

"What time are you off?" I asked.

"Midnight, sir."

I smiled. "Too bad. I was going to offer you some champagne, Amanda, but we'd better make it another time. And I'd appreciate if you wouldn't report Nathan's imbibing to his doctor."

She blushed, not sure if I was joking.

"Please tell your relief we've moved in," I said. "We got our furniture on sale but had to remove it from the showroom today. The building manager agreed to let us in a couple of days early."

"Certainly." Amanda glanced at Nathan. "I'll enter it in the logbook so all the shifts will know."

Her boss nodded his approval.

"Thank you," I said. "A pleasure to meet you."

She backed out into the hall, beaming at all of us, and closed the door.

"Glad to see you've got more women in uniform," Nakayla said.

Nathan shrugged. "You don't have to convince me. Women develop a better rapport with the clients. Good for business."

He drummed his fingers against the side of his glass. "But I wish I'd known her name."

"You've got more than two hundred employees," I said.

"No excuse. Good business also means good rapport with your workers. As soon as she said Amanda, I remembered her story. I waived a policy when we hired her."

"What policy?" Nakayla asked.

"When someone comes onboard full time, they have to be available to work any shift—some are eight hours, some ten, some twelve. Amanda couldn't work during the day."

I eased back into my chair. "Why not?"

"She has a quadriplegic husband. Her mother stays with him in the evening or overnight. The mother has a job during the day, and it would cost Amanda more for in-home medical care than what we can pay her. They've had a tough time."

"How'd it happen?" Nakayla asked.

"On their honeymoon of all things. He slipped on the diving board at the resort and cracked his neck on the edge. Hawaii I think." Nathan sighed. "A young couple flies away to paradise with their whole future ahead of them and then they come back with that future and their dreams shattered."

Suddenly the champagne didn't taste so good. I looked down at my left leg. Beneath the fabric of my pants, a cold mechanical device replaced the living bone and flesh blown away in Iraq. But I could walk. And I could use my arms. I had nothing to complain about.

"You were good to hire her," I said.

"What else could I do? Her husband, Matt, had worked for me for five years. I'd seen her photograph but never met her until today, because I agreed to the waiver while I was in the hospital."

"So she's new," I said.

"Yes. And since we only provide security here from 4:00 PM to 8:00 AM, she can keep this as a consistent assignment. About the most excitement she'll see is helping someone who's locked out of his office."

"That would be Sam," Nakayla said.

"I don't doubt it." Nathan set his glass down again, empty this time. "I need to get home before Helen calls out the state troopers." He stood and Nakayla and I rose. "And I suppose you have things to do."

Nakayla slipped into her shoes. "Right. I need to put the file in order. The empty one we're reserving for our first case."

"Don't worry," Nathan said. "Asheville has more than its share of secrets." He winked. "And maybe I will have a referral or two." He kissed Nakayla on the cheek and patted me on the shoulder. "Take care of each other."

As the echo of his footsteps faded down the hall, I looked around the office. We'd had the deliverymen set the furniture in the appropriate rooms, but nothing had been properly placed. Nakayla and I could start positioning desks and chairs, or—

She caught me eyeing the Coleman cooler and the magnum of champagne half buried in crushed ice. "You know what I think?"

"I'd be crazy to guess."

"And that's what I'm thinking. We must be crazy." She took my hand and led me to the window.

In the deepening dusk, Pack Square had quieted to a few tourists gathered around the base of the Vance Memorial where a duo playing banjo and fiddle tried to eke out an extra dollar in their open instrument cases. I couldn't determine whether the longhaired street musicians were male or female, but the faint strains of "Cripple Creek" told even my untrained ear that they were a long way from the masters of mountain music like Doc Watson or the Kruger Brothers.

"Blackman and Robertson," Nakayla whispered. "Is Asheville ready for us?"

"Blackman and Robertson. Has a nice ring to it."

"So does Laurel and Hardy."

I reached across her waist, took her other hand, and turned her to me. "Having second thoughts?"

Her dark brown eyes searched my face. "Are you?"

"No. I know we're crazy."

She kissed me on the lips, confirming our shared diagnosis. "Then maybe we'd better get back to the asylum."

I gestured toward the cooler. "But we have the champagne."

"Bring it. If I drink another glass here, Amanda Whitfield's next round on patrol will really give her something to enter into her logbook."

◇◇◇

The asylum was what we called my apartment building. It had opened in 1891 as a grand hotel, the Kenilworth Inn, during the time when George W. Vanderbilt was creating his mammoth Biltmore Estate and the adjoining Biltmore Village. Destroyed by fire in the early 1900s, the resort had been rebuilt and later converted into an army hospital for veterans of the First World War. Various incarnations included a sanitarium and a mental institution. Hence, the asylum.

Several years ago, a conscientious developer had saved the Kenilworth from demolition. The grounds and architecture still carried the impressive grandeur of Asheville's gilded age, and pulling up to the stone porte-cochère at the end of the expansive lawn made me feel like I was arriving at my mansion rather than my relatively inexpensive one-bedroom apartment.

The pleasant evening had lured residents out on the front lawn. Some walked dogs, and a younger group of middle-schoolers tossed a Frisbee. Everyone enjoyed the cool temperature and invigorating mountain air. Overhead, the clouds had cleared and stars began popping out as the sky turned from purple to black. I was tempted to suggest we sit in the Adirondack chairs clustered on the grass and swap the bottle of champagne back and forth like two alley winos who'd won the lottery.

But, as we walked from our cars, the tinge of pain in my stump told me I needed to remove my prosthesis. The day had been long, and the night promised to be much more intriguing than the ordeal of shopping for office furniture. I wanted to be comfortable, and Nakayla was one of the few people with whom I could be my whole self regardless of whether I had one leg or two.

Nakayla Robertson and I had been brought together by the murder of her sister, Tikima. In the course of solving that crime, we'd barely escaped with our lives. Now I couldn't imagine life without her—either as my new business partner or my bedmate. She wanted to proceed more cautiously, keeping her own house in West Asheville and limiting our lovemaking to the occasional overnight.

I tried not to think that her hesitancy to begin a more intimate living arrangement was because she had doubts about an interracial relationship or because she feared involvement with a wounded vet still coming to grips with his mutilated body. Nakayla sensed my insecurity, and more than once she'd assured me she simply needed some time to adjust to the recent upheavals in her world: the loss of her sister, the discovery of a family fortune, and the limitless possibilities of her future. She wanted to choose from those possibilities unclouded by grief or romantic passion.

For me, pleasure trumped pain no matter how emotionally vulnerable I might be. Clouding my grief with romantic passion seemed the perfect antidote to all I'd been through the previous six months.

Nakayla took the champagne as I unlocked the door to my apartment. We stood in a long, narrow hallway where the aura of institutional sterility clung to the walls and doors. Sometimes I awoke during the night and heard the creaks of the old structure sound in rhythmic waves as if white-clad nurses still scurried from room to room, ministering to those whose minds were as connected to reality as the ghostly footsteps of their long-departed angels of mercy.

Nakayla kissed me gently behind the ear and whispered, "I'll get the glasses while you slip out of something uncomfortable."

I went to the bedroom where I could remove my artificial leg along with the sleeve and sock that served to attach the device and create a snug fit. Plus champagne in bed seemed the perfect way to pick up where Nakayla and I had left off at the office.

I folded my pants over the chair at my small desk and noticed the red light flashing on the answering machine. The caller ID displayed an unfamiliar number with a 973 area code. I had no idea who was calling me or from where. I punched the play button and sat on the bed.

As I reached to release my prosthesis, the voice stopped me cold. The last time I'd heard it had been the last morning my left leg had been my own.

"Hey, bro. The Blackwater swill wants to drown me. They know where you are and they'll take more than your leg next time. Don't call. I'm going to earth." A beep signaled the end of the message.

Although I sat on a mountainside in Asheville, North Carolina, the horror of Iraq suddenly reached through the phone and grabbed me. The beep hadn't ended a message. It began a nightmare.

Chapter Three

"Are you all right?" Nakayla stood in the bedroom doorway, a glass of champagne in each hand.

"I'm okay." I hit the release on my leg and set the prosthesis on the floor.

"Well, you look pale as skim milk." She cocked her head and eyed me with concern. "Who was that on the phone?"

I wanted to say nobody, but she knew better. "Just a guy I served with."

She sat beside me, and I took one of the glasses.

She glanced at her watch. "You need to call him back?"

"No." I sipped the champagne and tried to regain my composure.

"Bad news?"

Nakayla probably thought I'd received word that one of our buddies had been killed. My first reaction was to lie, tell her the call was nothing more than a friend checking in. However, I was the one wanting a closer relationship, and shutting Nakayla out would be a step backwards. She read me too well. She wouldn't press me, but I'd be building a wall rather than a pathway between us.

I set my glass on the nightstand and took off my shirt. "Play it and then we'll talk."

I removed my sock and sleeve while Nakayla listened to the message. Wearing only my underwear, I leaned against the headboard and massaged the tender end of my damaged leg. The surgeons had managed to save several inches below the knee, which meant greater mobility with a more natural gait. But my body weight was still being borne by flesh never intended for such a load.

"Is he talking in code?" Nakayla asked.

"No, but it only makes sense if you know the context."

Nakayla began to undress. "Who is he?"

She had the body of a dancer, lean, lithe, and muscular with hardly a blemish on her light cocoa skin. My throat went dry and speaking became difficult. Had Nakayla been after government secrets, I would have given her the roster of the CIA.

"Calvin Stuart," I said. "He's a warrant officer in my unit."

"He's still in, then?"

"Yes, but he must be back from his tour. The phone number has a U.S. area code. I don't know where."

"He sounds black," she said.

"Yes. From up North. New Jersey I think."

Her last stitch of clothing dropped to the floor and she slid in the bed beside me. As she ran her fingers up and down my arm, she asked, "What's Blackwater swill?"

"Gee, you say the most romantic things."

"Talk is cheap, big spender."

"And you're a woman of action."

"We'll see. Maybe not."

"That's extortion." I wrapped my arm around her and she nestled into my side.

"So call the cops," she whispered.

"I'm a private investigator, lady. I even have a license."

"You show me yours and I'll show you mine."

I stared her in the eye. "I've seen all I need to. You've convinced me."

"Good." She laid her head against my shoulder, her soft hair brushing my cheek. "I'm listening."

"Blackwater swill. That's the name we coined for the suspects in a case I was working."

"Blackwater? The same company whose men were killed in Iraq?"

"Yes. But I'm not sure that Blackwater was involved in my case. They provided private security, both on corporate and government contracts. Some were heavily armed bodyguards with better weapons and vehicles than our troops. We'd gotten a tip that some of their former employees were conducting their own interrogations. They'd pick up suspected insurgents, but instead of immediately turning them over to the military, they'd have a go at them first."

"Why?"

"To get information."

"And you said you didn't think Blackwater was involved."

"The more I investigated, the more I believed we were dealing with rogue operatives. Ex-Blackwater employees who now worked their own deals. That's why we called them Blackwater swill—garbage flushed out of the company. Informants told us they were Blackwater, maybe out of resentment, maybe because to an Iraqi the private security forces were all the same. Our leads came from civilians who'd been interrogated and released. Civilians who claimed to have been tortured."

Nakayla raised her head. "Was our government paying contractors to do that?"

"No. That's why we got the case. After Abu Ghraib, we didn't want another incident of abuse fanning the flames of insurrection." I paused and remembered the concern on the face of the military prosecutor at our initial briefing. He'd wanted the problem quietly but thoroughly exterminated.

"But this was happening outside government forces?"

"Didn't matter. Everything reflected back on us. And there was some testimony that military personnel collaborated in the illegal interrogations."

"What were they trying to learn?"

"Anything they could about treasure. The location of any cache that contained valuables worth smuggling out of the country."

"And they'd found some?"

I shifted my weight, moving up in the bed so that Nakayla's head rested against my bare chest. "Oh, yes. Remember in the early days immediately after Saddam had been deposed how the widespread looting went unchecked across the country? Banks, museums, palaces, hospitals, and any other buildings that held anything of value were ransacked. The consequences of Mr. Rumsfeld's horrific blunder in not sending in enough troops to restore order amid the chaos of his so-called victory. Mission Accomplished—the biggest lie ever foisted upon the American public." I looked down at where my left leg ended in a calloused stump and the bitterness of that loss swept over me.

Nakayla must have felt me tense. She rubbed her palm across the flat of my stomach and sighed. "How much is still out there?"

"God only knows. Plenty. Gold, drugs, artwork, jewels, you name it. Enough to drive the treasure seekers to use whatever means necessary if they thought they could get a lead on a hiding place."

"And when your friend Calvin said Blackwater swill wants to drown him, he meant they're trying to kill him?"

"Yes, but Calvin has a flair for the dramatic."

Nakayla sat up. "But why would they be coming after you? Revenge?"

I shook my head. "I don't know. I was injured before we gathered enough evidence to make major arrests. Calvin must have continued on the case, and he's just being super-cautious by warning me. For him, it's only been six months since we worked together. For me, it seems a lifetime ago."

"Why wouldn't he want you to call him?"

"I suspect he called from a cell phone. He's probably cut it off so his location can't be traced. Going to earth means he's in hiding."

Nakayla frowned. "Blackwater's headquartered in North Carolina, isn't it?"

I'd forgotten that, and the knot in my stomach drew tighter. "Yes. But don't worry. I have absolutely nothing they want."

Nakayla snuggled into me. "But you have something I want."

Later, in the darkness, as Nakayla's rhythmic breathing signaled she was sleeping, I kept replaying one sentence from Calvin's message over and over in my mind: "They know where you are and they'll take more than your leg next time."

Nakayla left for home at seven-thirty the next morning so she could shower and change clothes. We planned to meet at the new office at ten to arrange furniture before the phone company installed our lines and Internet service. We'd missed the deadline to list our agency in the Yellow Pages, but Nathan Armitage had hooked us up with his company's web designer. We'd have our own domain with links to and from Nathan's company. We'd also purchased two laptops with satellite wireless support and a heavily encrypted, password-secured FTP site for storing the photos, documents, and videos we might generate during the course of an investigation. We had everything we needed except a client.

Before leaving the apartment, I used a reverse search on the Internet to check the ID number left by Calvin's call. No name was listed, but the area code encompassed a number of cities in New Jersey. If Calvin was on leave, he must have gone to familiar territory where he had contacts he could trust. I had no idea what steps he was taking to eliminate the threat.

As a chief warrant officer, I'd taken the lead in pursuing the evidence in what we'd tagged as the Ali Baba case. The name came from the ancient Arabian folktale "Ali Baba and the Forty Thieves," because the threads of the investigation entwined into a pattern that indicated the existence of an organization systematically locating, consolidating, and smuggling loot. We suspected a linked network of caches and were following informants back to their central command. I was hoping to find the "Open Sesame" magic word that would unlock the master "cave" holding the identity of the cadre of thieves. Calvin's call suggested we'd been closer than I realized.

I did a walk around my Honda CR-V before getting in. It had been my first purchase after receiving the money from my parents' wrongful death claim, and it still had that new car smell. Nothing seemed to have been disturbed. No grease marks near the hood latch or scratches on the door lock. Car bombs were a fact of life in Baghdad, and you learned to eye every vehicle with suspicion.

Asheville was an unlikely spot for such a crude killing device, and I feared my imagination was running wild. If someone were out to assassinate me, a quick shot to the head would be more efficient. Locating me would not be difficult. Calvin's warning that "they know where you are" wasn't particularly ominous. It wasn't like they'd undertaken some sophisticated tracking operation to hunt me down. When Nakayla and I had solved the murders of her sister and an Asheville cop, we'd been plastered all over the media, from the *New York Times* to Fox News. Between that publicity and my earlier testimony before a Congressional committee about the deplorable conditions at Walter Reed Hospital, testimony that had gotten me shipped to the V.A. hospital in Asheville, I'd had plenty of opportunity to reveal information that would have incriminated any number of thieves. Still, on my drive up Biltmore Avenue to my office, I spent as much time looking in my rearview mirror as the road ahead.

I stepped on the elevator for the short lift to the third floor. Two middle-aged men got in on either side of me. Each held a briefcase and a cup of coffee. Their dark suits, crisp white shirts, and conservative ties pegged them as lawyers in one of the firms in the building. We nodded an unspoken "good morning," and I relaxed. Assassins wouldn't have both hands full unless they planned to club me with a briefcase and scald me to death. As I left the elevator, one of the men said, "Have a good day, Mr. Blackman." My fame hadn't been so fleeting that my face wasn't recognized.

I would have a good day. I was a professional, and this first morning on the job gave me a renewed sense of purpose. I wasn't as formally dressed as the attorneys, but my blue blazer, open-necked pink dress shirt, and tan slacks were fashionable enough for me to meet with any potential client with confidence. I had a Blackberry clipped to my belt, a P.I. license in my wallet, and years of investigative experience in my head.

What I didn't have was a weapon. My credentials from North Carolina included the right to carry a concealed weapon. Nakayla owned a small .25 caliber semiautomatic pistol, but my sidearm had been the property of the U.S. government. Later in the day, I planned to purchase a suitable handgun and side holster.

A square white box sat on the floor outside our office door. It was no more than six inches by six inches. I approached it warily. Neither Nakayla nor I expected any deliveries. I bent down beside it and saw the logo for the City Bakery Café on the lid. Beneath it and written in blue ink were the words: "Sorry to have bothered you. Welcome! Amanda Whitfield." Our security guard had gone to the trouble to come back, and even though she had a passkey, she'd chosen not to enter our office. Or maybe the person who brought it didn't have a key. That possibility sent a mental alarm ringing.

My bad leg didn't bend so well so I dropped to both knees and leaned over the box. Then I put my nose close to the seam of the lid and sniffed like a dog. If the contents were an explosive device, someone had gone to the trouble to use materials that smelled like freshly baked muffins.

"Are you okay?" A woman's voice came from behind me.

I felt my face flush. She couldn't see my embarrassment. Her view would have been of my butt sticking up in the air. "Ummm" was all I could manage. I tried to rise but my artificial leg didn't want to flex enough to get both feet under me.

"Sir?" she asked more urgently.

"Contact. I dropped a contact." It was the second thought that popped in my mind after I discarded morning prayers. "Oh, here it is." I reached out and grabbed an imaginary lens by the door. I pretended to moisten it in my mouth and then insert it in my eye.

I swung around so that I was sitting on the floor. Above me stood an attractive woman I guessed to be in her mid-thirties. She had short brown hair and wore a brown pants suit with white running shoes. In one hand she held a thermos; in the other, a small shopping bag with the heels of her dress shoes showing over the edge. She looked at me suspiciously and I knew my nose-sniffing-the-box-lid antic hadn't gone unnoticed.

"That City Bakery Café makes the best muffins." I struggled to my feet and offered my hand. "I'm Sam Blackman. Blackman and Robertson. We're just moving in."

She smiled. "Of course."

I didn't know whether "of course" meant she'd heard we were coming or that Sam Blackman and behaving like a dog went together like a burger and fries.

"I'm Cory DeMille. I work for Hewitt Donaldson." She said the name as if I should know it.

"Is that a law firm?"

She laughed. "Sort of. If you count one lawyer as a firm. Hewitt Donaldson's a person. I'm his paralegal, and we have an administrative assistant. Hewitt works solo, often for other firms. He's a defense attorney. The best in town."

To me defense attorney translated into potential client.

"Well, I'm a private investigator. The newest in town."

Behind Cory, the elevator doors opened and Nakayla stepped into the hall.

"And this is my partner, Nakayla Robertson."

Cory turned around, and I saw Nakayla's eyes narrow.

"We've met on a few depositions," Cory said. "Will insurance fraud be your specialty?"

"No," Nakayla said coolly. "Finding the truth will be our specialty."

"Then I wish you luck. Most clients don't want the truth. But if anyone can find it, I'm sure you and Mr. Blackman will sniff it out." She looked from Nakayla to me. "Anything we can do to help you get settled, our office is just down the hall."

"Thank you," I said, and took a step backwards to let her pass. The crunch of my foot smashing through the box of muffins almost drowned out her "You're welcome."

We started with Nakayla's office, arranging her desk so that she faced the window overlooking Pack Square. Then plastic protective covers were removed from chairs, lamps unboxed, and a filing drawer positioned as a credenza. We worked steadily, keeping our conversation focused on the task at hand.

I preferred my office to be the mirror image of Nakayla's. With my back to the window, I could get some work done. Otherwise I'd spend my days gazing at the square and mountains behind it, finding the vista an easy excuse to avoid work.

When the basics were in place and we took a breather in the more comfortable furnishings of the central waiting area, I asked Nakayla the question that had been on my mind all morning. "Why don't you like Cory DeMille?"

"Was I that obvious?"

"Maybe not to the average person. You forget I'm a trained detective."

"Who observes all, if you don't count blueberry muffins."

Amanda Whitfield's gift had been smashed flat and became the first item to land in Blackman and Robertson's wastebasket.

"I'm serious," I said. "Is she someone we should stay clear of?"

"No. I'm just not nuts about her boss. Hewitt Donaldson will do whatever he can to get people off. When I was at the Investigative Alliance for Underwriters, I had to testify in court against some of his clients. They'd submitted fraudulent medical claims that anybody could see were forgeries. I'd observed his clients performing physical activities that the phony claims stated would be impossible due to pain and suffering. During cross-examination, Donaldson went after me like a pit bull, basically calling me a liar and a pawn of the big insurance companies."

"Who were you working for?"

Nakayla glared at me. "A big insurance company. What of it?"

"And did his clients get off?"

"No. They were convicted."

I laughed. "Then I guess the jury saw Donaldson for what he was, a desperate defense attorney grasping at straws." I leaned forward in the new chair. Nakayla was curled up on the leather sofa, and I realized we had each staked out our territory. "One of my best friends in the service worked as an advocate for defendants. Whenever I had to testify at a tribunal, I dreaded his cross because he was doing his damndest for his client. He once told me if he could rattle a prosecution witness, then the emotion unleashed usually undercut the facts of the testimony. It was advice I took to heart, although there were times I'd liked to have jumped out of the witness chair and punched him."

"Well, I guess Cory's all right," Nakayla conceded. "And if she works with Donaldson, he must not be a total jerk."

"That's the spirit."

"On the other hand, I work with you." She grabbed a decorative pillow and threw it at me.

Before I could escalate the battle, a knock sounded from the door.

The AT&T serviceman entered pushing a cart with boxes of phones and small spools of wire. "Is this Blackman and Robertson?"

"We are," I said, "and we're ready to be connected to the world."

Since we'd placed our desks close to the existing outlets, the man took less than fifteen minutes to install everything.

"Here are the manuals for your phones." He set them on my desk. "They're simple enough to understand. Each line lights up when in use."

"Okay," Nakayla and I said together.

"You have AT&T voicemail?"

"No. We have an answering service."

"Oh." He looked as dejected as if we'd run over his dog.

"We might add it later," Nakayla said.

"Good. I can set it so it doesn't pick up till after a large number of rings. You know, in case your service can't get to it." He pulled a sheet from his clipboard. "If you'll just initial the order form.

And here's a card with your four numbers on it. I've sequenced the three voice lines to roll over in ascending order."

Nakayla signed the form while I memorized the phone numbers. Now we'd need to order business cards.

"Does directory assistance have these numbers in case anyone should ask for us?"

"Definitely. All I need to do is activate the lines at the junction box on this floor and you're good to go. I'll call when they're hot."

In not ten minutes, the first line rang. I picked up and heard him say, "Good on that one. Leave the line open and I'll keep calling to check the rollovers."

All three lines lit without a problem.

"I'm coming back to check the other fax/DSL line with my meter," the tech said.

Before he returned, the first line rang again. "Blackman and Robertson," I said, winking at Nakayla.

"Sam, that you?" The voice creaked like dry wood.

"It is."

"This is Captain."

"Good to hear from you. How'd you get the new number?"

"Information. Listen, you guys open for business?"

"Yes, and you're our first call."

"I know you're busy, but I'm worried about Ethel down the hall. You think you could come talk to her?"

I had no idea who Ethel was. "Sure. What's it about?"

"She won't tell me. Just that she's got something weighing on her heart and it will kill her before she dies."

I let the convoluted logic of the statement pass. "And you think I can help?"

"She asked for you, Sam. All she said was get me that man who found Thomas Wolfe. F. Scott Fitzgerald needs him."

"Captain, is she mentally alert?"

"Of course not. What should I tell her?"

"That I'll be by this afternoon."

"Great. And be sure and wash your hands."

"Well?" Nakayla asked, as I hung up the receiver.

"Dust off the file. We've got our first case."

She beamed. "Who is it?"

"F. Scott Fitzgerald."

She stared at me, completely speechless.

"So where's the washroom on this floor?"

Chapter Four

Captain, whose real name was Ron Kline, lived at Golden Oaks, a retirement community atop a mountain in Arden, a small town outside of Asheville. The octogenarian was actually a retired Army colonel, but he'd been a captain in the Second World War and claimed it was the highlight of his military career, the time when his command meant the most to his men and his country. In his old age, he'd reverted to his favorite rank as a nickname.

Nakayla and I had first met Captain several months ago when we were tracking leads in the murder of Nakayla's sister. The title aptly described his role as chief organizer and motivator of his fellow Golden Oaks residents. Nothing got by Captain, and if someone named Ethel had a problem, Captain would take care of it.

Nakayla had decided to let me handle this initial interview on my own while she made another run to Office Depot. Chances were that Ethel Barkley just wanted fresh ears to hear an old story and there would be nothing for us to do other than say "how interesting" and "we'll get back to you." The only mystery might be why Captain wanted me to wash my hands.

A guardhouse stood sentry between the split of entrance and exit lanes at the foot of the road up to Golden Oaks. A crossbar blocked my way, and instead of an officer on duty, security had been reduced to an intercom box on a pole and a video camera mounted under an eave of the roof. I reached out my window and pressed the button by the speaker.

"Welcome to Golden Oaks," a woman said. "How may I help you?"

"Sam Blackman to see Captain Kline."

"Certainly, Mr. Blackman."

The bar immediately rose. It's good to know important people in high places.

The road merged to two lanes and twisted up the mountain at least half a mile in its ascent. Perhaps that extra elevation closer to heaven was comforting to some of the occupants of what Captain once called the extended waiting room for a funeral home.

I parked the CR-V in a visitor's spot and saw Captain waiting for me in front of the entrance to the main building. He leaned against his walker like a thoroughbred at the starting gate of the Kentucky Derby, but he didn't risk cutting across the well-tended flowerbed to intercept me. I quickened my step in case his enthusiasm to see me got the better of him. We exchanged our customary greeting, a brisk military salute.

"Sam, you're working that leg of yours like a champ. I should get two of them and throw away this glorified towel rack." He bounced his walker up and down on the sidewalk for emphasis.

"Who are you kidding? Everybody knows you only use it to fend off the ladies." I was only half joking. With a ratio of six women to each man, any male in Golden Oaks with a pulse was a hot prize.

Captain laughed and whipped his walker around with military precision. "Follow me. Ethel's waiting."

I hurried to catch up. "Why'd you ask me to wash my hands?"

"Because she'll want to see them. Ethel's a strange one. You just hold your peace. She'll let you know when she wants you to talk."

We stopped outside the closed door to one of the apartments at the end of a ground-floor wing. The name Ethel Barkley had been engraved on a brass plate centered beneath the peephole. On the wall to the left hung a memory box, a foot-square display case with a glass front that protected photos and personal mementos. The box served to share the occupant's history with neighbors and provide opportunities for conversation; in the Alzheimer's unit, the memory box became the means for a resident to find his or her room and to hold onto a fleeting identity.

If Ethel suffered from early dementia, it wasn't severe enough to cause her transfer out of the independent living section. Her display contained a black-and-white picture of a young woman that had been taken in the 1930s or '40s. A mammoth stone wall filled the frame behind her. She stood with one foot on the running board of a luxury convertible crafted by some long defunct automaker. Another photo showed the woman, slightly older, with a young man and a boy and girl. The woman held the girl, who couldn't have been more than two, on her hip, and the man had the boy by the hand. The lad wore a cowboy hat and chaps and must have been around five. I assumed I was looking at Ethel with her husband and children. They posed in front of a small bungalow. The mountain background suggested the picture had been taken somewhere in the Asheville area.

A larger photo showed the woman much older and seated in a group shot with two younger adults and four kids from pre-teen to toddler—grandmother surrounded by her family. All of these pictures were arranged around a headshot of an elderly lady whose wrinkled face bore but a faint resemblance to the young woman beside the vintage convertible.

Captain rapped on the door with his knuckles. "Might take her a spell to answer. She dozes in the afternoon." He turned to go.

"Aren't you going to introduce me?"

He headed down the hall and called over his shoulder, "Son, you know your name, she still knows hers. This way she won't have to ask me to leave."

I waited a few minutes, straining to hear any sound of movement from within. Then I knocked again, louder than the Captain. The door immediately opened.

Ethel Barkley peered up at me. She couldn't have been more than four-and-a-half feet tall and the thick lenses of her glasses made her more owl than person. Her bony left hand clasped the ends of a green shawl that draped around her stooped shoulders and covered a floral print housecoat.

"You from Captain?"

I nodded.

She reached out and grabbed my forearm, not in greeting, but for a brace as she leaned into the hall. She looked one way and then the other before pulling me inside. "Sorry to keep you waiting," she said. "My ears play tricks on me and I'm too short to see out the peephole."

Her apartment had two mismatched armchairs, a burgundy velvet loveseat, and a dinette table with two wooden chairs set under a heavily curtained window. A small kitchen lay off my left and a closed door on the right must have sealed off her bedroom and bathroom.

"Let's sit by the light," she said.

I followed her to the table and sat in the chair she indicated. I expected her to open the curtains, but she bent over and retrieved a goose-necked desk lamp that had been sitting on the floor. She set it between us and twisted the flexible neck so that the rounded metal shade kept the light from our eyes and concentrated on the bare wood of the tabletop.

"I'd like to see your hands," she said. She stuck out her own with the palms up, expecting my compliance.

So Captain knew this would be part of her routine. Fortunately, I'd taken his request to heart, even scrubbing under my fingernails. I held my hands a few inches above hers, palm to palm. Grabbing my wrists, she turned them over. Then she leaned forward in her chair, hunching over the table and bringing her face to within a few inches of my skin.

"Good," she said under her breath. "Napoleonic in both." She hooked my right thumb with her left hand and bent it back, arching my palm even closer to her thick lenses. With the fingers of her right hand, she rubbed it as if trying to smooth out the surface. For a few minutes, she made only faint clucking sounds as she extracted some meaning from what appeared to be a meaningless crisscross of lines. Then she dropped that hand and repeated the entire process with the left. "You'll do," she said, and looked up at me for the first time since we'd sat down.

"I'll do for what?"

"The mission. You're not perfect, but you're acceptable."

"Mrs. Barkley, I'm the one who has to accept this mission. I have to know what we're talking about." Even though I'd been brought up to respect my elders, this woman annoyed me. She was assuming I'd do her bidding. And why wasn't I perfect? And what did my hands have to do with anything? Ethel Barkley had crossed into a realm I didn't care to follow. Next she'd pull out a Magic 8 Ball and ask me to use it during interrogations.

Instead of taking offense at my tone, she laughed. "The hands never lie. You've got strong, intertwined heart and head lines with veins running beneath them. The analytical and the emotional in conflict. You're constantly torn between two poles. Your blood flaring up and cooling down. Serves you well but it can also be your undoing."

I was now annoyed and unnerved because she'd read me like a book. I wondered if Captain had given her insights to use in her palmistry shenanigans.

"There's the question of expense, Mrs. Barkley. Sometimes a potential client discovers that the cost of mounting the investigation outweighs the value of a successful solution."

She flicked her hand, dismissing the possibility. "You don't care about money. That's not what motivates you. Your Napoleonic lines in both hands are subjugated by your quest for the ideal."

"The ideal?"

"The way you think things should be. Righting a wrong is more important to you than collecting a fee." Her gaze returned to my hands, now resting on the table. "But you don't like to show people that side. You're wary they'll take advantage of you."

Now I smiled. "Like asking me to investigate a case without paying me."

Her thin, gray eyebrows arched above her glasses. "I didn't say I wouldn't pay you. I said you'd be motivated by righting a wrong."

"So, a crime is involved?"

"Yes."

"And you want me to discover who committed it?"

"Sorry. I don't remember your name."

"Sam Blackman. And I'm not a descendant of Napoleon."

Although I'd suspected Ethel Barkley of dementia, this was the first time she looked confused.

Then her face brightened. "Napoleonic lines, Mr. Blackman, don't refer to genealogy. They're your head and heart lines. That's what Laura Guthrie called them. She's the one who taught me to read."

"Your school teacher?"

"Laura taught me to read hands. She entertained the guests at the Grove Park Inn. Mr. Fitzgerald called her his dollar woman."

"F. Scott Fitzgerald?" Finally we were getting to a connection with Captain's phone call.

"Yes. He named her that because she read his palm for a dollar. Then he hired her as his secretary." Her eyes lost focus as if she were looking back across the years. "Laura's dead now or I'd have her fix it for Mr. Fitzgerald."

"He's dead too." I said, just to make sure we were intersecting somewhere on the same plane of reality.

Ethel clicked off the light. "But that doesn't make him any less a victim."

"When did this crime occur?"

"1935."

"1935? Mrs. Barkley, that's nearly seventy-five years ago. I'm sure any statutes of limitations expired long ago, not to mention the guilty party."

"There you're wrong, Mr. Blackman. The guilty party is very much alive." She patted the back of my hand. "She just read your palm."

Her smile wilted and in the dim light I saw magnified tears well up behind the thick lenses.

"And there's no crime worse than betrayal, Mr. Blackman. A betrayal has to involve trust, even love." She took a deep breath and the air caught in her throat. "I betrayed Mr. Fitzgerald and I'm counting on you to make it right."

Ethel Barkley got to her feet and took slow, short steps to the bedroom door. She opened it and disappeared into the gloom. I heard the squeal of a drawer, and then she returned, her right hand clenched in a fist. Instead of sitting, she stood beside me so we were at eye level.

"Take this," she said. She dangled a small key in front of my face. "It unlocks a safe-deposit box at my bank." She studied the tag attached to the key by a string. "Wachovia. The banks keep getting bought up so I can't remember the names. The box number is written on here."

I took the key and saw the name and a number. "Is this a main branch?"

"Yes. On Haywood Street. I haven't been there since I gave up my driver's license."

"You want to go with me?"

"No. I'll call the bank manager and let him know you're coming."

"He'll allow access to your safe-deposit box based on a phone call?"

She nodded. "All pre-arranged. I have to give him a password. So do you. Can you go this afternoon?"

"Yes. What am I getting?"

She moved around the table and sat. "A metal lockbox, not much smaller than the safe-deposit box. Bring it here this evening. After six would be best. We eat early and if I'm not at my usual table, folks will wonder why."

"That's it?"

"For right now. And, Mr. Blackman, keep this between us. There are certain people who would love to get possession of it." She got up again. "I'd better get you something to put it in. Everybody in this place is always snooping in other people's business."

She returned to the bedroom. A few minutes later, she emerged carrying a folded bag with stiff twine handles. "See if this is big enough."

I opened a shopping bag that could hold at least four shoe-boxes. The logo for Ivey's Department Store was printed on the heavyweight paper. "This should work. Maybe I'd better get your phone number in case I run into any problems." I pulled a notepad out of my coat pocket. "And I'll give you the one for my cell if you need to reach me." I tore a sheet from the pad, jotted down my number, and slid it across the table. Then she told me hers.

I stood and slipped the key in my sport coat. "Until this evening." I reached out and shook her hand. Then I looked at my palm. "Good Napoleonic lines, huh?"

She smiled. "Mr. Fitzgerald's dollar woman would be impressed."

I turned to go.

"Your fee, Mr. Blackman?"

"We can talk about it later, when you require more than a courier."

She shrugged. "See, money isn't important to you." She clasped her hands in her lap and looked up, the tension in her narrow face clearly visible. "But I'm a ninety-year-old woman and if something were to happen to me, there's a gift in the lockbox. From Mr. Fitzgerald. I want you to have it."

"What is it?"

"I don't know. But I'm sure it's very valuable."

She had to see my confusion.

"Another woman had sent it to him," she explained. "He refused to accept it. Told me to get the package out of his sight and for all he cared I could keep it."

"And you never opened it?" I asked.

"Mr. Blackman, no woman wants a rejected gift. But like you said, we'll talk about it later."

"Yes, Mrs. Barkley." I thought I'd been dismissed.

"You'll want the password," she said.

"Sorry. What is it?"

Her smile returned. "*The Great Gatsby.*"

Chapter Five

In the blocks encompassing the heart of Asheville, traffic could be as congested as any city in the nation. Even though we were between tourist seasons—after Labor Day and before the invasion of the "leaf-peepers" for the October foliage—there were no parking places to be found on either Haywood Street or Patton Avenue near the bank. I found a spot in the deck behind the Pack Library and started the short walk to Wachovia. I'd take the chance that Ethel Barkley's lockbox wouldn't be too heavy to carry back.

The late afternoon temperature hovered in the low seventies. Shadows came early as the western ridges of the Blue Ridge Mountains rose to meet the setting sun. A cool breeze dispersed the fumes of the crawling vehicles and created the illusion that human technology couldn't harm Mother Nature.

Asheville was a growing city of 70,000-plus, attracting out-of-state retirees who wanted mountain homes and a migration of NewAgers who claimed to be drawn to an ancient Appalachian vortex humming beneath Asheville like a giant crystal on steroids, a convergence of mystical forces and dimensions that eluded scientists and the rational world. Ethel Barkley and her palmistry qualified as a senior NewAger, a homegrown original hybrid of both camps.

Between the two extremes lay the locals, the mountaineers whose ancestors had settled the hills centuries before and who now found their land values and taxes soaring. Some of the young people who had moved away could no longer afford to return. When Thomas Wolfe wrote *You Can't Go Home Again*, he didn't mean because you couldn't buy a house.

Thomas Wolfe. His legacy had played a part in the murder of Nakayla's sister, and Ethel Barkley must have thought I specialized in literary celebrities. What had she done to F. Scott Fitzgerald that caused her to feel such guilt? Perhaps there was something in her safe-deposit box she didn't want revealed at her death. Something she feared her family would discover. If my mission were to destroy evidence of a crime, could I safely do that even if the crime dated beyond the limits of prosecution? Or could I be liable for prosecution myself and risk the loss of my license? Sam Blackman, the record-holder for the shortest career as a private detective in the history of North Carolina.

I realized my musings had taken me several blocks without once thinking about my leg. The V.A. doctor had told me the unnaturalness of the prosthesis would fade as my body reprogrammed nerves and muscles, but this was the first time I'd gone so far without being aware of balance and stride, aspects of my walking that usually required conscious effort to perform.

I noticed the other pedestrians around me. None of them paid any attention to my wobbly gait. I was glad to be just another guy on the sidewalk with a folded shopping bag tucked under my arm, a forgettable figure who looked as normal as the pleasant September Tuesday.

"They know where you are." Calvin Stuart's words rang in my head. Ethel Barkley had driven my Army buddy's warning from my mind. Maybe I wasn't forgettable to someone, and, despite my assurances to Nakayla, the unease created by Calvin's call returned. My senses sharpened and I looked over my shoulder. My ability to walk might be improving, but how fast could I run?

The bank lobby had a customer service desk separate from the tellers' counter. A young man of Asian descent wearing a badge with the un-Asian name of Hubert looked up from his computer terminal and smiled. "Welcome to Wachovia," he said with such sincerity I almost believed him. "How can I help you?"

"I'm looking for the manager."

"Is Mr. Tennant expecting you?"

"Yes. I'm representing one of your customers. She should have phoned ahead."

Hubert picked up the phone next to his keyboard. "And you are?"

"Sam Blackman."

He gave me a second look. Either the manager had alerted him or he recognized my name from the summer's news coverage. He pushed an intercom button, paused a second, and then said, "Mr. Blackman is here."

Before he could return the receiver to its cradle, an office door opened along the sidewall and a beefy man in a short-sleeved dress shirt and blue paisley tie strode toward us.

He was still twenty feet away when he called, "Mr. Blackman. So good to meet you." He extended his right arm in more of a docking maneuver than a handshake. I stepped forward to meet him lest his momentum knock me over. He squeezed my hand with such enthusiasm that I was afraid any future reading of my palm would be more like deciphering a crumpled newspaper. The man was probably in his late forties and might have been a football player in his earlier years. Now his muscular block of a body was in danger of going to fat.

"Thank you for seeing me, Mr. Tennant."

"Call me Ross," he insisted. "And it's no trouble at all. Let me say how glad we are that you're with Wachovia."

The light bulb went off in my head. Ross must have done a quick check on me. I'd deposited the bulk of my parents' wrongful death settlement in a money-market account in the Wachovia branch in Biltmore Village. About half a million had been wired to an offshore account in the Caymans where Nakayla and I could begin the careful process of converting her assets into cash, but that still left over two million dollars yet to be more traditionally invested. To Ross Tennant, I wasn't Sam Blackman the detective; I was Sam Blackman the millionaire.

"And I'm very pleased you're helping dear Mrs. Barkley," Ross continued. "What a sweetheart."

"You've been out to see her?"

He shook his head. "No. She came in to meet me. Must be nearly ten years ago when I first became manager." He glanced down at his hands and I suspected Ethel had given him a most memorable interview.

"Did Mrs. Barkley tell you what I needed?"

Ross glanced around the lobby. "Let's step into my office."

The furnishings were nice but not lavish. He pointed to one of four chairs at a small conference table in a corner opposite his desk and then he closed the door behind him. "Mrs. Barkley said you'd be bringing the key to her safe-deposit box." He wedged into the chair across from me. "Do you have it?"

I pulled the key from my coat pocket and laid it on the table.

Ross eyed it appreciatively. "And there's something else."

"Not that I know of." I waited for the frown to appear on his ruddy face. "But *The Great Gatsby* sends his regards."

"Excellent." He clapped his hands. "She's quite the character, isn't she?"

"One of a kind." I thought for all he knew, Ethel Barkley could have been my grandmother.

"I'm glad she's seeking your advice, Mr. Blackman."

"Please call me Sam."

"Sam." He leaned against the table and lowered his voice. "I've tried to get her to be a little more aggressive with her funds. Not that she should be in anything risky at her age, but rolling CDs every ninety days isn't earning the interest she should." He laughed. "I'm not saying she's not a profitable client for the bank, but I'm looking out for her best interests." He paused. "Just like we would be looking out for yours."

I wasn't certain if his point was about Ethel or a sales pitch for my investment account. "I'm sure Mrs. Barkley has confidence in you, but she has her own reason for doing things her way." I figured that comment was accurate although the reason could be a sign in her tea leaves or a wayward line in Ross Tennant's palm.

"Exactly." His gaze returned to the key. "I just wanted to assure you if there's anything in her safe-deposit box, stocks, bonds, or other securities, that she wants converted, I'd be happy to set up a consultation with an advisor from our Private Wealth Management Group."

"I'll mention that to her."

He looked up, all smiles. "And remind her she's close to the breakpoint where management fees are further reduced and interest rates increased."

"Right. What's that amount again?"

Ross hesitated, weighing whether he was revealing too much of Ethel Barkley's personal finances. He must have decided if the breakpoint was already public information, then he wasn't violating her confidentiality. "Five million."

Ethel Barkley would have no problem paying my fee. I picked up the key. "I'll see what I can do."

Ross Tennant got to his feet. "I'll escort you to the vault. You'll need to sign in and out, and since you're not the designated holder of the box, I'll counter-sign the log with you."

I stood. "Mrs. Barkley said only I was to have access."

He raised his big hands apologetically. "Of course. You'll enter on your own. There is a counter with individual dividers. You can examine the contents in complete privacy."

He led the way to the rear of the bank, slid back a wall of shiny metal bars, and crossed into the vault area. A podium held an open logbook just inside the door. A security guard sat at a desk beside it.

"Mr. Blackman will be bringing out some items, Ralph."

The guard looked at me. He wasn't part of Nathan Armitage's company. "Do you need to borrow a bank bag, sir?"

I shook out the shopping bag. "I think everything will fit in here."

The guard whistled. "I'll be. Ivey's. I haven't seen one of those in years. I used to have night duty there before the store closed."

"They were bought out, weren't they, Ralph? Must be close to twenty years ago."

"Yep. If a day."

Great. So much for not drawing attention to myself.

"Well, give Mr. Blackman what he needs." Ross signed the book and handed me the pen. As I wrote my name, he said, "The safe-deposit boxes are in the first room on the right. Let Ralph know when you're finished and I'll come back." He left, and I sensed his disappointment that I hadn't asked him to accompany me.

The safe-deposit box matching the tag on the key was on the lowest level and appeared to be one of the largest available. The front must have been at least a foot square. I feared the trek back to the car might be more than I'd bargained for.

The lock turned with a slight squeak and metal scraped metal as I pulled out the drawer. A box fit snugly inside, but I knew this couldn't be what Ethel wanted me to bring her. This box was the property of the bank. I lifted it free. The weight must have been around fifteen pounds. It closed with a latch, not a lock. I carried it to a counter on the opposite wall and set it down between two privacy screens. If Ethel didn't remember that the box belonged to Wachovia, then I might have to empty the contents into the shopping bag.

I flipped up the clasp and raised the hinged lid. Like one of those wooden Russian dolls, another box lay inside. The metal had long ago lost any sheen and the dimpled surface of its top showed other objects had at one time banged against it. There was just enough room to wedge my fingers along the sides and pull it free. I set it directly in front of me.

The dimensions were roughly eighteen inches in length, ten inches in height, and ten inches in width. Just below the lip of the lid, a release button with a slot for a key provided a modest hindrance to anyone attempting to pry the top open. To the right of the lock, I saw an irregular bulge that started on the lid and continued over the side. This wasn't a protrusion of the metal, but some other material adhering to it. I turned the box on its side. Clunks sounded as the internal contents shifted.

Someone had poured molten lead over the seam of the lid. The dull gray blemish was about the size of an egg yolk and its unbroken surface showed no one had opened the box since the hot lead had cooled. Like wax dripped over the closed flap of an envelope, the soft lead had been pressed with a recessed seal. In the bright fluorescent light of the bank vault, the raised design stood out with toxic clarity. The marking was simple and chilling.

A swastika.

◇◇◇

"Please don't hesitate to call on me if I can ever be of assistance." Ross Tennant made the offer as he held open the front door of the bank.

"Thank you." I could only nod my appreciation since both my hands clutched the bag with the Ivey's logo to my chest. I didn't trust the twine handles.

I got tired during the walk to the car. The weight of the box seemed to increase with each step. Pain in my stump began to grow as perspiration soaked the sleeve and changed the fit of my limb in the prosthesis' socket. I'd stop by the office where I kept a spare sleeve. Maybe I could find a packing carton big enough for the lockbox so Mrs. Barkley's neighbors wouldn't think Ivey's was back in business.

I set the shopping bag on the floor in the hall, logo facing the door, and knocked. No answer. Nakayla either hadn't returned from Office Depot or she'd gone for the day. I glanced at my watch. Five-fifteen.

"Good afternoon, Mr. Blackman."

I jumped. Amanda Whitfield stood behind me. Her soft rubber soles hadn't made a sound.

"Sorry. I didn't mean to startle you." She looked down at the bag. The end of the lockbox was clearly visible. "Can I help you with that? It looks heavy."

"No thanks. Just getting my key and then I'll slide it inside." I turned to the door, not wanting to get into a conversation.

"Have a nice evening. Remember I lock the doors at seven." She continued down the hall.

I felt guilty that I'd been so abrupt. "Amanda," I called. She stopped and faced me.

"Thanks for the muffins," I said. "They were delicious."

She smiled. "I'm glad you liked them. Last night I pulled a double shift and the bakery down the street was just making their first run when I got off. My husband loves their muffins for breakfast."

"You worked sixteen hours?"

"My relief, Jack Mountjoy, got sick yesterday afternoon. I'm covering for him again tonight. The work's easy." She laughed. "As long as I can stay awake to make my rounds." She looked at the bag again. "You sure you don't need help with that?"

"Positive. It looks heavier than it is. Just some old files I'm putting in our new cabinets."

"I'm glad you're here, Mr. Blackman. I know you and Ms. Robertson will be a big success."

I thanked her and watched her continue on her rounds. Her good spirit was all the more remarkable for the hardship Nathan Armitage had told me she endured.

Nakayla had set several bags of office supplies on my floor. One of them was large enough to conceal the lockbox and I figured carrying a bag from Staples was better than from a defunct department store.

I'd started putting away legal pads and assorted manila envelopes when my cell phone rang. I recognized Ethel Barkley's number.

"Mrs. Barkley?"

"No, Sam. It's Captain. Ethel had me call. Told me where this number was in her apartment."

"What's wrong?"

"Oh, she's okay. We think she skipped her meds this afternoon. Probably got excited that you were coming. She doubled up her missed dose right before supper and on an empty stomach it made her woozy."

"Did she fall?"

"Nah. She kinda passed out at the table. No big deal."

I had an image of old people stepping over Ethel to get to the buffet line. "I'm supposed to come see her tonight."

"That's what she said. And she's madder than a wet hen because Golden Oaks' policy states she has to stay in the assisted living unit for observation. She should be out first thing in the morning if everything's normal. She's already ornery again. A good sign."

"Will you call me?"

"I could but Ethel asked me to pass this number to the front desk. They'll be the first to know when she's back in her room."

I glanced down at the Staples bag holding the swastika-sealed lockbox. The sooner I got rid of it, the better both Ethel Barkley and I'd feel. "Okay. Tell them to call as soon as she's released, no matter how early."

"Roger, that."

"And tell Ethel everything went fine, and to get a good night's sleep."

"Will do, Sam. I told her you were the man for the job, whatever it was."

Captain had probably been on enough missions in his military career that he wasn't the least bit curious about what Ethel's had been for me.

A few minutes later, Nakayla's number flashed in the caller ID window.

"Where are you?" I asked.

"Coming in on Broadway. I picked up two printers on sale at Office Depot. Can you meet me in front of the building and help me unload them? I'll treat you to dinner."

Even though my back and leg ached from toting the lockbox, I couldn't refuse her offer.

We spent an hour hooking up printers to our laptops, aligning ink cartridges, and trouble-shooting the multiple features. Then we organized the rest of the supplies Nakayla had purchased so that tomorrow morning we'd be ready for business.

"How about Tupelo Honey Café?" Nakayla asked.

The restaurant was a favorite on College Street, a few blocks away.

"If we can get in. It's nearly seven."

The restaurant didn't take reservations and the wait could be long.

Nakayla grabbed my hand. "So, we'll have a drink and you can tell me about our first case."

We'd spent the setup time reading printer directions and I'd yet to mention anything about my meeting with Ethel Barkley.

I resisted her tug toward the door and instead pulled her back to my office. "Let me show you something first. I don't want to talk about it in the café."

I led her around my desk and then pulled the lockbox from the bag.

"Oh, my God. What's in it?"

"I don't know."

Nakayla bent down and ran her fingers quickly over the swastika as if it might bite her. "Is this old lady a Nazi?"

"How should I know? She didn't goose-step or shout *seig heil!* She said she betrayed F. Scott Fitzgerald and that something in this box was going to make it right."

"What are you going to do with it?"

"I was supposed to bring it to her tonight, but Captain called and said she's not feeling well. I'll take it to her in the morning." I slid the lockbox back in the bag.

"Shouldn't you notify the authorities?"

"About what?" Now I was the one tugging her toward the door. "It's not illegal to have a World War Two souvenir."

"If that's all it is."

"Look. Ethel's a bit nutty, but harmless. If I find Adolph Hitler's stamped passport to Argentina in there, I'll be sure to report it."

"Then why didn't you want to talk about it at Tupelo Honey."

"Because pinot noir and the word swastika don't go well together." I opened the office door and nudged Nakayla into the hall. "Besides, I don't want anything to distract you from my terrific Napoleonic lines."

"Your what?"

"Sorry. You'll have to wait. I don't want to overwhelm you before dinner."

She punched me in the side. "I've heard enough of your lines, hotshot. Here's mine. I've changed my mind. You're picking up the check."

Chapter Six

And so I'd picked up the check, polished off the wine, and now crouched over a body in our office.

"Nakayla?" My voice quivered. I reached up the wall, feeling for the light switch. The overhead fixture came on instantly, but I needed a few seconds to comprehend the horror before me.

Amanda Whitfield sprawled like a rag doll, her neck bent at such a wicked angle that I suspected there was no point in calling for an ambulance. I checked her carotid artery for a pulse and tested for a pupil reaction, but my initial assessment had been correct. The poor woman had died instantly when someone snapped her neck like a dry twig.

I heard footsteps behind me, then a gasp.

Nakayla leaned against the doorjamb and raised a hand to her throat. "What happened?"

"I don't know." I stepped into my office and flipped on the overhead light. The bag with Ethel Barkley's swastika-sealed box was gone. "Let's get back in the hall. This is a crime scene. Use your cell to call the police."

The police department was less than a hundred yards away and within five minutes two uniformed officers burst from the elevator. I recognized them, but I couldn't tell them apart. Patrolmen Ted and Al Newland were identical twins. Their uncle worked as a homicide detective. I hoped his nephews would put in a back-channel call to Curt Newland so Newly would be the first of Asheville's investigative team to arrive.

"The victim's in the office," I said, and glanced at their nameplates to keep them straight.

"Did you call for an ambulance?" Ted asked.

"No. She's clearly dead. I didn't want medics contaminating the scene."

Al nodded. "I'll go in and check things out. Ted, call Uncle Newly."

"Tell him it's the night watchman," I said. "She never got her gun out of her holster." I let Al pass by me to enter the office alone.

Ted had been on his cell phone less than a minute when he waved me over. "He wants to talk to you."

"Newly," I said, skipping past a hello. "She's Amanda Whitfield and works for Nathan Armitage. Someone broke her neck."

"Jesus, not Mandy." His voice choked on the words.

"You know her?"

"Yes. She and her husband were in school with the twins. Ted and Al were ushers in their wedding."

I turned around to see Al coming out of the office. His face was chalk white. Tears sparkled on his cheeks. He whispered "Mandy" to his brother. His twin shook his head in disbelief and pushed by him. Nakayla understood the crime scene had become intensely personal and went to comfort Al who leaned against the wall, his face now buried in his hands.

"They're taking it hard," I told Newland. "How soon will you be here?"

"Ten minutes. I'll call the crime lab from the car. Tell the twins to cover the building entrances. Tell them no one comes in or out. I'll bring in backup."

I realized Detective Newland was putting me in charge. "Okay. Anything else?"

"Sit tight. I'd like you to go over the scene with me. Let me know if anything's missing."

I knew what was missing, but I didn't say it over the phone. Client confidentiality was an important tenet of a private investigation. I'd promised Ethel Barkley that I'd keep her so-called mission between us. But, I hadn't bargained on murder, and my military career of serving the interests of justice outweighed the obligation I felt to a ninety-year-old woman and a Nazi lockbox. I would tell Detective Newland everything that had happened, but I'd also inform Ethel Barkley that the mission had failed.

"Got it," I assured him. "See you in a few minutes."

I relayed Newland's request to his nephews and they left to take up their positions on the ground floor.

"So we wait," Nakayla whispered, as if afraid of disturbing the dead.

"Not for long. Detective Newland and his reinforcements will be here soon."

"I'm tired of standing," she said, and sat on the hall floor, resting her back against the door.

My stump hurt and I eased down beside her. I stretched both legs straight in front of me.

Nakayla locked her hand in mine. "Who knew we had the lockbox?"

"Ross Tennant, the bank manager. Also some guard named Ralph. I suppose anyone in the bank lobby could have seen me coming out of the safe-deposit room with a full bag. And Amanda saw the box outside this door. She must have heard something on her rounds and gone in to investigate." I had the sick feeling that she might have seen the wastebasket with the crushed muffins inside. A totally stupid and irrational concern that I couldn't shake. Had Amanda thought we didn't like them? "I've got to check something."

"Aren't we supposed to stay clear?"

"This will just take a second." I opened the door and stayed close to the wall farthest from Amanda's body. I'd dumped the muffins in the wastebasket in the corner nearest the window. In the dim light from the outside street lamps, I could see a fresh trash liner. Thankfully, the cleaning crew had been through before Amanda. That fact could also help narrow the timeframe for the murder.

"Sam, I hear a door opening." Nakayla hurried into the office.

"Whoever it is can't leave the building."

Without hesitation, Nakayla stepped back in the hall. I joined her and we became a barricade blocking the way. The corridor in front of us turned right and we couldn't see around the corner. The sharp clicks of a woman's heels grew louder.

Cory DeMille appeared, walking briskly, her attention focused on straightening the running shoes in her shopping bag while juggling her thermos. She looked up and jumped at the sight of us.

"My God, you scared me to death." She laughed nervously. "Blackman and Robertson are certainly putting in the late hours." Her voice rose, as if she wanted someone else to hear the words.

"I'm afraid we're all going to be putting in late hours tonight," I said. "The police are sealing off the building and no one can leave."

Her face paled. "What's happened?"

"Tell whoever's in your office to come out here and I'll tell you."

She didn't argue, but walked back to the corner and yelled down the hall. "Hewitt, come quickly. Something's wrong."

Within a few seconds, a man bolted around the corner. His stringy gray hair draped to his shoulders and a pair of reading glasses dangling from a cord around his neck bounced against his chest. In a rumpled white linen shirt and beltless tan slacks, he looked more like an aging, overweight rock star at a beach cabana than the lawyer his paralegal described as the best defense attorney in town.

He eyed Nakayla and me with suspicion. "What's the trouble?"

I didn't mince words. "Amanda Whitfield, the security guard, has been murdered. She's in our office."

A strangled cry caught in Cory Demille's throat. She reached out and steadied herself against the wall.

Hewitt Donaldson stood rock solid. His eyes narrowed as he studied Nakayla and me. "You've called the police?"

"Yes. You can relax. We didn't kill her."

He took a deep breath. "The police will want statements." He turned to Cory. "Why don't we wait in the office where you can sit down."

She nodded. "I'm okay. But I just can't believe it."

Donaldson looked at me. "You're Sam Blackman, right?"

"Yes. This is my partner, Nakayla Robertson."

"Would you get us when the police arrive?"

Nakayla took a wobbly step forward. "Can I join you? I feel a little faint."

I grabbed her arm to steady her and tried to look concerned. Nakayla's instincts had been sharper than mine. She wasn't going to let them be alone together in case they suddenly needed to concoct a story.

"Certainly, my dear," Donaldson said. "Let me help you."

He took Nakayla's other arm as I released her. "Can I bring you anything?" he asked me. "Water? I keep some scotch handy if you need something stronger."

"No, thank you."

"I'll be back to keep you company." Donaldson took each woman by the hand and walked between them to his office.

A few minutes later I heard a loud clatter of rolling wheels and bumping metal as if a train had started rumbling down the hall. Donaldson returned, pushing two desk chairs that seemed intent on going in opposite directions.

"These damn things are like runaway grocery carts." He shoved one over to me and plopped down in the other. "No sense standing and waiting."

"Thanks." I maneuvered the chair in front of the door and sat.

"Glad to meet you, Sam," Donaldson said. "Wish it was under better circumstances."

"Yeah. Amanda seemed like a good kid." Although she couldn't be much younger than me, Amanda had a little girl quality that her uniform couldn't disguise. Anger burned in my chest and I was glad Newland was giving me some part to play.

Donaldson must have read my mind. "Are you going to be involved in the investigation?"

"Officially, no. But Detective Newland's on his way and he's been open to my opinions before."

"He ought to be. You saved their bacon."

I let his jab at the police pass. "I can work in ways they can't. Newland's all right."

"I suppose he's the best of the lot," Donaldson said without enthusiasm. "Any idea why this happened?"

Warning bells sounded in my head. I realized I could be talking to the potential attorney for the murderer. If Hewitt Donaldson were the best defense lawyer in town, then he would be looking for every possible angle to clear his client.

"No. Maybe someone saw us moving in and thought they'd heist our new stuff."

"Anything missing?"

"I haven't had a chance to go through everything. As soon as I saw the body, Nakayla called the police. We're keeping the crime scene pristine." It was my turn to give an informal grilling. "Did you and Cory hear anything?"

"No. We were going over deposition videos for a trial tomorrow."

"You were quiet. I didn't hear a sound in the hall."

Donaldson grinned. "Good. I like a skeptic. We were listening on headsets because I don't want there to be a sound in the hall for just anyone to hear." He glanced at his wristwatch. "Cory had to meet her fiancé at the airport. The connector from Charlotte doesn't get in until nine. I hope she left a message for him to take a cab."

He looked past me to the door. "Any sign of a break-in?"

"No. And I'm positive we locked up."

Donaldson ran his tongue across his gapped teeth. "Well, that raises the ugly possibility of an inside job. Maybe Amanda stumbled onto someone she knew and that sealed her fate."

Before I could comment, the elevator doors opened and Detective Newland squeezed out followed by two other plain-clothes officers, three uniforms, and a crime lab tech pushing a cart of supplies. The men had been packed so tightly in the elevator there couldn't have been much room left for air to breathe on the ride up.

Unlike Donaldson, Newland wore his gray hair in short, springy curls, but they were just as disheveled. "Sam, we got here as quick as we could." Newland cast a sharp stare at Donaldson. "Congratulations, Hewitt. I knew you could out-chase the ambulances but this is the first time you've beaten the police."

"Not in a courtroom."

"His office is on this floor," I said, trying to defuse their petty bickering. "He and his paralegal are waiting to give their statements."

"Fine." Newland turned to the two plain-clothes men. "Chip, you and Jim escort the esteemed counselor back to his office and see if you can arrange to question him and his associate separately. If there's no room, take them to the station."

Donaldson got up. "Would one of you gentlemen bring Sam's chair? I don't want to break up a set."

I rose and let a detective push the chair after the flamboyant attorney.

"I hate to think how many crooks that bastard's gotten off," Newland muttered. "Let's boot and glove. Jenkins, do a pass with the video camera and then stills."

The crime lab tech handed me latex gloves and shoe covers similar to those worn by the staff in an operating room. As soon as the three of us were ready, Newland opened the door.

"Follow me, Sam. We'll check Amanda first and then you tell me anything that's missing or out of place." He stepped inside. "You can hit the lights."

I switched on the overheads, and this time Amanda looked even more frail and broken on the floor.

Newland halted. "Poor girl." He squared his shoulders and knelt beside her. "No sign of blood. No sign of a struggle. It's like she dropped from a gallows and was hanged by invisible rope."

"If she'd been headed into my office, someone could have come out of Nakayla's and surprised her from behind." I walked back to Nakayla's open door. "The drawers are pulled from her desk."

"Anything taken?" Newland asked.

"Nothing to take. The drawers just held supplies. We only moved in yesterday."

"What about computers?"

"The laptop and new printer are there." I crossed the reception area and edged around Newland where he still knelt by Amanda's body.

My desk drawers were also pulled out. Printer paper, empty hanging files, and paper clips littered the floor. Like Nakayla's, my laptop was still docked with its desktop monitor and connected to a full-sized keyboard.

"I see only one thing missing," I said.

Newland's face snapped up, his brown eyes quizzing me. "What's that?"

"A lockbox I was holding for a client."

He scrambled to his feet and walked around my office, careful not to step on the items on the floor. "Where was it?" He searched as if the location should be obvious.

"Tucked behind my chair. It was hidden in a Staples bag. Nakayla and I went to dinner and it seemed better to have it locked in the office rather than leave it in the car. I'd come back to pick it up."

"You don't have a safe?"

"Not yet. Till this afternoon I didn't have a client."

Newland put his pen to his notepad. "Who's the client? And don't give me that crap about confidentiality. This is a murder case, not some philandering husband dipping his wick all over town."

"Ethel Barkley. You know her?"

"I don't think so. What's in the lockbox?"

I shrugged. "I haven't a clue. My job was to bring it to her."

"Where can I find her?"

"Golden Oaks in Arden. She's ninety and not going anywhere. In fact, she's in their infirmary. That's why I couldn't deliver the box tonight."

"Where'd you get it?"

"Wachovia down on Patton. Check with Ross Tennant. He's the manager."

Newland kept his eyes focused on his pad and continued writing. "Describe it."

"Gray metal. Kinda beat up. About a foot and a half long. I'd guess ten inches high and wide. Internal locking mechanism with a release button."

"You try it?"

"Yeah. It was locked. Ethel Barkley must have the key."

Newland tapped his pen on his pad impatiently. "Who else knew the lockbox was here?"

I repeated the list Nakayla and I'd discussed earlier.

After Newland jotted down the names, he asked, "The old lady tell anyone else at the retirement center what you were fetching?"

"I don't think so. She's very secretive. She might not be totally connected to reality."

Newland flipped his pad closed. "And we don't know whether her lockbox was the target of the break-in. Every drawer was still pulled out."

"Maybe the search was for the key," I said. "Or Amanda could have come in, been killed, and the bag with the lockbox was the easiest and quickest thing to take."

"What do you think?"

I shook my head. "I think we'd better turn up some hard evidence. The only thing we know is it wasn't a break-in."

"Maybe someone forced Amanda to open the door." Newland looked down at the dead woman. Reinforcements had arrived and mobile crime lab techs began dusting and lifting prints. Two men gently rolled Amanda's body over.

"Here's something under her," one of the techs said. His gloved hand pinched a black circle about the size of a nickel. "A button." He passed it over to Newland.

The detective knelt again and studied Amanda's uniform. "Definitely not off her clothing. Does it belong to you or Nakayla?"

I examined the button. Hard plastic with four thread holes. It was too big for a shirt button unless it came from outdoor wear like one of those flannel or wool shirts that adds an extra layer without the heavier weight of a jacket.

"I don't recognize it," I said. "Better show it to Nakayla."

"Drop it in an evidence bag," Newland said. "Where is Nakayla?"

"She was in Donaldson's office keeping an eye on the paralegal."

Newland smiled. "Smart move. Your idea?"

"Hers."

His smile broadened. "Can't hide homegrown talent. Well, I won't keep you two any longer than necessary. Have Nakayla look at the button. Then each of you come to the department and write up a statement."

"One other thing." I motioned for him to step back into my office where we'd have more privacy.

"What?" he asked.

"In addition to the lock, the stolen box had a lead seal covering the seam of the lid with the imprint of a swastika."

Newland's notepad flipped open so fast I felt a breeze across my face. "I'll need to talk to your client right away."

"She's supposed to be released to her room in the morning. Okay if I tell her you're coming? I'd like to explain why. And I don't think bringing her to the station straight from the infirmary is a good idea."

"All right. We'll go there about eight-thirty tomorrow. I don't want to sit on our best lead."

"Fine," I said, but like the smart little pig battling the big, bad wolf, I hoped to get to Ethel Barkley an hour earlier.

It was nearly ten-thirty when I drove the CR-V into the rear parking lot of my apartment building. The back of the once grand Kenilworth Inn offered the quickest entry for residents. I parked along the dark edge of the lot and walked through drizzling rain across the asphalt, dodging puddles of water that had collected in the pavement's depressions. A fast-moving line of thunderstorms had dumped an inch or two of rain while Nakayla and I'd been finishing up at police headquarters.

We'd submitted our signed statements, and then I'd had the unfortunate task of phoning Nathan Armitage to tell him of his employee's death. Right now, he and the Newland twins were making a personal visit to Amanda's mother and quadriplegic husband, and as tough as the evening had been for me, carrying such bad news to a family already burdened with tragedy would be far worse.

The Kenilworth Inn sat like a royal castle atop the knoll of a mountain. I looked up at the random pattern of rectangles created by the lighted windows of those fellow tenants who were still awake. The slope of the land meant I had to climb a flight of exterior stairs to reach the ground floor, but I'd found the ascent less exerting than walking across the expansive lawn from the front parking spaces.

As I reached the hand railing, a featureless silhouette moved in the murky shadows of the bordering shrubbery.

A gruff voice whispered, "Blackman. Another step and you're a dead man."

I froze, my blood chilled more by the sound of my name than the threat. This was no random mugging. Someone had lain in wait for me.

"Hands out to your side. Now!"

I snapped my arms at right angles, wishing they were wings.

"Turn away from me."

I pivoted to face the parking lot. The rustle of leaves signaled that my assailant came closer.

"Take a step back and then lace your fingers behind your head."

I used my good leg to test the soft ground, but my prosthetic foot snagged on an exposed root and I struggled to keep my balance.

"Easy. Keep it nice and slow."

He had ordered me into the shadows where the spill light couldn't penetrate. If he meant to shoot me, I didn't understand why he hadn't pulled the trigger as I started up the stairs.

"What did you do with it?" The voice was so close to my ear I could feel hot breath on my neck.

"Do with what?" I asked.

The cold steel of a pistol pressed against the back of my skull.

"Don't be cute. You got it out. We want it back. Or the cash. Or the account numbers."

"The lockbox was stolen," I said.

"What's in the account?"

"I have no idea what you're talking about," I said. "Somebody broke into my office and stole the lockbox. End of story."

The gun muzzle pressed harder against me. "No. The end of the story will come if you don't give us back what you took from us."

"Tell your Nazi friends I don't have it!"

Across the parking lot, a pair of headlights flared and an engine revved to life.

"Damn it," muttered the man behind me.

I stiffened, expecting the pistol to fire at point-blank range. Instead, a fist smashed into the small of my back and pain seared through my kidney. A thrust against my shoulders propelled me over the curb and sent me sprawling onto the asphalt. As my face scraped the pocked surface, I managed to look back and see a man in a black shirt and pants running for the woods. Then beams swept across me and a car squealed to a stop a few yards from my head.

I twisted around and squinted against the glare of the headlights. The vehicle's door opened and the driver stepped out.

"Well, Chief, you just gonna lay there, or you gonna invite me in for a drink."

Chapter Seven

"And then when you didn't go up the stairs I got suspicious." Calvin Stuart swirled the ice in his glass of scotch. "Nice to be the cavalry to the rescue for once."

He sat across from me at my dining table and stared at his large, black hands. They gripped the glass tighter and for a second I feared Calvin would break it. Through gritted teeth, he said, "I should have been there for you at the checkpoint."

"And what? Gotten killed? We could have had ten more guys there and the outcome would have been the same. They had Iraqi uniforms and came close enough to make us sitting ducks for the first rocket grenades."

Warrant Officer Calvin Stuart had been part of my team. I knew he felt guilty that he'd been in the infirmary the morning we'd been hit. But if I'd had a choice between him being with me then or being with me tonight, the present beat the past.

I reached out and grabbed his wrist. "Cal, you were here when it counted."

He nodded, took a deep swallow of scotch, and leaned back. "And I told you to watch your back."

"That you did." I shifted in my chair and winced. My back hurt like hell.

"You sure you don't want me to take you to the ER?"

"I'm fine. I'm more interested in how you wound up in my parking lot at ten-thirty."

Calvin rose, as if what he had to say couldn't be expressed unless he was in motion. He stood a good six inches taller than me, nearly six-four, and though we were both in our early thirties and had enlisted in the U.S. Army out of high school, Calvin came late to the Criminal Investigation Detachment. He'd transferred about a year ago from prison administration duties, even though it extended his Iraqi tour. He'd told me he'd been fortunate not to be tied to any of the abuse scandals, but the taint of those gross injustices was spreading from the guilty to the innocent. Calvin saw no future down that military career path. I'd found him to be a good soldier, if not a little cocky. But he'd always deferred to my judgment, and jokingly accepted his subordinate role. In short, I liked the guy.

"The Ali Baba case," he said. "I called you because I picked up a tail here in the states."

"You're on leave?"

"Such as it is. Six weeks. I'm a rotation statistic so the Pentagon can claim they're not keeping personnel in Iraq too long. Of course, I'll head right back."

"Who's following you?"

He stopped pacing and grabbed the back of his chair. "Who do you think, Chief? If the swill's got the connections to smuggle booty out of Iraq, they can certainly find me in Paterson, New Jersey."

"That's where you were?"

Calvin started pacing again. "At my grandmother's. I noticed this guy parked down the block. Even though I've been out of the hood for years, some things never change. You sense when someone's not where he's supposed to be."

"You confront him?"

Calvin looked at me like I'd grown an extra ear. "And do what? Let him know I made him so he could shoot me down in the street? Man, I was packed and out the back door so fast I'd covered twenty yards between saying good and bye to Granny."

"Is that when you called me?"

"No. This was last Saturday. Monday my grandmother phoned nearly in hysterics."

"Yesterday?"

"I guess it was. Seems longer. Granny found her cat on the stoop, dead with a noose around its neck. She read me the note: 'Tell your big buck and Blackman to return what's ours or they're next.' I told Granny to catch the next bus to Philly where she can stay with her sister and not to leave till I said so."

"What the hell does that mean?"

Calvin whipped the hard-backed chair around and straddled it. "They think we plundered their cache. The one you were headed for when you were ambushed."

"How do you know?"

"Because three days later when my runs had stopped and I could walk without shitting myself, we went after it. Charlie and Ed were dead, and you'd been flown stateside, so I led some MPs to the site hoping to catch the bastards. That storage shed behind the contractor's motor pool was empty."

We'd tagged some ex-Blackwater men as possible actors in the Ali Baba operation and traced them to a construction company who'd hired them for private security. A tip had told us about the storage shed.

"What about the suspects?"

"Gone. Disappeared like a desert mirage. But one local laborer said he saw them the night after you were attacked. Screaming, cussing, guns drawn. He hid because he didn't know what they were going to do."

"How many?"

"He said three. We'd pegged two, Lucas and Hernández, but it stands to reason there would be a third, either working higher or lower. We know Lucas and Hernández are fired Blackwater employees and working independent."

"Did the laborer understand what they were saying?"

"Not really. He spoke very poor English. I was questioning him through an interpreter. He said someone had ripped them off."

"Who?"

The tension in Calvin's face eased into a cold smile. "The informant pointed at me. 'Black man,' he said. I understood those words well enough."

"They thought you robbed them?"

Calvin gave a humorless laugh. "Oh, the MPs jumped on that all right. The interpreter got him to explain that he didn't mean me, but someone like me. He thought they were accusing a black guy."

"That description doesn't help much."

"No," Calvin agreed. "Uncle Sam's definitely an equal opportunity employer. But what if the words they'd been screaming hadn't been black man but Blackman? You, Chief—the guy they knew was onto them. The guy I think they tried to kill earlier."

I wasn't buying it. "We were attacked by insurgents."

Calvin raised his hands, palms out as if pushing me into reconsidering. "Maybe. Maybe not. We must have been getting close to cracking the case. You think our perps couldn't have paid for a hit? Hell, they could easily get freelancers from a militia or even a legit Iraqi unit if the price was right."

I felt weak. A cold numbness grew in my belly. If what Calvin said was true, then the Iraqi insurgents in stolen uniforms who'd attacked the checkpoint had been targeting us. The men weren't on a random assault. They were hired assassins. Hired by Americans. And they'd killed Charlie Grigg and Ed Cuomo, two of my best buddies, and left me walking on a mechanical leg.

Calvin got up and poured more scotch from the bottle on my kitchen counter. "This guy who jumped you, did he say anything?"

"He accused me of taking something. Cash, I guess. He wanted the cash or the account numbers."

"What account numbers?"

"Hell, I don't know."

Calvin leaned against the counter, towering over me. Although he wore black jeans and a dark green golf shirt, his military bearing wasn't disguised. "Look, Chief, here's the way I see it. We got a tip on the storage shed. It sounded reasonable because the two guys we're onto perform private security for the construction company."

"The tip was your source," I reminded him.

"Yeah, and the little worm had been reliable since his prison days." Calvin shook his head. "But I think he conned me this time."

"What do you mean?"

"Someone knew we were going to search that shed and he emptied it. But I don't think that fact was shared with everyone in Ali Baba. While you were being taken out at the checkpoint, the loot was being moved. The attack on us was a ruse to give someone cover. Why move it if we were never supposed to get near it?"

"Aren't you arguing against your own theory? They got wind of our investigation, relocated their cache, and then we had the bad luck to be at the wrong place at the wrong time when the insurgents attacked."

"Okay, Chief. Then why does my witness see our suspects raising holy hell at the storage shed? Why's my grandmother got cat food she no longer needs? Why are you going to be pissing red for a week while your kidney heals?"

I felt sure Ethel Barkley's lockbox was the reason I'd been jumped, but I didn't have an answer for Calvin's other two questions. I saw the logic of his theory. "So, someone in the conspiracy betrays his partners and says we did it. We stole from the thieves before our official search of the premises."

"And if a hit had been planned, so much the better," Calvin said. "We're dead and can't argue otherwise."

"But how would we have smuggled their booty out? They had guards."

"Who better to know that anybody can be bought," Calvin argued. "Ain't nobody more suspicious than a thief. They'd just project onto us what they'd do." He arced his arm in a semicircle. "Look at this place. Damn, you drive up and it's bigger than the Plaza Hotel in New York. I know you're getting disability, but is anybody going to believe you can live like this?"

"Yeah," I said. "It's an old hotel and a converted hospital that was saved from the wrecking ball. What I pay in rent wouldn't get me a closet in Manhattan."

"And you opened a new business. That takes dough."

"How'd you know?"

"Same way I found your apartment. Google. Got your phone number from information, reverse-looked up your address, and checked new business licenses for Asheville. All from a computer in the Paterson library. I flew in tonight, rented a car, and pulled in your parking lot about ten minutes ahead of you. If I can do all that from a public library, what do you think our Blackwater swill friends are capable of?"

"Okay. You've made your point," I said. "But you've got to know something. A young woman was murdered in my office tonight and something I was holding for a client disappeared. Everything the guy who attacked me said can also apply to that case."

Calvin scowled. "But don't you see? It's got to be them. They just made a mistake."

"Maybe. And you've got to be careful not to force facts into your theory. My client warned me people were after the item I was keeping. I let her down, and I have to deal with that."

"What are you going to do?" Calvin asked.

"Tell the police what happened. They're investigating a local homicide, not an international conspiracy. My attacker could be their man."

Calvin balled his right hand into a fist and punched his left palm in frustration. "I don't know, Chief. I thought you and I could work this together—for Ed and Charlie." He looked down at my left leg stretched out from under the table. "And for what you've been through."

"We can do both. But the police need to be involved. They'll concentrate on their angle and we'll work ours." I thought about what Calvin had told me about his grandmother. "And I'll need to warn my partner. If someone's been watching me, then they might think she's got information."

Calvin's eyebrows lifted. "She?"

"Nakayla Robertson. She's an experienced insurance investigator."

He nodded thoughtfully, but I couldn't tell where those thoughts were leading.

After a few seconds of silence, he said, "Is there anything that could have set these bastards off, given them the impression you did rip them off?"

I stared at him, suddenly remembering he was a trained interrogator. "You don't think—"

"No, man," he interrupted. "You're so squeaky clean you make the Boy Scouts look subversive. But it ain't about what I think."

He was right. We had to put ourselves into the heads of our enemies. "I came into some money," I admitted. "Actually a lot of money."

"Mind if I ask how much?"

"Close to three million."

He whistled softly. "Where'd you land that kinda stake?"

"A lawsuit. My parents were killed in a wreck at the same time I was being airlifted out of Iraq. The driver of the moving truck that hit them had failed a drug test, but the company put him behind the wheel anyway."

Calvin laid a hand on my shoulder. "I'm sorry, brother. I really am. But you can see how it could look to someone who just saw bank accounts. Anything offshore?" His dark brown eyes were inquisitive, not suspicious.

"No." I paused, as if trying to come up with a helpful suggestion. "I did take a short vacation trip to the Caymans when my parents' settlement was finalized. And a trip to New York to talk to a family friend about investments." True, except the Cayman trip set up an offshore account for Nakayla and New York connected me with buyers of assets who could wire funds to the Cayman account. That information wasn't mine to share with anyone, but if the Ali Baba conspirators had tracked my movements, what other conclusion would they draw?

Calvin rolled his eyes. "Jesus, man, why couldn't you have gone to Disney World? Your trips are as good as a confession."

"I don't like talking mice."

"And now you've got an infestation of rats." He looked at his wristwatch. "You going to call the police tonight?"

"No. There's nothing for them to do. I'm sure the guy outside covered his tracks. I'm meeting the lead detective first thing in the morning."

Calvin returned to his chair and leaned across the table. "Look, Chief. Let's keep me out of this for now."

"Why? You're right about Ali Baba's possible connection. The police need to know that."

"But Ali Baba doesn't know I'm here. If they've got a tail on you, then I can spot them. We'll bring in the locals when we've got something to hand them. Otherwise, if I wind up in a police report, no telling who'll see it."

Calvin raised a good point, but I had to give Newland a reason for considering something so improbable as an Iraqi-based conspiracy murdering a woman in Asheville, North Carolina. "I'll tell him about your phone call to me. And that someone attacked me, but a car coming into the parking lot scared him off. That should be enough to put him in the game."

Calvin nodded. "I can live with that. And, believe me, living's no small task when dealing with these people."

I gestured to my sofa. "You need a place to crash?"

"Nah. Not worth the risk of being seen here in the morning. I'll find a cheap motel close by. What time you rolling out tomorrow?"

I looked at my kitchen clock. It was nearly midnight. "I'm going to see my client as soon as I get word she's available. Early, I hope."

"Give me the location. I've got GPS in the rental."

I went to the phonebook by the kitchen extension and looked up the address for Golden Oaks. "Need anything else?"

"I'm good for now," Calvin said.

"You carrying?"

"Oh, yeah. I checked a bag just so I could bring some friends." He lifted his pant leg and showed me a snub-nosed .32 pistol in a calf holster. "I left my serious girlfriend in the car. A little too warm to wear a jacket over my shoulder holster."

I thought about the permit to purchase a handgun that lay in the desk drawer of my bedroom. I'd gotten it a month ago from the Buncombe County Sheriff's Department after filling out the application and going through the five-day waiting period. I'd also been issued a permit to carry concealed. Tomorrow I'd put both of them to use.

"How will we stay in touch?" I asked.

"If I need you, I'll get to you. If you need me" —he paused, looked around the room—"you mind if I check the bedroom?"

"Go ahead." I followed him down the short hall.

He left the light off and pointed to the two windows over-looking the front of the apartment building. "If you want me, put those blinds halfway down. If you're in the car, park and leave the windows halfway down."

"And if it's raining?"

He laughed. "Then you'll get wet."

We walked back to the kitchen and living room area. "Have you let anybody in the Detachment know about the threats?"

"Yeah. I wired a report Saturday after I spotted my tail, and the word came down to consider it part of the hazards of the investigation. A couple of new men are working the Baghdad side, but I'm the only one in the states. We're stretched so thin nobody else will be assigned, unless I wind up dead."

"Not a good way to get new help."

"But now I've got the Chief on my side. You're still the best." He gave me a bear hug, and then slipped out the door, closing it before I could follow him into the hall. He left me with a lot to think about.

My first concern was for Nakayla. She could be a target just because of her close association with me. Late as the hour was, I called and woke her. I gave a condensed version of my conversation with Calvin and warned her to be careful. I promised to meet her at the office as soon as I finished with Ethel Barkley.

The other person I trusted was Nathan Armitage. He not only knew everything about Nakayla and me, he also ran western North Carolina's largest protective security firm. If Calvin and I were going up against Blackwater-trained operatives, I wanted more than the Asheville Police Department on my side. But, it was late and Nathan was still recuperating from a gunshot wound. He'd have to keep till morning.

I deadbolted my door and closed the blinds. Calvin's signal was like something out of an old spy movie. He must still be keeping his cell phone inoperable and untraceable. I'd be careful with what I said on mine.

I removed my leg and stripped to my underwear, too tired and sore to bother with pajamas. I slid between the cool sheets and hoped to fall asleep quickly.

Two images kept tormenting my mind: the body of Amanda Whitfield crumpled on my office floor like a child's discarded doll, and the swastika stamped on the lockbox, a symbol of death and destruction that made the Ali Baba conspirators look like shoplifters.

Sick or well, Ethel Barkley was going to give me the information I wanted.

Chapter Eight

I asked Ruth, the clerk on duty at the Golden Oak's front desk, to ring Ethel Barkley's apartment and tell her I'd arrived. Ruth had called at seven to let me know Ethel was being released from observation. If the woman thought my seven-thirty appearance to be a little early, she didn't comment, but immediately made the call. She probably knew Ethel well enough not to be surprised by anything the old lady might be up to.

My working day had started when I telephoned Nathan Armitage at six. He was awake, drinking coffee, and reading the Asheville *Citizen-Times* account of Amanda's murder. I'd told him I'd been attacked but I didn't want to get into it over the phone because some very sophisticated players were involved. He agreed to meet me at my office at ten.

I found Ethel Barkley standing outside her door waiting for me. The previous afternoon, she'd been wearing a housecoat. This Wednesday morning, at a time when most of her neighbors were probably still sleeping, she had on a lavender dress my great-grandmother would have called "Sunday-go-to-meetin'." She didn't look like a woman who had fainted the night before. I could see the welcoming smile fade from her face as she realized I was walking toward her empty-handed.

"Are you okay, Mrs. Barkley?"

"What happened?" Her voice shook. "Wouldn't they give it to you?"

"We need to talk." My harsh whisper frightened her.

"Do you want your money first?"

"The police will be here in less than an hour."

Her magnified eyes behind the glasses seemed to double in size. "The police? You went to the police?"

"They came to me. Now let's step back inside before someone else hears your business."

I gently took her arm and guided her into the apartment. Her weight, light as it was, fell against me, and I feared she might stumble before I could get her seated. My blunt statement about the police shocked her more than I'd intended, and I decided to proceed more delicately. I didn't want her fainting again.

I eased her down on her loveseat. "Would you like some water?"

"No." She took a deep breath and squared her frail shoulders. Wariness replaced the panic in her eyes. "Why the police?"

"Someone broke into my office last night and stole the lock-box. They murdered the night security guard, a young woman who was working two shifts to support her invalid husband."

Ethel Barkley shuddered and a sob caught in her throat. "No. They wouldn't have. Not after all these years."

"Who are they?"

"I don't know. They never came." She looked around the room as if seeing things beyond my senses. "Maybe now they have come. How could they have known I sent you?"

She and I may have been asking the same questions, but I for one couldn't pull the answers out of the air.

"The swastika, Mrs. Barkley. The one on the seal. I saw it."

"So?" She looked up at me without a trace of guilt.

"So? Well, the Nazis—"

"Nazis? What Nazis?" Then she made a small "O" with her mouth and got to her feet. "No. It's a good luck omen."

"Not for at least thirteen million people."

"*The Great Gatsby,*" she said, as if that explained everything. She walked to a bookshelf across the room.

I was ready to jump up and catch her, but her balance was steadier. She pulled out a green volume and flipped through the pages.

"Here it is," she said, and handed me the old book. "Read where it's underlined."

I studied the yellowed page. "The door that I pushed open, on the advice of an elevator boy, was marked 'The Swastika Holding Company,' and at first there didn't seem to be any one inside."

"What's The Swastika Holding Company?" I asked.

"In the story, it's owned by a Jewish man named Wolfsheim. A friend of Gatsby's."

"Jewish?"

"Mr. Fitzgerald said the swastika was just a good luck charm."

I flipped to the front, turned the flyleaf, and read Charles Scribner's Sons and a copyright date of 1925. I held a first edition of *The Great Gatsby* that was certainly worth a chunk of change. But I didn't know history well enough to place the adoption of the swastika by the Nazis with the publication of Fitzgerald's novel. The symbol was ancient, and before Hitler's rise to power, it had been used by many cultures. Ethel Barkley's assertion of its "good luck" power had merit, but the fascist dictator had tainted the symbol forever.

"Did F. Scott Fitzgerald write that in the book?"

"No. He told me himself."

I couldn't help but sound skeptical. "You spoke to F. Scott Fitzgerald?"

"Yes. Well, he was talking to some reporter about it when I was in his room."

I must have looked even more doubtful.

"At the Grove Park Inn," she said. "I worked on the fourth floor. Mr. Fitzgerald was in 441. A real gentleman. We'd talk sometimes." She frowned. "When that woman wasn't with him."

"His dollar woman?" I remembered Mrs. Barkley's reference to the woman who'd taught her to read palms.

"No. That was Laura Guthrie, his part-time secretary. I'm talking about that Texas hussy who threw herself at him. She's the one who sent him the gift he wouldn't accept."

"The gift that's in the lockbox?"

"Yes."

We'd finally gotten back to the most pressing topic.

"The police will want to know what's in it," I said.

"That's none of their business."

"It's part of a murder investigation. If there's jewelry or negotiable securities, then maybe someone will try to sell them. The police will be suspicious if you're secretive."

She seemed to ponder my point for a few seconds. Then, from out of the blue, she asked, "Would you like some tea?"

"No, thank you." I couldn't keep the exasperation out of my voice. "I'd really like to understand what's going on with the lockbox before the police arrive."

"Yes. Maybe I'd better brew a large pot." She headed for the kitchen and I had no choice but to follow. "Sorry," she said, "I don't have coffee. Upsets my stomach. And I think better with a cup of tea." She held an electric kettle under the kitchen faucet and filled it. "My son bought me this. I got too forgetful. Left the burner on in my house and the kettle melted. Got so hot the kitchen counter started smoldering. Lord, it would have burst into flames if the cat hadn't come back in the bedroom wailing to beat the band. I was listening to Rush Limbaugh. You like his program?"

"No. I've never really listened to him."

She set the kettle on the power pad and flipped it on. "Me neither. After that day. I figure he nearly got me killed. My brother Hugh would have liked him. Hugh lived and breathed politics." She pulled a porcelain teapot and box of teabags from a cabinet. "All I have is green so that will have to do."

"I don't care for any," I repeated. "Are there valuables in the lockbox that can be sold?"

"Hugh was the one who was so excited when he heard I met Mr. Fitzgerald. He bought me his book so I could get it autographed. Did you see?"

"No."

"Well, he did it. I felt sorry for him. His wife going batty and all. She was up in Baltimore that summer and he was down here for his health, or so he said. He was bad to drink. The bellboys would smuggle in beer and the management didn't like all the carrying on."

"What year was that?"

"1935."

The same year as her alleged crime, I thought. "And you worked at the Grove Park Inn?" Nakayla and I'd been up to the mammoth stone hotel and spa a couple of times for a sunset drink. The resort dated to the early 1900s and had lured the famous and the infamous to Asheville for generations. Now the photograph of the girl in front of the stone wall that I'd seen in Ethel Barkley's memory box made sense: the picture of her had been taken beside a section of the inn.

The old woman gave a wistful smile that shed years from her face. "I was eighteen. It was my first real job. Even though I was only changing sheets and cleaning rooms, to be around such glamorous people set a girl's fancies flying."

I wondered if those fancies had included the author. "And there's something else in the lockbox that belonged to Fitzgerald?"

Her worn yellow teeth bit her lower lip as she nodded. "Hugh wanted to know what Mr. Fitzgerald was writing and who he was seeing. My brother was nearly seventeen years older and I adored him. As a young man, he'd loved the Jazz Age, the smart people who came in by train, the dancing, and the parties. He made friends with everyone in the grand hotels. Then the stock market crashed."

"Did your brother lose a lot?"

"No. Hugh didn't have that kind of money. He was a lawyer and helped support Mother and me. Our father had died in a railroad accident when I was thirteen. Hugh saw what the Depression had done to this town. Even my high school had to close for awhile."

The boiling kettle cut off and Mrs. Barkley poured the hot water over three teabags dangling in the pot.

"The tourists still came," I said.

"Yes. But their money stayed in New York and Chicago banks. Development stopped. Hugh said Roosevelt used the crisis to grab power. Then he recognized the government of those Russian Communists and turned our country away from God."

The woman was zoning out again. I wondered if Detective Newland would have any better luck getting a coherent statement.

"What does that have to do with F. Scott Fitzgerald?"

She looked at me with surprise. "Everything. Hugh said Mr. Fitzgerald had defined an age and maybe he could be enlisted to bring the country to its senses."

I began to see a glimmer of logic in her rambling. "Your brother wanted you to spy on Fitzgerald? Get something to use against him?"

"No," she said sharply. "Hugh wanted to know what he was thinking. Mr. Fitzgerald would leave papers out in his room or keep talking with guests when I was present. I told Hugh I thought he didn't care much about politics one way or the other. Then partway through the summer, Mr. Fitzgerald checked out. I think he went back to see Zelda in Baltimore or to New York. I cleaned his room and found a large envelope that had fallen behind his bed. It was filled with manuscript pages. There was no address on the envelope, so I didn't know if he meant to mail it or used it to keep the pages together."

"What did you do?"

"I took it to Hugh. I expected him to read it and give it back." She took two cups and saucers from a shelf and poured from the pot. "Let's sit down."

I took the unwanted tea without protest and joined her at the table where yesterday she'd studied my palm. At least there were no loose leaves to read at the bottom of my cup.

"Your brother didn't return it, did he?"

"No," she whispered. "I begged him to, but Hugh said if it was that important, then Mr. Fitzgerald wouldn't have left it. He said it was a story, and just because Mr. Fitzgerald didn't want it, didn't mean it wouldn't be valuable some day."

"You must have gotten it back if it went into your lockbox."

She took a sip of tea and then hesitated before speaking. "That was Hugh. He kept a safe-deposit box under my name. There were some financial difficulties at the time and he didn't want his name to appear."

"Then why didn't you give the envelope back?"

"Because Hugh kept the key. When Mr. Fitzgerald returned in a few weeks, he asked if I'd found any papers in his room. I had to say no or he would have thought I was a thief."

He would have been right, I thought. "And this all happened in the summer of 1935?"

"Yes. Mr. Fitzgerald shed himself of the Texas woman. He moved in and out of the Grove Park a couple times. The next summer he returned and put Zelda in Highlands Hospital. I was courting my husband Terrence by then and working a different part of the Grove Park."

"What did your husband do?"

"He was an accountant. I met him through Hugh."

I thought about Ethel Barkley's net worth. "He must have been a good one."

"He was smart. In the forties, we bought a little place on Sunset Mountain close to the Grove Park. When I sold it two years ago, I couldn't believe the price."

"And you have other investments, I'm sure."

She shook her head. "No. But the house brought enough that I can stay here the rest of my days." She turned up her palm. "Even my lifeline doesn't go on forever."

I was confused. How much money had her house brought? "Mr. Tennant at the bank told me he could find a better rate of return on your CDs."

Her expression darkened. "Mr. Tennant should mind his own affairs. That's money in trust, not mine." She looked away and I barely heard her whisper, "Has the time come?"

"Mrs. Barkley, you said they never came. Who are they?"

She kept silent.

"Were they friends of your brother?"

"I'll know them when the time comes."

There was that phrase again: when the time comes.

"Mrs. Barkley, you told me you're ninety and your lifeline doesn't go on forever. What will happen to the trust and your lockbox when you're gone?"

She set her cup on her saucer. "My son and nephew will take it, and I don't know what to tell them. Hugh didn't say." Her tears started again. "But I don't want Mr. Fitzgerald's papers found as part of my property. You've got to get them back to their rightful owner."

"Did anyone else know about them? Your children?"

She shook her head. "Terrence and I had a boy and a girl. Sarah died when she was ten. Polio. One of the last cases before that Dr. Salk invented the vaccine. My son Terry's retired in Charlotte. We wanted more children, but my husband was killed in a car wreck."

"Did your brother have children?"

"Only one son. He's four years younger than Terry. My brother didn't marry till he was over forty. Hewitt was born during the war."

I felt a tingle down my spine. "Hewitt?"

"Yes. But Hugh couldn't have told him anything. He died before his child was born."

"Was your brother named Hugh Donaldson?"

She smiled. "You know about him?"

A knock came from the door. Detective Newland must have arrived.

Ethel Barkley glanced over her shoulder and then back to me. She lowered her voice. "Was this a test?"

Chapter Nine

I went with Ethel Barkley to her apartment door. Detective Newland and another officer he introduced as Tuck Efird stood on the threshold. Efird looked to be in his late thirties, a good twenty years Newland's junior.

"How long have you been here, Sam?" Newland asked.

"Long enough to tell Mrs. Barkley about the theft of her property and that she needs to cooperate in any way she can."

"And I certainly will," she exclaimed. "Terrible about that woman. Just terrible." She stepped back to give the two men room to enter. "Would you gentlemen like tea?"

"No, thank you," they replied in unison.

"Fine. It'll just take a minute."

I winked at Newland. "Wash your hands."

He wasn't amused. "I think we're going to have to compare notes on this one."

"Yeah. She's a live one all right. I'll be at my office." Then the thought struck me. "Am I okay to return?"

Newland nodded. "Crime lab went over everything. Tape might still be up, but you're clear to enter. If you notice something any of us missed, call me."

I shook his hand. "Thanks. We'll catch up later." As I stepped into the hall, I called, "Goodbye, Mrs. Barkley. I'll be in touch." I didn't wait for a response. She was Newland's problem now.

I glanced at my wristwatch. Five after eight. Newland had gotten there earlier than he said. I wasn't planning on being at the office until nine, and the strange conversation with Ethel Barkley had been unsettling. The woman couldn't be dismissed as a nutcase, but just when I thought she was making sense, she would fly off on some tangent. What was history and what was delusion? The oldest and possibly sharpest mind in the building might help me navigate through her maze of fact and fantasy.

A plaque on the door read "The Mayor." I knocked below it.

"Come in," said a familiar, raspy voice.

Harry Young sat in his customary spot on his sofa with his wheelchair parked close at hand and his crutches within reach. Young in name only, Harry approached his one-hundred-and-a-half birthday next month. At his age, he'd reverted to a preschooler's arithmetic when birthdays are proudly calculated in fractions.

Like me, Harry had lost a leg—the right one in a bear trap when he was twelve. Eighty-eight and a half years later, his ancient skin had grown so thin he could no longer wear a prosthesis, and he hobbled around his apartment as best he could. But his mind was as sharp as a new razor, a database of Asheville's history that Nakayla and I'd already drawn upon to discover her sister's killer.

Harry looked up from his morning paper. From the shake of his head, I knew he'd read about Amanda Whitfield's murder.

"What happened, Sam?" He patted the cushion beside him, inviting me to sit.

I shook his thin, dry hand and then twisted against the arm-rest to face him. "We don't know. She must have interrupted someone who was searching our new office. The police have determined that the cleaning crew came through about seven-thirty. I returned around eight-thirty. The medical examiner's report won't be completed for a day or two, but preliminary indications suggest she was killed shortly after eight. That matches the schedule of her rounds."

Harry licked his cracked lips and turned away. "As long as I've lived, the cruelty of human beings never ceases to amaze me."

We sat quietly for a few seconds as Harry must have let his thoughts wander back through his century. "And then," he added, "I never cease to be amazed at our capacity for kindness. What a mixed-up species we are."

"You won't get any argument from me."

The old man tapped the front page of his paper. "With this going on, why are you here?"

I had to smile at his insightfulness. "I need your help, of course."

He pushed the paper aside and his eyes brightened. Nothing pleased Harry more than to feel useful. "I don't know what I can do, but just tell me."

"This is between us. Don't even tell Captain."

He nodded. "Mum's the word."

"I'd been asked to bring the contents of a safe-deposit box to Ethel Barkley."

"Ethel? She tied up in this?"

"I don't know. The contents turned out to be a lockbox. I brought it back to my office, and it was the only thing taken."

"No fooling. Who'd be prying into Ethel's belongings?"

"We don't know if anybody was. Her lockbox was the easiest and fastest thing to take. But we can't ignore the possibility it was the target."

"Have you told her?" he asked.

"Yes, and she's talking to the police now."

"Well, what do you want from me?"

I leaned closer. "Tell me about her. Can I believe what she tells me?"

"Depends." He chuckled. "Shortly after she came here, she read my palm. She said I'd live to be ninety-two. I laughed at her because I was ninety-eight."

"Ethel was right. You lived to be ninety-two."

Harry slapped his thigh. "By God, that I did. So maybe there's more truth in what she says than I give her credit for."

"She told me she learned to read palms from a woman at the Grove Park Inn."

"No reason she'd make that up." He looked down at his wrinkled hands. "Ethel sets a lot of stock by what she sees in these lines. And I remember the Grove Park used to have people whose job was to entertain the tourists."

"She said this woman's name was Laura Guthrie and that she was F. Scott Fitzgerald's secretary."

Harry scratched the side of his face. "I knew a Laura Hearne folks said knew Fitzgerald. I think she wrote something about him, but that was years ago."

"And Ethel worked at the Grove Park?"

Harry shook his head. "I got no call to deny it. Back in the Depression, the hotels were about the only places offering good steady work."

I remembered Ethel Barkley's remark about her brother's perspective on Roosevelt and on Asheville's hard times. "Did you know her brother, Hugh Donaldson?"

"I knew of him." He laughed. "We didn't exactly run in the same circles. He was a lawyer and I worked in the Biltmore dairy, mostly looking at the south end of northbound cows."

"Seems like an attorney would be indistinguishable in that crowd. How come you remember him?"

Harry straightened as if I'd offended his pride. "Just because I worked in a barn didn't mean I couldn't read the newspaper. Hugh Donaldson was a hotshot defense attorney and handled some of Asheville's biggest cases."

"Really? His son's a defense attorney."

Harry shrugged. "Don't know nothing about the boy, but I guess he must be cut from the same cloth."

"Ethel said her brother was killed when his son was a baby."

"Yep. I recall that well enough. Car wreck. Hugh Donaldson and Terrence Barkley skidded off Macon in an ice storm. Both died instantly."

"Ethel's brother and husband died in the same accident?"

"Yep. Hell of a thing. A couple of days before Christmas. Must have been 1944, because the war was still going on. They'd been at a benefit for the Red Cross or something like that."

"In Macon, Georgia?"

Harry squinted at me. "Georgia? No, Macon's the road that runs up Sunset Mountain to the Grove Park Inn. Funny what you remember. The newspaper said their car wound up crashed against a tree just a block from Terrence Barkley's house. Poor Ethel probably heard the crash." He looked at his palms again. "What good's all the tomfoolery of reading the future if you can't see something like that coming?"

I didn't have an answer. But if Ethel Barkley had nearly five million dollars and a lockbox worth killing for, then someone had planned her future very well.

I got up. "If you think of something about Ethel or her brother, would you let me know? No matter how insignificant it might seem to you."

"That's all I do is sit and think. I could use a little action."

"Then keep an eye on Ethel. There's something not right about her story." Her words "They never came" resounded in my head. Who was she talking about and did Amanda Whitfield's body mean someone had returned? Was the old lady in danger? "Harry, I don't want you to breathe a word about the lockbox, but tell Captain that Ethel could be at risk."

"That true?" He frowned.

"Yes, and until we find Amanda Whitfield's killer, Captain should watch over her. He's the one who had me see her in the first place, so he'll not be surprised at the request."

Harry's face brightened with a broad grin. "Captain's the man for the job. I can help him organize it."

"Good. And you take care."

I left Harry energized with his task. The Golden Oaks residents would soon be taking strolls up and down Ethel Barkley's hallway in seemingly natural wanderings.

Somewhere my own security guard, Warrant Officer Calvin Stuart, should have his eye on me. I hoped he'd be as effective as Captain's brigade.

◇◇◇

Nakayla and I had settled into our office conference positions, she on the sofa and I in an armchair. She listened to my recap of the conversations with Ethel Barkley and Harry Young without interrupting. When I finished, she sat quietly, her brow furrowed and her eyes locked on some image in her mind.

"So, what do you think?" I asked.

She cocked her head and gave me a critical appraisal. "You've spent fifteen minutes talking about Ethel Barkley's lockbox and not one second about a man holding you at gunpoint. If your friend Calvin hadn't shown up, Nathan and I could be planning your funeral."

"Maybe I don't like to think about it."

"Maybe you'd better."

She was right, but I didn't have any ideas as to how to pursue a faceless assailant who left no clues. My only threads came from Ethel Barkley and the names she had given—names of dead people. Tracking them would be an exhumation of information.

"Did you see Calvin this morning?" she asked.

"No. But that doesn't mean anything. If he's doing his job right, I won't see him."

"How much are you going to tell Newland?"

I'd been mulling that question since last night. "It's nine-thirty. Nathan will be here at ten and I'll give him the complete story. Newland and I need to compare notes on our conversations with Ethel Barkley, but I'll honor Calvin's request to omit him from any official report. Newland will be privy only to Calvin's warning phone call."

Her mouth scrunched in disapproval. "You sure that's a good idea?"

"Newland has his plate full investigating Amanda Whitfield's death, and I don't think the Asheville Police Department is prepared to go up against covert-trained mercenaries."

"And you and Calvin are?" Her sarcasm left no doubt as to her opinion.

"No. But we've got Nathan Armitage and a secret weapon."

"And what would that be?"

I glanced around the room as if looking for eavesdroppers, and then I slid onto the sofa beside her. "You," I whispered. I leaned in to give her a kiss, but she hopped up, leaving me smooching the air.

"Then I'd better get to work researching the names Ethel Barkley gave you." She stopped in her office doorway and turned around. "Don't you think it's odd that Ethel's nephew is on our floor and the day we meet him, his aunt's lockbox disappears?"

"Yes, but he's a lawyer and this building is crawling with them. I'm sure he didn't see me bring the box up."

"Someone else could have told him," Nakayla said.

"Maybe. But then being on our floor would still be a coincidence."

Nakayla folded her arms across her chest. "Coincidence? Aren't you the guy who told me a coincidence should always be the last explanation accepted?"

I knew Nakayla didn't like Hewitt Donaldson. I hadn't dismissed him from my consideration, but the police had already taken his statement and would be checking his alibi. "The fact that he and Cory DeMille were still in the building works in their favor. I find it hard to believe they would calmly wait in their office for over an hour after committing a murder a few doors down the hall."

"And wouldn't a crafty lawyer anticipate your reaction? Use it to eliminate himself from suspicion?"

She had a point. I stood and put on my sport coat.

"Where are you going?" she asked.

"To pay a visit on our neighbor. I want Hewitt Donaldson to know we're concerned about his welfare."

I walked down the hall and around the corner. His door held a window of frosted glass with a brass plate mounted on the wood beneath it that read "Hewitt Donaldson, Attorney-at-Law." I turned the knob without knocking and walked into a reception room about the size of our central office.

Behind a desk, a woman typed furiously at a computer and spoke without looking up. "Can I help you?"

From the angle of her head, I couldn't tell if she was young or middle-aged. Straight jet-black hair covered the profile of her face and draped over her shoulder.

"I'd like to see Mr. Donaldson," I said.

"Impossible. He's due in court in ten minutes, and if I don't finish typing his notes, he might as well walk in there buck-naked."

"Then the jury would see he has nothing to hide."

Her fingers froze and she barked out a laugh so loud the glass pane in the door rattled. "Jesus, God, don't ever say that. Hewitt'll do it."

She swiveled in her chair and smiled at me. Her face was narrow and coated with white makeup, except for the dark eyeliner accenting her blue eyes. If she was going for a look to startle clients, she succeeded.

"Hewitt'll do it," I repeated. "Catchy phrase."

She turned back to her computer. "Yeah. Too bad it won't fit on his license plate."

"What's he got now?"

She said, "N, O, T, hyphen, G, I, L, hyphen, T."

I smiled. "How foolish of me to even ask."

"Now if you'll excuse me," she said, and hunched over her keyboard.

"Two-minute warning," Hewitt Donaldson bellowed from somewhere down the hall behind her.

The free-for-all atmosphere of the office was contagious.

"Sorry," I shouted. "My fault. I'm distracting her."

"You're as crazy as he is," witchy woman muttered.

I heard a door open and footsteps pad down the hall. Hewitt Donaldson bounded into the room. He held a pair of black dress shoes in his left hand and a briefcase in his right. His long gray hair was pulled back in a ponytail, and his dark blue suit, white shirt, and perfectly knotted burgundy tie could have clothed a corporate lawyer for Exxon.

"Sam, what's up? Have the police arrested someone?" He plopped down in a chair along the wall and started putting on his shoes.

"No, they haven't. I thought I'd check in and make sure they didn't hold you all night. How's your paralegal?"

"Cory's not here. That's why things are crazy this morning. We've got closing arguments, and I foolishly told her we'd be all right without her. The police finished with us about ten-thirty, but her fiancé's plane still hadn't landed. They couldn't get off the ground in Charlotte because of thunderstorms. Hell, might have been two in the morning before he landed."

"Well, you look good."

He tapped his head with a finger. "Psychology. The whole case I've dressed like a model for Good Will, but today I want that jury to know Hewitt Donaldson is attired for a come-to-Jesus session. I'm walking my client down the aisle and turning him over to their wisdom and compassion. The D.A.'s gonna look like he's always looked, but Hewitt Donaldson and his message will be something special." He tied his shoe with a flourish.

"Is that a trick you learned from your father?" I asked.

The change in his expression came so swiftly I felt like I was suddenly looking at a different person. His jaw tensed and his dark eyes bored into me. "What do you know about my father?" The challenge in his voice rippled through the room, and I heard the clicks of the receptionist's keyboard abruptly halt.

"Nothing," I said. "I was talking to someone about last night and mentioned you'd been working in your office. The person said you were a lawyer just like your father."

Donaldson jumped to his feet, one shoe on and one shoe off. "I'm not like my father. Never have been and never will be." He raised his hand, a trembling finger pointing at my chest. "My father's death was the best thing that ever happened to me because if he hadn't died, there's a good chance I'd be in jail for killing him."

The vehemence of his words and the passion with which he spit them out left me speechless. I just stared at him. He breathed heavily, like a sprinter at the end of a hundred-yard dash. He looked from my face to his pointing finger and blinked, as if surprised by the sight. His hand fell to his side.

"Sorry. I owe you a beer and civil conversation. I'm upset. About last night. About not being ready this morning." He sat and pulled on the second shoe. "Shirley, hit print and give me whatever you've culled from my notes. I'll make it work."

The woman, who looked no more like a Shirley than I did, punched a couple keystrokes and the printer behind her whirred to life.

I felt my cell phone vibrate on my belt. "Good luck with your closing argument," I said. "Maybe we can grab that beer sometime."

"Yeah," he said, without looking up from his shoes. "We'll do that."

Outside in the hall, I recognized Harry Young's number.

"Hi, Harry," I said.

"Sam, this is Harry." The old fellow had a little trouble understanding caller ID.

"Yes. How are you?" I kept walking to my office.

"Good. Say, I remembered something after you left about Hugh Donaldson's car wreck."

"What was it?"

"Hugh and Ethel's husband had been over in Hendersonville at a Christmas party."

"So they'd been drinking," I guessed.

"No. The newspaper had been clear about that. Like I told you, it was organized by the Red Cross."

"Okay. What was so special about it?"

"Maybe nothing. But it was a party at the work camp over there." Harry paused as if I was supposed to know what he meant.

"A migrant work camp in December?"

Harry cleared his raspy voice. "No. A German work camp. Hendersonville had a POW prison outside of town. Hugh and Terrence had been visiting the captured soldiers."

Instantly Ethel Barkley's explanation of the swastika as a good luck charm lost all credibility.

What had I gotten myself into?

Chapter Ten

"One, we have a mysterious lockbox with a swastika. Two, a son who despises his father and works next to the office where a guard was murdered and the lockbox stolen." Nakayla raised the fingers of her right hand one at a time as she ticked off each point. "Three, the father who died in 1944 after attending a party for German POWs, and four, the father's sister who now has nearly five million dollars and knows a secret about the missing lockbox she wants to keep hidden." Nakayla unfolded her pinkie and held her open palm in front of my face. "And, last but not least, a gang of thieves in Iraq who think you've ripped off their fortune, who probably know you've set up an offshore account, and will torture you before killing you. Am I leaving anything out?"

I forced a grin. "Don't forget Ethel Barkley says I have a long lifeline."

"Right. This from a woman who worries about the ghost of F. Scott Fitzgerald."

"I guess that about sums it up. What have you learned in the last ten minutes while I was dancing with Donaldson?"

Nakayla shook her head in disbelief. "Other than my partner might as well have a target on his back?" She glanced down at a notepad in her lap. "I searched the Internet for Laura Guthrie and Laura Hearne and found Laura Guthrie Hearne. She was described as having briefly been a part-time secretary to Fitzgerald."

"Good. So there's some truth to Ethel's statements."

"Yes. An article by her in the December 1964 issue of *Esquire* is mentioned as well as a book by some guy named Tony Buttitta entitled *The Lost Summer: A Personal Memoir of F. Scott Fitzgerald.*"

"Can we get them?"

"The Pack Library should have them."

"What about the authors?"

"I'm sure they're both deceased," Nakayla said.

"Harry's not."

Her brown complexion darkened. "Right. I'll see what I can dig up. Maybe the Grove Park Inn has a staff historian who can confirm Ethel's story."

"Sounds like a good excuse for a drink on the Inn's terrace," I said. "What about Hugh Donaldson?"

"I was just getting started when you came back with Harry's German POW news. Hugh Donaldson and Asheville on Google got over twenty-five thousand hits. I added lawyer and it dropped to fifteen thousand, but lawyer's a common word and not specific enough. I'll need to get a more targeted database."

"Did you try Hugh Donaldson in combination with Nazi?"

Nakayla rolled her eyes. "Now why would I do that? You just got the information from Harry. I'm not a mind reader, especially of someone who has such a weak transmitter."

I'd learned not to get in a putdown match with her. She beat me every time.

A knock on the door saved me from needing a clever comeback. Nathan Armitage entered.

"Good morning." A sheen of perspiration coated his pale face. He used both hands to carry an oversized brown leather satchel. As soon as he stepped inside, he set it on the floor.

"What have you got in there?" I asked. "Barbells?"

Nathan snapped his right index finger up to his lips and shook his head. I shut up and cut my eyes to Nakayla.

"The poor guy just got out of the hospital, Sam. Give him a hand."

Nathan winked at her and closed the door behind him. "We bought some extra hard drives for the company, and I thought you could use a few. Heavy suckers. You can never have enough data storage." He flipped the releases for the two latches and they sprang back with loud clicks.

"Thanks," I said, not sure what game we were playing.

Nakayla went to her office and returned with a pen and legal pad. "You can bet I'll be the one keeping everything organized." She handed the pen and paper to Nathan as she spoke.

She and I stood beside him as he wrote three words: BUGS —KEEP TALKING.

"I spoke with Detective Newland this morning," I said. "I don't think he has any leads."

Nathan sighed. "I didn't get home till three this morning. Amanda's husband and mother are heartbroken." The pain came through his voice. He wasn't acting. He pulled a silver case out of the leather satchel and silently flipped open its latches. Then he extracted a black box from a foam rubber liner. Other pieces of electronic gear lay in form-fitting cavities.

"I've hired a nurse to stay with them," he continued. "At least until we figure what the next step will be." The box was a couple inches thick and the height and width were slightly larger than his hand. He pressed a button on the bottom and a small light on the top began flashing red pulses. He moved forward and the frequency increased from about one every second to rapid fire. When he reached the phone on the end table, the light burned steadily.

Nathan held up one finger and moved past us into my office. "The funeral probably won't be before Saturday since the medical examiner still has the body." The light started blinking again, and then glowed solid red over my phone. Nathan held up two fingers.

"We'd like to go," Nakayla said.

"That's kind of you." Nathan returned across the reception area into Nakayla's office. Again, the indicator light stayed red over her phone. Nathan clicked the device off. "The drives all work with firewire so they're interchangeable between your laptops. And they're password encrypted. You can each have one behind your dock."

Nathan took the antisurveillance device and knocked it into Nakayla's phone, forcing the receiver off the cradle. "Oops. Sorry." He picked up the instrument and popped off the front of the earpiece. He slipped his finger inside and pried out a black object the size of a nickel. Cupping it in his palm, he walked to the electronics case, lifted out a dull gray cylinder no bigger than a bicycle grip, unscrewed the top, and dropped in the object.

Nathan no longer bothered with conversation, but performed the identical procedure with the other phones. Each one yielded the same eavesdropping bug. Then he took a larger piece of equipment, adjusted some dials on its face, and walked the perimeter of all the rooms, paying particular attention to the wall sockets and lighting instruments. When he was satisfied, he turned off the hardware and relaxed.

"Okay. We're clean, but there must be a relay transmitter somewhere." He walked to the window overlooking Pack Square and scanned the streets. "I don't see a van or car with an unusual antenna."

"What made you think we were bugged?" I asked.

"You. You didn't want to go into detail over the phone, and you said they were sophisticated." He gestured toward the three capsules. "Judging from the electronics, you're tangling with a formidable foe."

Nakayla sighed. "Not exactly the first case I'd been hoping for."

"We should turn these transmitters over to Newland," I said. "Amanda could have interrupted someone planting the devices."

"Or the phone man could have done it," Nakayla said. "He was in yesterday morning."

"Pull the work order he left us and get his name," I said. "And we'd better check the connector room on this floor where he activated the lines."

Nathan sat in one of the armchairs. "Tell me everything and I'll try to help with a game plan."

I went through all of the events: last night's gunman, Calvin's surprise appearance, the strange conversation with Ethel Barkley, Harry's memories, and the reaction of Hewitt Donaldson. Nakayla filled in the details about Laura Guthrie Hearne and the initial verification of Ethel's claim to have known F. Scott Fitzgerald.

"When are you going to see Newland?" Nathan asked.

"No set time," I said. "He doesn't know I've got new information, and I wanted to talk to you first."

Nathan touched the tips of his fingers together under his chin and thought for a moment. "My advice is to see him immediately. We don't know if we're dealing with one case or two. I understand your friend Calvin's wish to work unfettered by the local authorities, but I don't want Newland and his boys stumbling into something unprepared."

"Neither do I."

"So, what exactly is our case?" Nakayla posed the question in a manner that told me she wanted a serious answer.

"I can tell you what's not our case," I said. "Amanda Whitfield's murder."

Nathan nodded. "As much as the police like you, they can't have you second-guessing them. That one's theirs."

"But we can try to recover our client's property."

Nakayla slid forward on the sofa and pointed her finger at my chest. "Our only case is keeping you alive." Fire sparkled in her eyes. "Mrs. Barkley's lockbox doesn't even come close."

"No one wants me to stay alive more than I do. We've got to flush them out in the open if we have any hope of catching them. I know how these Ali Baba people think. They're crafty, merciless, and greedy. Their greed might be their undoing."

"Which makes you little more than bait," Nakayla argued.

"If I hide, then we don't know where they are. But if I'm openly pursuing something, then they'll want it too."

"What if they have it?" she asked.

"Depending upon what it is, they could be even more curious." I thought about the three electronic surveillance devices sitting neutralized in Nathan's special containers. "If someone was monitoring Nakayla and me this morning, he heard us talk about Ethel Barkley's stolen lockbox and five million dollars. That's enough to pique anyone's interest. We know from the bank manager her funds are in rolling CDs but our enemies don't."

"Doesn't putting that much money in CDs strike you as unusual?" Nathan asked.

"Not if access to them is more important than yield."

Nakayla had taken the legal pad and pen and started making notes. "I'd like to know if she owns them outright or if there's a more complex structure."

"Like what?" I asked.

"I don't know. Some sort of trust or tax shelter that keeps that amount of money off the radar screen."

Nathan scratched the side of his face and mulled over Nakayla's point. "There might be a way to look into that. Ethel's husband was an accountant and her brother was a lawyer. Put them together and you've got a license to steal."

"How would we find out?" I asked.

"A probated will is a public document. Unless Hugh Donaldson was the proverbial cobbler without shoes, he should have had his affairs in order. The same for his brother-in-law."

Another family member leapt to my mind. "Would Hewitt have had access to those papers?"

"Sure," Nathan said. "His mother probably kept a copy. We should check on that as well."

I got to my feet. "Good. Then we agree. We'll focus on keeping me alive—"

"Amen," Nakayla interjected.

"By pursuing Ethel's lockbox and the story behind it. Nakayla, you head up the research and Nathan can follow the legal trail and keep us bug free."

"I'll see if I can find a relay transmitter and then leave the detectors," he said. "You'd better sweep your homes as well." He picked up one of the cylinders holding a surveillance mike. "Let me keep this. Give the others to Newland when you assure him you're staying clear of his murder inquiry."

"And Calvin Stuart?" I asked.

Nathan shrugged. "You know him. I don't. Play it as you see best." He paused and his eyes narrowed. "But if you keep him out of the information you give Newland, then be careful not to share anything with Calvin that you learn in confidence from the police. If all this wraps up in one neat package, you don't want to be the guy in the middle who played favorites. And you sure don't want to be the guy in the middle who winds up dead."

Nathan stood and walked to his satchel. "So, I got you a little business gift." He bent down and pulled out a pistol. A bright red bow encircled the barrel. "I know Nakayla likes her .25 Colt, but I thought you'd want something with a little more horsepower."

I took the gun. The balance felt good and the weight light.

"A Kimber Ultra Carry II," Nathan said. "I prefer it for concealment. Less than five inches tall and weighs a little over a pound. Small, sweet, and deadly. The clip holds only seven rounds but the forty-five caliber silvertips have the stopping power to get the job done." He reached back in the satchel. "But just in case, here's an extra magazine and two boxes of ammo. I also got you a Galco shoulder rig that you can exchange if it's not comfortable. I like it because the gun's horizontal under your arm. You can draw it quicker."

"This is too much, Nathan. I can't accept it."

"Of course you can." He patted me on the back. "Especially if you ever want a referral out of my company." He stretched out the double loops of the harness with both hands. "Slip these on and we'll adjust it. The gun's under your left arm and the extra magazine fits in a sleeve below your right."

The rig fit well, and when I put on my sport coat, only a slight bulge on my left side gave any indication that more than my ribs lay underneath.

Nathan stepped back and admired his creation. "Looks sharp, doesn't he?"

"Like he's ready for the private-eye episode of Project Runway," Nakayla said. "A regular Tim Gunn."

I buttoned my jacket. "Let's not get carried away. The cover of GQ will suffice."

Nathan turned serious. "Both clips are full, but I didn't load a round into the chamber. I belong to a pistol club that has a practice range off the road to Weaverville. I gave them your name for a guest pass. I don't want the first time you fire it to be a life or death situation."

"I'd as soon that day never came," I said.

"Me either." Nakayla handed me our copy of the phone work order. "The installer's name was Vince Freese."

I folded the sheet and slipped it in the inside pocket of my jacket. "I'll give it to Newland, although I doubt the guy had anything to do with the bugging."

"Right now we can't rule out anybody or anything," Nathan said. "So watch your back."

I patted the pistol under my coat. "Don't worry. I'm armed and dangerous."

"That's exactly why I'm worried," Nakayla said. "When you get overconfident, then you are dangerous—to yourself."

Chapter Eleven

"Well, I don't know whose tale is stranger, yours or Ethel Barkley's." Detective Newland rocked back on the rear legs of his chair and folded his arms across his chest.

We sat opposite each other at a table in one of the police department's interview rooms. Newland's partner, Tuck Efird, leaned against the wall by the door, a bemused smile playing across his lips.

I ignored him and focused on Newland. "The woman may be a little dingy, but enough kernels of truth seemed to be sprinkled through her story that I'm not dismissing anything out of hand."

"Especially when you've got a hand with such great Napoleonic lines," Efird said.

I glared at him.

"Hey, that's what she told us," Newland said. "And then you throw in Ali Baba and the Forty Thieves and a Nazi treasure chest."

I tapped the surveillance mikes sitting on the table. A larger transmitter rested beside them, the device Nathan found attached to our junction box. "These didn't come from Radio Shack."

Efird's smile broadened into a grin. He walked behind me and gently squeezed my shoulders with his long fingers. "Relax, Sam. We tease the guys we like. But I have to tell you, this is the most bizarre set of circumstances I've seen."

I tilted my head back till I could look him in the eye. "The only thing I see is Amanda Whitfield's body. I don't give a damn how bizarre the circumstances might seem to you."

Efird jerked his hands from my shoulders like I'd become electrified. The front legs of Newland's chair hit the floor with a bang.

The older detective leaned over the table. His blood-shot eyes held mine with a pained look.

"Sorry," I said. "That was uncalled for. I know you want her killer as much as I do."

Newland's gaze went to Efird behind me. Whatever response his partner gave him must have been a signal to let it go. "Okay. Now what about this army buddy. How's he fit in?"

The detective had zeroed in on the point I was least comfortable discussing. I didn't want to lie to the man. He was counting on me to do everything I could to help him.

"Calvin gave me the warning when he came stateside. He'll work the case his way, but I don't know how much support he'll be able to give us."

"Does he know about the attack on you?"

"Yes."

"And Amanda's murder?"

"I've briefed him on what we know."

Newland nodded. "I'm not one to get into a turf war, but it's a local murder case, not a theft and smuggling incident ten thousand miles away."

"According to Calvin, we lost two buddies and I'm walking on a metal pole because of that incident."

Again the detective's tired eyes appraised me, and I sensed we reached an understanding.

"Where's Calvin now?"

"I don't know." I told the truth. I didn't know where Calvin was at the moment. "It wouldn't surprise me if he showed up here."

"Have you got any pictures of these Blackwater guys?"

"Ex-Blackwater," I corrected. "Calvin might, or I can get a message to Baghdad. You've got my rough description of Hernandez and Lucas. I can work with a sketch artist."

"Why not go straight to Blackwater?" Efird asked. "Their headquarters are in North Carolina. A call from the state police should get their attention."

Newland looked at me. "What do you think?"

"Blackwater's a tight-lipped outfit. They like to play by their own rules. But we're in the States now. The downside could be your having to give up too much information to get their cooperation."

"Was Blackwater aware of your Ali Baba investigation?" Newland asked.

"Yeah. I suspect they were doing a little investigation of their own. When you run a private army, you like to keep your dirty laundry hidden."

Efird walked around to the same side of the table as Newland and slid into a chair. "Sounds like you don't care for Blackwater."

I shrugged. "My career in the U.S. Army was spent in upholding the honor of my country by seeing that our soldiers obeyed our laws. Now we're outsourcing military operations to so-called contractors who lobby our spineless Congress for immunity from civil prosecutions while refusing to submit to the jurisdiction of the armed forces they claim to be part of. They wrap themselves in the flag while setting themselves above the law."

I felt the old anger boil up against the politicians and ideologues who threw around terms like sacrifice and patriotism to muzzle anyone who challenged them.

Newland closed the notepad in front of him. "Like turning over our police work to Nathan Armitage's rent-a-cops without holding them to our code of conduct."

"Except in this case, Nathan's rent-a-cop is the victim. I trust him a hell of a lot more than anyone from Blackwater."

"We'll bear that in mind." Newland shot a sideways glance at his partner.

"That we will," Efird agreed.

I realized I'd accomplished all I could for the moment. "So, how can I help?"

"Tell us what you're up to," Newland said without hesitation. "We know you're not going to sit on the sidelines."

"Ethel Barkley is my client. I'm going to try and recover what she entrusted to me."

"And if you find it?"

"Then I guess you can take it from her. But you won't get it from me without a warrant."

"We're on the same side here," Efird said.

"Absolutely. The side of the law. So have the warrant ready." I stood. "In the meantime, I expect you'll give Ethel a grilling about her husband and brother partying with the German POWs."

"Among a few other things," Newland said. "Where will you be?"

"Somewhere in the past." I reached for the doorknob, and saw it swing away.

Ted and Al Newland stood in front of me. The twin on the left leaned in. "Uncle Newly, can you come out a second?"

"I was just leaving," I said.

"You probably ought to stay." The other twin stuck out his arm like a tollgate and I stepped aside as Detective Newland left.

When the door closed, Efird said, "Something bad's going down."

"Why do you say that?"

"The twin called him Uncle Newly. They're more formal at work. The only time I've heard the boys lapse into the family names were when they were under pressure. More specifically, during a shootout."

And they wanted me to stay. My mind jumped to Nakayla. The night before I'd endured intense agony when I thought she lay dead on our office floor. Was she all right now?

In less than a minute, Newland returned. His grim expression confirmed Efird's fear. "Well, we won't be interviewing Ethel Barkley. They found her in her apartment. Somebody smashed in the little old lady's skull."

◇◇◇

Three sheriff's deputy cars lined the circle in front of the entrance to the main lobby of Golden Oaks. The crime had occurred in the county, and the jurisdiction of its investigation would probably require interdepartmental cooperation. I'd driven separately from Newland and Efird, but they'd put me between two Asheville patrol cars whose flashing lights and sirens cleared traffic.

I parked beside a fire hydrant, figuring the authorities had better things to do than give me a ticket, and followed Newland and Efird into the building. Just beyond the front desk, residents stood in silence, some leaning on walkers and others on canes. Death was a frequent visitor, but murder shocked them. Captain stood in the center of the crowd and shook his head. He gestured over his shoulder with his thumb, signaling that he'd like to speak with me later.

Two deputies leaned against the wall outside of Ethel Barkley's door. Newland and Efird knew them. Newland asked me to hang back while they spoke. The four men formed a huddle, and after a few minutes, Newland waved me to join them.

"This is Sam Blackman," he said. "I have no doubt a case he's working ties into Barkley's death and the murder of Amanda Whitfield. I can vouch for him."

"You want him cleared for the scene?" one of the deputies asked.

"Yeah. But first we want to hear what you've got."

The deputy looked at his partner.

The other officer shrugged. "I don't think the Sheriff will have a problem." He winked at me and stuck out his hand. "Everybody knows Sam Blackman. I'm Todd Kramer. Pleasure to meet you."

We shook and I repeated the process with Deputy Clint Settle.

"From what we understand," Settle began, "the residents had started some kind of patrol to guard Mrs. Barkley. We don't know why."

"I suggested it," I said, and deferred to Newland.

The old cop cleared his throat. "I'll fill in the details later, but, in short, Sam was holding a lockbox that belonged to Barkley. When Amanda Whitfield was murdered last night, the lockbox was the only item taken from Sam's office."

Deputy Kramer whistled softly. "And now Barkley's dead."

"We don't know what's in the lockbox or if the same person came here and killed Barkley," Newland said. "Why do that if they possessed the lockbox? And how'd they get past the security gate and Sam's unofficial patrol?"

"Flowers," Deputy Settle said. "There was a delivery van that brought a vase of flowers. The driver said he was supposed to give them to Mrs. Barkley personally."

"Who from?" Efird asked.

"That's the interesting part. The card reads, 'I promise I'll find who took it,' and it's signed Sam Blackman."

A shudder ran down my spine. Someone had used my name to gain entrance to Ethel Barkley's apartment. Someone had worked very quickly.

"What time was this?" Newland asked.

"About eleven." Deputy Settle pulled a notepad from his chest pocket. "A Dorothy Jefferson saw Ethel Barkley admit him and close the door. She described the man as quote—'one of those foreigners.' The front desk said he was possibly Hispanic, but no one remembers an accent. His van was the typical Ford Econoline, white without any company name or logo."

"Somebody get a plate?" I asked.

"I checked," Settle said. "Their video camera at the front gate only tapes the incoming lane and North Carolina doesn't have front license plates. Wouldn't have mattered. They don't run a security recording."

"We'll need to contact all the rental companies," Newland said.

"Did he tell everyone the flowers were from me?" I asked.

"Yes," Settle said. "And everyone knew Ethel'd had the front desk call you this morning and that you'd been by to see her. They thought you were very sweet to send flowers."

"Damn," Efird muttered. "How'd he know you came to see Barkley?"

"The bugs in the office. Nakayla and I talked about her and her money this morning before Nathan discovered them."

"And we came to see her right behind Sam," Newland said. "Somebody thought the old lady knew something."

"When did the deliveryman leave?" I asked.

The two deputies looked at each other. "Nobody knows for sure," Settle said. "The Jefferson woman got worried when fifteen minutes passed and the guy never came out. She knocked on the door, but there was no answer. She went for help. By the time they got someone with a passkey, another five minutes had gone by. When they opened the apartment, they found Barkley dead in the bedroom, and no deliveryman."

"Windows?" Newland asked.

Settle nodded. "The one in the bedroom was unlocked and the screen ajar. Ethel Barkley's apartment faces the rear woods where someone could slip out the window unnoticed. No one saw the van leave, and at eleven-thirty there's a lot of incoming traffic as visitors arrive for lunch."

Newland scowled. "So from eleven to eleven-thirty we have an unidentified man on the premises, and for approximately twenty minutes of that time he was in our victim's apartment."

"Yes," Settle agreed. "He could have killed her immediately or only a few seconds before the Golden Oaks staff member entered."

Newland turned to Efird. "I think it's time we examine the crime scene."

Efird carried a black satchel that made him look like a country doctor. "Mobile lab on the way?"

Settle nodded. "It's coming from the north end of the county. Should be here in about thirty minutes."

Efird opened the satchel and handed me gloves and shoe covers. At the rate I was going through them, I'd be wise to stock my own.

We found Ethel Barkley on her bedroom floor, face down with her thick glasses protruding from under her forehead. She wore the same lavender dress I'd seen her in less than six hours earlier. A large splotch of congealed blood matted her white hair into a tangled clump against her skull.

The wrinkles on the bedspread showed someone had either sat or lain on top of it. A pillow had been pulled from against the headboard and tossed by the closet door. While Newland and Efird bent over the body, I took a closer look at the pillow. A damp spot in the center slightly darkened the white linen. It wasn't blood, but appeared to be saliva with traces of mucus.

If Ethel Barkley's assailant had used the pillow to smother her, then why bash in her head? I saw the lamp from the nightstand on the floor a few yards from the body. The power cord had been jerked from the wall socket, indicating the lamp hadn't been simply knocked over during a struggle. The square, gold-plated base had the heft to inflict the fatal damage to Ethel's head.

The blow had probably hurled her forward, which meant she'd been facing the bedroom door, possibly making an attempt to escape her attacker. I glanced at the pillow and then knelt beside Ethel's outstretched right arm. Her little finger, slender as a child's, angled from her hand at nearly ninety degrees.

"He used the pillow to stifle her cries as he tortured her." I pointed to the dislocated finger. "Have the lab check the pillow-case."

"I wonder if she gave up what he wanted?" Efird asked.

Newland took a closer look at the damaged hand. "Hard to say. The most stubborn person I knew was my grandmother. You could have set her on fire and she wouldn't budge once her mind was made up."

"Especially if Ethel Barkley was protecting something she valued more than her life." I got to my feet. "Where are the flowers?"

We found them in a clear glass vase in the kitchen. Twelve cut carnations—the kind of bouquet you could buy at any large grocery store. The hand-printed message with my forged signature was clipped to a stem; the paper was an unlined three-by-five note card.

"These guys improvise fast," Efird said.

Newland turned to me. "They murdered two women in cold blood. If they didn't get what they want here, they'll come back to their next best source."

"Me," I said.

"Or your partner, Nakayla. Anybody else you talked about before you found those bugs?"

"I know we discussed Hewitt Donaldson and that Ethel was his aunt." A disturbing thought flashed. "And I told Nakayla Calvin Stuart had warned me." I'd said more than that. I'd told her Calvin had scared off the man who attacked me. Now they knew Calvin was in Asheville. I'd have to get word to him as soon as possible.

"We need to learn as much about these guys as fast as we can," Newland said. "Maybe we can set up a conference call with your friend."

Efird shook his head. "I still think we should put some pressure on Blackwater for information. Demand anything in their personnel records that can help us. Hell, these guys might have relatives or girlfriends in this part of the state."

"I'll see what I can do about contacting Calvin." I left them in the kitchen and walked over to the table where Ethel had read my palm. Except for the horror in the bedroom, nothing in the apartment looked amiss.

I dialed Nakayla's cell as fast as I could. Her voicemail picked up. "Phone me as soon as you can. You're in danger." Then I tried the office, but the answering service took the call. I left a message for her to call immediately. Where was she?

I pulled *The Great Gatsby* from the bookshelf. Ethel might have had many secrets, but this was the one I knew. A folded piece of yellowed paper lay tucked near the back. The place it marked was the swastika page she'd showed me. I unfolded the sheet and saw a handwritten poem. The paper hadn't been there yesterday. I slipped it into my coat pocket as Newland and Efird entered.

"What did you find?" Efird asked.

I held out the book. "*The Great Gatsby*. That was the password I had to give the banker for access to the safe-deposit box. And here's the passage she marked about the swastika." I showed them the underlined sentences and noticed the letter "T" in the first word "The" was circled.

"Ethel told me Fitzgerald gave it to her." I turned to the title page and we all read the inscription: "To Ethel—my palmist-in-training. May your future always be bright."

"There might be other notations," I said. "If you want to sign it out to me, I'll go through it."

As I expected, Newland balked. "No. I'll earmark it to be dusted by the lab. Given her fixation on Fitzgerald, we ought to go over all her books. But I'll segregate this in an evidence bag and give you permission to examine it at the station."

"Fair enough. Listen, I'm trying to alert Nakayla about what's happened, but I can't find her." I started for the door. "And what about Hewitt Donaldson?"

"Let us contact him," Newland said. "He's probably the best source for information on Ethel Barkley's next of kin."

"You need to warn him. Anyone who bugged my conversation with Nakayla might decide Donaldson knows something about the lockbox."

Efird glanced at his watch. "It's after one. If he's in court today, he's probably on recess. Much as I despise the slimy bastard I guess I'd better give him a heads up."

"I know some of the residents here," I said. "If it's okay with you, I'll check with them before I leave."

"Knock yourself out," Newland said.

I found Captain in the lobby. He broke away from his friends and we sat beside the dormant fireplace near the dining hall.

"Sam. I'm so sorry."

"That wasn't your fault, Captain. The guy got past the front desk."

"And we were the last line of defense. In the army, that meant failure wasn't an option."

I smiled at him. "In the army, Dorothy Jefferson wouldn't have been your sentry. And I hope she's not taking this as hard as you are."

He rubbed his hands together in nervous agitation. "She's pretty broke up. But I told her she did what she was supposed to. She came and got me and I had maintenance let us in." He sighed. "But we were too late."

"These men are smart and ruthless. Golden Oaks isn't equipped to go against that kind of enemy."

"There you're wrong. We notice things here. Hell, not much else to do but observe life."

"Okay. I understand. Maybe Dorothy shouldn't have waited fifteen minutes before becoming alarmed."

Captain fidgeted in his seat and then slapped his hand against the walker beside him. "Not Dorothy. Me. I saw the guy come to the front desk. I heard him ask for Ethel and say he was delivering flowers from you. I thought what a thoughtful person you were to treat her so nicely. I also thought it was odd he wore gloves."

"Gloves? Well, he was carrying plants."

"Not work gloves. These looked like kid leather. Driving gloves or maybe shooting gloves. Not the kind you'd expect to see on a flower deliveryman."

"Umm," was all I could say.

"Yeah. I knew as I pushed this walker as fast as I could to Ethel's room what those gloves meant. The guy didn't want to leave fingerprints. And I was just too stupid to put it together when it counted."

I stood and stepped beside him, laying a hand on his bony shoulder. "And I should have been more careful what I said, because whoever killed Amanda Whitfield also bugged our office. I did know whom we were up against, Captain, and my carelessness cost Ethel her life. But they'll pay. You have my word."

He reached up and patted my arm. "I wish I could watch your back."

"Between you and me, I've got somebody from my unit doing just that. We've both got a score to settle."

I left Captain and returned to my car. I tried Nakayla's cell again. Still no answer. She might have been at lunch and not heard her phone. I left another urgent message for her to get in touch. Then I pulled the paper from my pocket and read what I'd found in Ethel's book.

"The Commander Comes Riding in with The Dawn.

And behind Him His Legions Resplendent in Silver!

YES, The Silver Shirts are marching!

Christ Men! Grim men! Men of stamina, men of mettle, old men, young men, Lords of High Courage, Chamberlains of Valor

The Silver Shirts Are Marching!"

What the hell was this? Some poem of F. Scott Fitzgerald's? It certainly didn't sound like anything the celebrated author of the Jazz Age would write.

A shadow passed over the paper, and I set it on the passenger seat as if it were no more important than a laundry list. Efird knocked on my window.

"Nathan Armitage is at headquarters. He spotted someone tailing your partner."

"Is Nakayla all right?"

"As far as I know. The guy gave him the slip at a restaurant, but not before Armitage managed to retrieve the glass the man had been drinking from." Efird smiled. "He wasn't wearing gloves."

"Are you going there now?"

"Yes. Newland will stay here and coordinate the scene with the Sheriff's Department and the lab. I thought you might want to talk to Armitage. Hear if his description sounds like one of your Ali Baba thieves."

I was tempted, and I appreciated being included, but the poem I'd read was unsettling. So was the fact that someone was following Nakayla and I didn't know where she was. I wanted to get to her as soon as I could. And I had to reach Calvin Stuart. He didn't know our enemies were aware he'd come to Asheville.

"Thanks," I said, "but I've got an appointment with my partner. I'll check back later this afternoon."

"Okay. By the way, we got word that your telephone installer, Vince Freese, has been with the company for over twenty years. He's their employee of the month. We can't see him as the guy."

"He was a long shot."

"Yeah. Well, stay safe." Efird headed for his car.

Stay safe. Right. Two murdered women. A killer stalking Nakayla. And now an army of religious zealots called The Silver Shirts. Were they real or poetic imagery? And if they were real, where were they marching? More important, was I in their path?

Chapter Twelve

Instead of taking I-26 back to Asheville, I used Highway 25, which ran through Biltmore Village and passed near my apartment. I kept phoning Nakayla but stopped leaving messages. I didn't know where to look for her so I decided to set the signal in my window in hopes of reaching Calvin and bringing him up to speed on the day's developments.

After placing the bedroom blinds midway down, I checked my answering machine and heard one voicemail: "Sam. Hewitt Donaldson. I just got the word about my aunt. Any chance we can meet for that beer this evening? My cell's 555-0871. I'm heading back to court but leave me a message as to if, when, and where."

The time identification on the machine said the call came at 1:29. Less than fifteen minutes earlier. If Detective Efird had contacted him after I left Golden Oaks, then Donaldson must have immediately telephoned. I wondered whether Efird had mentioned Ethel Barkley's missing lockbox.

I sat on the bed and changed out the sleeve for my prosthesis. Although the calendar read September 12th, the thermometer had risen to August levels. I'd perspired to the extent that the damp sleeve against my stump had become an irritation. A dry fit meant I'd be more comfortable as the afternoon progressed and there was no telling when this day would end.

The V.A. doctor had provided me with two artificial limbs: one designed for daily routines such as normal walking and office work, and a second for more strenuous activities like hiking or even running. I thought of it as having two cars: a cushy-riding sedan for interstate travel and a four-wheel-drive with a tighter suspension for off-road adventures. I opted to continue with the Cadillac/Lexus mode of transportation.

My cell rang as I started to lock the apartment. When I saw Nakayla's ID flash on the screen, I stepped back inside and closed the door. "Where are you? I've been worried sick."

"Outside Pack Library. I just picked up your message."

"Have you seen Nathan?"

"No. Did he find more bugs?"

I was irked that Nathan hadn't warned her.

"He left me a voicemail," she added, "but when I saw how many times you'd called I skipped over him."

"Someone's been following you. Nathan spotted him at a restaurant but then lost him. I guess Nathan lost you too."

"Must have been the Early Girl Eatery. I grabbed a quick lunch and brought a book to read. I'd turned my phone off in the library and forgot to turn it back on. I should have been paying more attention to what was going on around me."

"We all should have. Someone murdered Ethel Barkley."

Nakayla gave a sharp gasp. "In her apartment?"

"Yes. Stay in the library. I'll meet you there." I flipped my phone shut and clipped it on my belt. Then I popped off the Kimber's restraining strap and snatched the forty-five from the holster. Nathan had been right. The horizontal ride cut the draw time in half. But a fast draw would be useless without the explosive impact of a bullet. I pulled back the slide action and loaded a cartridge into the chamber.

On a Wednesday afternoon, the library was sparsely populated. A few students came straight from school and huddled in whispering groups, but the majority of the patrons browsed the popular fiction shelves or used the computers.

Nakayla sat engrossed in a book in the reference section. Several other volumes lay stacked on the table near her elbow. She jotted notes on a legal pad, and the number of flipped pages showed she'd accumulated a significant amount of information.

I sat across from her and checked that no one else was within earshot. "Have you given up on the Internet?"

"No. The Internet led me to some very interesting resources." She tilted the book in front of her so I could read the title: *BLACKWATER—The Rise of the World's Most Powerful Mercenary Army,* by Jeremy Scahill. "Kind of scary. Erik Prince, who heads it, is either an extremely clever businessman or a right-wing Christian crusader."

"Maybe both. But I think in Iraq his people are trying to stay alive like everybody else. They just take more liberties in their methods, and that's like leaving a smoldering ember in a storehouse of gas cans."

"Their headquarters are in Moyock, North Carolina. Ever been there?"

"No. I'd never heard of the place till I talked to some Blackwater operatives in Baghdad. I think it's down east."

"The Great Dismal Swamp on the Virginia line. The name Blackwater comes from the dark brackish bog water."

"Sounds charming," I said. "Also fitting. With black water you can't see what's beneath the surface." I tapped the book. "When did this come out?"

"A few months ago." Nakayla tore a narrow strip of paper from the bottom of her pad and marked her place. She slid the book aside and picked up another. "Here's more corroboration for Ethel Barkley's story. The author had a bookstore in Asheville in 1935 and Fitzgerald befriended him."

The book was entitled *The Lost Summer: A Personal Memoir of F. Scott Fitzgerald.* I'd never heard of the author, Tony Buttitta.

"Does he mention Ethel?"

"I've only read the first few chapters." Nakayla turned to the top page of her legal pad. "He writes that Laura Guthrie Hearne was the dollar woman, and she read palms at the Grove Park Inn.

She was Fitzgerald's part-time secretary that summer. Fitzgerald was having an affair at the inn with a married woman he called Rosemary. Buttitta says that wasn't her real name. Laura Hearne wrote an article in *Esquire* in 1964 excerpting the diary she kept the summer of 1935. She also refers to the affair. Rosemary was evidently quite wealthy and blindly in love with Fitzgerald."

"Must be the woman who gave him the gift Ethel kept."

"And there was a third woman, a prostitute, whom Fitzgerald confided in."

I studied the black and white photograph of Fitzgerald on the cover. "Sounds like he was living in one of his own books."

"He was close to a meltdown. Zelda was institutionalized in Baltimore, and his writing career was on the skids. But he could still charm." Nakayla shook her head. "Like he did poor Ethel. Do the police know anything?"

"Not really. The killer posed as a flower deliveryman. We have a vague description of a white cargo van with a Hispanic driver. Captain's upset because he saw the guy wearing an expensive pair of gloves and feels that should have tipped him off. We know the police won't find any fingerprints."

"The gloves must have unnerved Ethel."

"Why?"

"She couldn't see his palms."

I hadn't thought about that irony. "I still feel an obligation to her, even though her case has taken a bizarre twist." I pulled the folded poem from my pocket. "Look at this."

Nakayla's forehead creased as she read through the verses. "Where'd you find it?"

"In Ethel's copy of *The Great Gatsby*. She stuck it where the swastika was mentioned. Maybe she pulled it out before she showed me the quote."

"The Silver Shirts. Any idea what that means?"

I took back the poem, scanning the lines again. "Hitler had his brown shirts. Maybe he had another level."

"A premium grade of thug?" Nakayla stood. "Let's do a quick Internet search."

We left the books and Nakayla signed in to use a computer. "Silver Shirts" netted 22,500,000 sources.

"Add Nazi to the query," I suggested.

"But look at this top recommendation—The Silver Legion of America." Nakayla clicked on it and a page from Wikipedia instantly appeared.

The summary sentence read, "an American fascist organization founded by William Dudley Pelley on January 30, 1933."

"Now we're getting somewhere." I slid my chair closer to the monitor. "Try the link to Pelley."

The screen refreshed with a lengthy biography that began with Pelley's birth in 1890 in Lynn, Massachusetts. A graphic to the side reproduced a WANTED poster with the black and white photograph of a distinguished looking man with a gray mustache and Vandyke.

"Looks like Pelley ran afoul of the law." Nakayla double-clicked on the poster and enlarged it.

The text beneath the photo was in fine print, but the capital letters "UN-AMERICAN" written before the word "activities" caught my eye.

"Oh, my God." Nakayla moved the mouse's cursor to the bottom of the poster and stopped it under the issuing official's name: Laurence E. Brown, Sheriff—Asheville, N.C. "Pelley was here."

We spent the next ten minutes speed-reading through an article that painted a fascinating portrait of Pelley. He'd grown up in New England, migrated to Hollywood, and become a scriptwriter. In 1928, Pelley had an out-of-body experience and claimed to have spent seven minutes in eternity speaking with the dead. He moved to Asheville, where he founded Galahad Press, Galahad College, and the League for Liberation. His teaching and writing were described as a bizarre mix of mysticism, Christianity, and politics, a dangerous and combustible concoction. When Hitler rose to power, Pelley saw that as a divine omen and founded the Silver League of America, commonly called The Silver Shirts. One year later, the League claimed 15,000 members in twenty-two states.

When Nakayla had scrolled to the bottom of the last webpage, she turned to me. "His life intersects some key points."

"The poem about a fascist cult certainly suggests a connection to the swastika-sealed lockbox."

"More than that." Nakayla wrote the number one on her legal pad followed by the word mysticism. "Pelley had some kind of paranormal vision and then came to Asheville. Mysticism is woven throughout this town's history."

"You think some crystal freaks are behind this?" I found the NewAgers' claims that the mountains around Asheville contained portals to other dimensions to be ludicrous.

Nakayla smiled. "I'm not drawing any conclusions. You told me Ethel Barkley learned to read palms from Laura Guthrie Hearne, who was Fitzgerald's secretary. The occult is playing a role we can't ignore."

"Okay. I'll concede there could be a link."

She patted the back of my hand. "That's what I like about you. You're so magnanimous."

"What else?"

She jotted down the number two and added writer. "Pelley wrote Hollywood scripts. Today having an extra-dimensional experience in L.A. might be as common as sneezing, but back then people would have looked at him as a nut. Maybe that's why he came to the mountains. But I doubt he considered himself any less of an artist. Living in Asheville with F. Scott Fitzgerald must have kindled a curiosity. I wonder if they met?"

Nakayla raised an interesting possibility. Part of my conversation with Ethel Barkley took on new meaning. "Ethel told me her brother wanted to know what Fitzgerald was writing. He said Fitzgerald had defined the Jazz Age and might be persuaded to do the same for a new age. What if it was Pelley's fascist age?"

"Fitzgerald would have been a voice that attracted attention." Nakayla wrote a third word on her list. Blackmail. "They might have approached Fitzgerald openly and when that didn't work, looked for a more underhanded way to get his cooperation."

"Has Pelley's name shown up in that guy's memoir?"

"No. But I've just started the Buttitta book. We can ask at the inn."

"The inn?" Nakayla had lost me.

She rapped her knuckles against her head. "Sorry. When you told me Ethel'd been murdered, I forgot to tell you. I've made an appointment to speak with a historian at the Grove Park Inn. I stepped outside to make the call and realized my phone was off. That's when I realized you'd been trying to reach me."

"Who is the historian?"

"Derrick Swing. He works with staff training and teaches a class on the inn's history."

"What time's the appointment?"

"Four."

I glanced at my watch. "It's three now. I think we should go there together."

Nakayla logged off the computer. "Nathan's voicemail warned me I was being followed. He said the man had straight blond hair. Average height and mid-thirties."

"Well, that's someone other than the Hispanic flower man. The police are running your stalker's prints. Maybe you should stay with me until we figure out what's going on."

I expected a smart reply, but Nakayla simply nodded. She was worried.

"We've got about forty minutes," she said. "What do you want to do?"

"See if you can find a connection between Pelley and Fitzgerald"

"What about between Pelley and Ethel's husband or brother?"

"Damn." I said the word louder than I should and saw the librarian at the research desk raise an eyebrow.

"What's wrong?" Nakayla asked.

"Hewitt Donaldson left me a message. I forgot to call him."

Nakayla rolled her chair back and stood. "You'd better see what he wants."

"He wants a beer. I could use one too. The Sunset Terrace at the Grove Park should meet with his approval."

"Then tell him five-thirty. We don't want to rush our conversation with Derrick Swing."

I left Nakayla at the reading table and headed outside to call Donaldson.

"Sam." Nakayla's urgent whisper stopped me. "Look at this."

I returned to the table and peered over her shoulder. Scrawled on small sheet of white paper were the words, "Chief—Things are coming to a head—now!"

"What's it mean?" Nakayla asked.

"Calvin got my signal. He's in the men's room."

"The men's room?" Nakayla looked at me from the corners of her eyes. "How do you know that?"

"Calvin's a wise-ass. He spelled a head as two words. Head's the nautical term for the bathroom. Stay here. I'll be back before we need to leave."

The men's room was downstairs on the lower level. An older man was washing his hands in the sink. I went to the far urinal, hoping I wouldn't have to fake using it too long. I heard the hand dryer blow for about thirty seconds and then the man left.

"Chief?" The whisper came from one of the three stalls.

I flushed and scanned them. All the doors were open except the one nearest the wall. I entered the stall beside it, wiped the seat with toilet paper, and sat. In case something went wrong, I wasn't going to get caught with my pants dropped around my shoes. I realized my hand had slipped under my sport coat and rested against the butt of my pistol.

"Busy day," I muttered, as if to myself.

"You're telling me." The whisper turned into Calvin's recognizable growl. "What the hell happened? You were sandwiched between two cop cars and I couldn't keep up with you."

"The woman who owned the lockbox stolen from our office was murdered."

Calvin whistled. "Damn. Two murders in two days. Have you any doubt it's Ali Baba?"

"Smells that way, but there's something else going on."

"Like what?"

"We think the old lady was hooked up with some fascist group in the 1930s."

Calvin slapped his hand against the stall. "God damn it, Chief. All the Nazis are dead. And we might be too if we don't nail these jokers."

"I know. I'm just trying to cover all the angles. Our offices were bugged. Anybody could have gotten information about our client."

"Bugged? Did you talk about me?"

The stall suddenly felt like a steel-walled confessional. "Yeah."

"Well, then what the hell are we doing hiding in the john?" He pushed open the door so hard it banged against the wall.

I stepped out and watched him pace back and forth in front of the sink. He wore loose black jeans and a dark blue pullover. He had no shoulder holster and I suspected one of his so-called girlfriends rode in the small of his back and another on his calf.

He balled his large hands into fists. "So I've lost the element of surprise."

"They would have expected us to reunite at some point. And now they've got the police to worry about."

Calvin walked over to me and pressed his thumb against my chest. "These local yokels couldn't find their own asses if you tattooed their names on each cheek."

"They've got fingerprints."

Calvin's eyes widened. "Really? I'd have thought those guys would be more careful."

"If they really are our guys. A friend spotted a tail on my partner."

"The black chick? I spotted her tail myself. Nice piece of merchandise."

"She's my partner." I said the words clipped and hard.

"Okay. No offense." He moved his hand to pat my shoulder and felt the butt of my Kimber. "All right, Chief. Now you're talking." He backed away and leaned against the sink counter. "What have the police got?"

"A glass my friend picked up that the guy used. He described him as mid-thirties, average height, and with blond hair. The police are checking the prints."

"Anything else?"

"The man who killed my client posed as a deliveryman and was described as Hispanic. So, we're dealing with two people."

"The Hispanic has to be Hernandez. The other guy could be Lucas."

"The Asheville police are requesting ID photos from the military and Blackwater. Have you got any with you?"

"No. I didn't expect my leave to turn into a manhunt."

The restroom door cracked open. "Go ahead, Todd," a woman said. "Mommy will be right outside."

A boy no more than four backed through the door. "No. You come with me."

"Mommy can't. This bathroom's only for big boys."

The lad turned around. His oversized Superman tee shirt hung to his knees. He saw me and bolted away, faster than a speeding bullet. As the door closed, he whined, "There's a man in there. I want to go to your potty."

Footsteps faded and I figured Todd's status as a big boy was a few months away.

Calvin punched the hand dryer and spoke just above its roar. "With the police running the show, what are you going to do?"

"Work the case I've got. Why was my client killed? What did they want?"

"Information about you." The dryer died and Calvin lowered his voice. "Maybe something in the lockbox made them believe she knew about your accounts."

"God damn it. I don't have any accounts."

Calvin held up his hands. "Okay. If you say so."

I stared at him for a second and then the light clicked on. "You checked me out, didn't you? Somebody thinks I'm dirty."

"Chief, you know how it is. The bad guys make wild accusations and the snitches pass them along."

I wondered if my wire transfer to the Caymans had been flagged. "All right. I'm guilty. Arrest me. I opened an offshore account because I didn't want all my settlement money in U.S. banks. Hell, I didn't know whether I'd even stay in the country." The last statement wasn't true, but I needed to push Calvin off this line of questioning.

He relaxed. "Like I said, Chief, you'd make a boy scout look subversive. Here's my theory. Ali Baba thinks you and I stole their treasure. They come after me and when I disappear they show up in Asheville. They bug your office and kill the poor security guard in the process. Then they take your client's lockbox. One of them attacks you outside your apartment demanding information about your offshore account, an account you now admit exists. Why did they kill your client? I don't have a clue. Maybe they thought she had information or there was something in the lockbox they didn't understand. These guys won't walk away if they smell money. They'll get it any way they can."

"And that's their weakness. Let's meet at my apartment tonight. You, Nakayla, and me. I'd like to come up with a plan to turn their greed against them. Then we'll bring the police in."

"The police? Why don't we get support out of Bragg?"

I weighed Calvin's suggestion and discarded it. "Too much paperwork and too long to bring them up to speed. We need help now."

Calvin didn't look happy, but he must not have had any other options. "Okay. What time?"

"Say, seven."

"What do we do till then? If I stay in this men's room any longer they'll start delivering my mail."

"Nakayla and I are going to the Grove Park Inn for a history lesson."

Calvin's face screwed up like he'd bitten into a persimmon. "History lesson?"

"Yeah. Something happened back in the 1930s that involved my client and that lockbox."

Calvin smiled. "Your Nazis?"

"Possibly. Our only solid lead is to F. Scott Fitzgerald when he stayed at the inn."

Calvin locked his eyes on mine. "*The Great Gatsby.*"

I was surprised. I hadn't taken him for the literary type. "Yeah. But the book came out ten years earlier. My client was enamored with it. *The Great Gatsby* was the password I needed to retrieve her lockbox."

He rubbed his hand across his chin. "Then there really could be more to this than the Blackwater swill."

"That's what I keep telling you. Keep an open mind and you might come out of this case with a promotion."

Calvin laughed. "Chief, I'll be happy to come out of this case alive."

Chapter Thirteen

Nakayla and I took my CR-V from the library. On the way, I dialed Hewitt Donaldson and got his voicemail.

"This is Sam Blackman. I'm headed for an appointment at the Grove Park Inn. Let's meet at five-thirty on the Sunset Terrace for that beer. Leave me a message."

"He might not like that I'm along," Nakayla said.

"Tough. You're my partner."

"How do you know he's hiring us for a case? It might be personal. You know, man talk."

"I don't like leaving you by yourself."

"Excuse me?" She turned in her seat to face me. "I can wait in the lobby where Nathan or one of his operatives is probably shadowing me. And if we're going to be partners, you're not relegating me to research at the library and running the office. I can carry my share of the field work." She zipped open her handbag and extracted her Colt twenty-five. "And I'm as armed and dangerous as you."

"Then heaven help us both."

As we twisted up Macon Avenue toward the inn, I thought about the car wreck that occurred over sixty years ago and left Ethel without a husband and Hewitt Donaldson without a father. Which of these curves had held the deadly patch of ice? And had the fatal accident somehow started a chain of events that culminated in Ethel's murder?

The Grove Park Inn and Spa jutted from the side of Sunset Mountain like a majestic castle. Countless rocks and stone boulders that could have built an enormous pyramid lay stacked in long horizontal rows to create a multistoried lodge in keeping with the grandeur and proportion of its Appalachian setting. Unlike more recent construction that perched atop the ridges with all the charm of warts on an elegant cheek, the Grove Park complemented its surroundings, from the muted brown and gray tones of its rock walls to the rustic red of the roof that matched the foliage of the fall hardwoods.

I didn't know much about the inn's history, other than it was built a few decades after George W. Vanderbilt established his Biltmore Estate. E.W. Grove had made millions off his patent medicine, Grove's Tasteless Chill Tonic, a treatment for the symptoms of malaria popular during the time when the disease plagued the mosquito-ridden South.

If I remembered correctly, Grove had come to Asheville for his own health and used part of his fortune to erect a resort that would appeal to wealthy people seeking rest and relaxation. Nakayla had told me he wasn't interested in attracting the sick. Instead, he bought many of the nearby "consumption houses" and either tore them down or converted them to regular residences to insure the vitality of the inn's image. Asheville's reputation as a haven for sufferers of lung ailments had grown to the point where the locals referred to Pack Square as Phlegm Square.

Derrick Swing could fill in those details, but I wondered if he had any insights into how my client, Ethel Barkley, managed to entwine her life with one of the most influential writers of the twentieth century and one of the most abhorrent political movements in human history.

I turned left off Macon and drove down a lane to the parking lot.

Nakayla pointed across me to where the valets met the cars of arriving guests in front of the main doors. "Derrick said to use the staff entrance. It's down the hill. Look for a long red awning."

The inn sprawled along the mountainside, adding new ground floors as the land sloped away. We spotted the awning and I found a parking place in the lower lot less than fifty feet away.

The waiting room inside the staff entryway held an assortment of mismatched chairs. Two young men were filling out employment applications at long tables. Bulletin boards on the walls displayed notices of the inn's policies and a variety of government regulations.

A woman wearing a staff uniform and carrying a clipboard came down a short flight of steps to our left. We caught her eye and she paused. "Is someone helping you?"

"Not yet," Nakayla said. "We're supposed to meet Derrick Swing at four."

"He's still in the classroom, but they'll be breaking up in a few minutes. You can wait outside the door if you like." She gestured to the stairs behind her. "Just follow the hallway."

We walked down a narrow corridor that had the feel of a tunnel and I knew we were heading underground where the nuts and bolts of running a resort were hidden from the patrons. A door opened a few yards ahead and a stream of people emerged. Some wore uniforms like the woman with the clipboard; others dressed casually, marking them as employees who either didn't interact with the public or hadn't gone on duty.

We stood to one side and let them pass. When the last person had exited, I followed Nakayla into a room set with folding tables and chairs split either side of a center aisle. They faced the far wall where a photograph of the Grove Park's exterior was cast onto a screen by an overhead projector. The wash of the room's fluorescent lights nearly obliterated the image. Bending over the table nearest the screen, a man in a light blue dress shirt and sharply knotted yellow tie was gathering note cards together.

"Mr. Swing?" Nakayla called.

The man looked up. He struck me as somewhere in his mid-thirties, but his blond hair and boyish grin could have shaved a few years off his actual age.

"Are you Ms. Robertson?" He walked down the aisle to greet us.

"Yes. But call me Nakayla." She shook his hand. "And this is my friend, Sam Blackman."

"A pleasure to meet you." He clasped my hand with a firm grip. "I'm Derrick." He motioned to a table just inside the door. "You're in luck. Today I was teaching a class on the history of the inn for some of our employees. I saved you copies of the PowerPoint presentation." He picked up two spiral-bound booklets and handed us each one. "You can use it for general background." He grabbed three chairs and set them in a circle. "We're fine to stay here. I understand you have some questions."

We sat and I looked to Nakayla to start the conversation. We'd agreed to be direct and honest about why we needed his help.

Nakayla folded her hands on the booklet in her lap. "As I said on the phone, we're trying to retrieve a lockbox for a client. It was stolen from our office."

He nodded, and his face grew as solemn as a stone. "I read about the woman who was murdered."

"Amanda Whitfield," Nakayla said. "The security guard."

"And you think it involves the Grove Park?" The concern in his voice bordered on fear. History was one thing but linking the inn to an active murder case was something else.

Nakayla shook her head. "Not directly. People who were guests or employees could play a role, but we're talking seventy years ago."

"I don't know how specific I can be. My knowledge of the inn's history is more general."

"Our client claimed to be an employee," Nakayla said. "I guess it's too much to hope you'd have personnel records that far back."

"From the 1930s? I'm afraid not. But your client should be able to provide enough details that I can validate her claim." Derrick's face brightened. "I love meeting the old timers."

Nakayla cut her eyes to me, seeking confirmation to give Derrick the bad news. I cocked my head slightly and she read my okay.

"Our client, Mrs. Ethel Barkley, was murdered this morning."

Derrick's jaw dropped. "She must have been in her nineties." He turned to me. "Who would kill an old lady?"

Maybe he thought I was more familiar with the seamy side of the world. "We don't know," I said. "The police are investigating. We're following through on our leads in an effort to assist them. But we need your help."

Derrick leaned forward. "What do you want to know?"

"Ethel said she worked here during the summer of 1935," Nakayla said. "When F. Scott Fitzgerald had a room."

"He was in and out that summer, and the summer of 1936 as well. He usually had room 441 or 443. He liked the fourth floor."

"Ethel Barkley said she worked the fourth floor."

Derrick shrugged. "She could have picked that information up anywhere."

I interrupted Nakayla's questioning. "Ethel had an autographed copy of *The Great Gatsby*. It was inscribed 'To Ethel—my palmist-in-training. May your future always be bright.'"

"Palmist-in-training?"

"Yes," I said. "She told us she learned to read palms from Laura Guthrie Hearne, who entertained the guests with her fortune-telling."

Derrick reflexively glanced at his own palms. "That's certainly possible. At that point, the Grove Park Inn had begun taking a more active role in providing diversions for the guests."

"It hadn't always been that way?" Nakayla asked.

"No. Grove's son-in-law, Fred Seely, was the real brain behind the operation of the inn. He and Grove modeled it after the Old Faithful Inn in Yellowstone National Park. None of the plans submitted by architects pleased Grove or Seely. Finally, Seely drew up his own sketch, using boulders instead of logs. He stunned everyone by promising he could build it in a year. They broke ground on July 9, 1912 and opened for business July 13, 1913."

"He missed by four days," I said.

"And you can be sure Seely wasn't happy about it. He was a tough taskmaster. The first two general managers quit after working only one year each. He laid down the law to everyone, including the guests."

"Would he and Fitzgerald have locked horns?" Nakayla asked.

"Yes. If Seely had still been in charge. He envisioned the inn as a place for wealthy people to enjoy rest and relaxation, peace and quiet. If guests got too loud in the Great Hall, a printed card was delivered asking them to be more subdued. Children were discouraged, dogs forbidden, no alcohol was served, and you couldn't run water in your room after ten-thirty."

"Not exactly the kind of place I'd expect to find the Father of the Jazz Age," I said.

"Things had loosened up by 1935. Seely and Grove had had a falling out. When Grove died in 1927, Seely was excluded from the will and any operations of the inn. Fortunately, he'd purchased Biltmore Industries from Edith Vanderbilt, George's widow, years before, so he set up shop right across the street. The buildings are still there."

"Must have been a bitter pill," I said.

Derrick smiled. "Seely kept a hand in the game. The heirs sold the inn shortly after Grove's death, and Seely worked as a consultant for the new owners. His austere philosophy had to give way to a more accommodating atmosphere." Derrick scratched the side of his face as he thought for a second. "Of course, Fitzgerald still taxed management's patience. He had the bellboys sneak in beer, which he considered a concession to cutting back on hard liquor. He had a very public affair with a married woman who was here caring for her sister, and people came to his room at all hours of the night."

Derrick's depiction matched what Ethel had told me. "Did he become involved in the local community?"

"No. But I think he was courteous to local writers and admirers. Thomas Wolfe didn't return to Asheville till 1937, so Fitzgerald had the literary stage all to himself."

124 Mark de Castrique

"Did he hold court with his admirers?"

Derrick shook his head. "Not really. Famous figures of the early twentieth century frequently came to the inn. Harry Houdini, Henry Ford, Al Jolson, Will Rogers, and almost every U.S. President. Fitzgerald was at the low point of his career. He'd even been given a literary obituary by the New York Post."

"How'd he afford to stay?"

"Friends with money. And he was selling the occasional magazine story, although he wrote very little while he was here." Derrick glanced at his watch. "Do you have time to see his rooms? One of them might be vacant."

I wasn't sure how that would help our investigation, but I was curious to glimpse where Ethel and Fitzgerald had met so many years ago.

Nakayla rose quickly. "That would be great, if it's no trouble."

Derrick waved a hand to one side. "No problem, unless they're occupied. We'll check the front desk."

He led us out of the classroom and up a long flight of stairs. We passed through a narrow door and stepped into a wide corridor. Rounding a corner to the right, we entered the Great Hall of the Grove Park Inn, virtually unchanged since its grand opening over ninety-four years ago.

The space had to be over a hundred feet long. Guests entering through the main entrance found themselves between two incredible stone fireplaces running the width of the opposite walls. In a few months, trunk-sized logs would blaze on the massive andirons and the sweet scent of wood smoke would mingle with the multitude of aromas generated by the inn's extravagant buffet.

Nowhere did the influence of the magnificent lodges of the Rockies appear more clearly than in this room, although the terrace off the rear didn't overlook jagged peaks and harsh bluffs. Instead patrons gazed at the ancient, rounded Appalachian hills shaped by eons of wind and rain and covered with a thick growth of hardwoods and evergreens. A hint of pink tinted the wisps of clouds, promising richer colors as evening neared. The view from the Sunset Terrace would be beautiful for my beer with Hewitt Donaldson.

"Wait here while I check with the front desk," Derrick said. "If one of Fitzgerald's rooms is available, we'll take the elevator." He pointed to the closest fireplace where a shaft had been built into its side.

Nakayla grinned. "I've always wanted to ride in that."

"If we get stuck, at least we'll be toasty." I walked over to a placard mounted on an easel that had been positioned where arriving guests could see it.

The banner across the top read: "The Fitzgerald—Sumptuous condominiums just steps from the Grove Park Inn Resort and Spa." Beneath the type, an artist's rendering showed an elegant beige stucco building adjacent to the inn and sharing the same spectacular view.

I tapped the word "Fitzgerald" with my finger. "The guy who was the bad boy when he stayed here is now a marketing brand name."

"And he'd finally have enough money to be *The Great Gatsby*," Nakayla said.

"How old was he when he died?"

"Forty-four."

"So much for his lifeline. But Ethel said the fortune-teller charged him only a dollar." I looked at my palm. "He should have paid more."

Nakayla took my hand and traced a path from below my wrist to the tip of my middle finger. "That's the lifeline I wish for you. But my magic's only good if you stay in Asheville. Fitzgerald had a heart attack in Hollywood. He shouldn't have left."

Hollywood. The place William Dudley Pelley worked before coming here to launch his fascist movement. What a time—the heart of The Great Depression with its politics of the New Deal, Communism, and Fascism all vying for loyalties. What had Fitzgerald found here amid the turbulence shaking the nation and the turmoil racking his personal life? Maybe the timelessness of the mountains or the strength of these stones that created both a shelter and a statement from a bygone age. A place where Jay Gatsby would have been at home.

I looked across the vast hall. Some people moved quickly, some strolled, and some sat in small groups or alone. For a moment I could see F. Scott Fitzgerald among them: a participant and an observer. And yet the scene would have been so different in his time. The cluster of businesswomen waiting for a table on the terrace would have disappeared, relegated to being escorted by their husbands. The black couple at the bar would have been washing glasses, not drinking from them. Nakayla and I couldn't have walked across the room holding hands without drawing icy stares or overt hostility.

Some things from the past were best buried.

"We're in luck." Derrick held up a magnetic keycard. "441 checked out this morning." He pressed the CALL button set in the stones.

As we entered, I asked, "Why's the elevator in the fireplace?"

"It saves space. And the rocks insulate the sound of the motor."

Nakayla laughed. "So you can ride the elevator after ten-thirty at night but not flush your commode."

Derrick shrugged. "Our elevator's in *Ripley's Believe It Or Not;* our commodes aren't."

"For being in the fireplace?" Nakayla asked.

"This one has three doors." Derrick swept his hand in an arc in front of him. "We came in the center, and there's a door to either side. Which one opens depends upon the floor. We're going to the left for the fourth."

Fitzgerald's room had a brass plaque on the door proclaiming its special heritage. Derrick keyed the lock and allowed Nakayla and me to enter ahead of him. I first noticed that the short entry hall had wooden dresser drawers built into the plaster wall. The room wasn't large and contained twin beds with slat headboards, a desk, and two wooden armchairs under a single window. Between the desk and the chairs stood an armoire, which I suspected housed a TV and cable box. On the wall hung photographs of Fitzgerald and various historical perspectives on his career and time in Asheville.

I ran my hand along the surface of the small desk. "Is this the same furniture?"

"The desk, chairs, headboards, and even the bathtub were in this room when Fitzgerald lived here."

"Didn't he also use 443?" Nakayla asked.

"Yes." Derrick walked to a door beside the desk. "It's adjoining. Occasionally he'd have them both as a suite, but this one was his favorite."

I bent between the chairs and looked out the window. "His favorite? He's facing the parking lot."

Derrick smiled. "Exactly. He'd sit here, and, while writing, he'd check out the young women entering the hotel. He'd note down those he'd want to meet later."

Nakayla spun around, taking it all in. "Amazing that you've been able to preserve everything."

"We did patch the bullet hole in the ceiling."

I looked up at the unblemished surface. "Fitzgerald had a gunfight?"

"No. The story is he discharged his handgun in a moment of passion."

"Gives new meaning to Mae West's question: 'Is that a pistol in your pocket or are you just glad to see me?'"

Nakayla winced. "Really, Sam."

Derrick politely let my remark pass and changed the subject. "Most of the Mission Arts and Crafts throughout the inn are originals. The grandfather clock in the Sammons Wing has been appraised at over a million dollars. Unlike the Biltmore House, we don't keep our treasures roped off."

"You must have one hell of a security team."

Derrick smiled. "Every employee. That's why I teach a class on the history. I want them to appreciate what we have."

"Fitzgerald didn't create any literary treasures in this room?" I asked.

"No. On top of all his other troubles, he severely dislocated his shoulder while diving at Beaver Lake. He was forced to wear a cast and couldn't type. He tried dictating his stories, but it didn't work out too well."

I turned to Nakayla. "Do you know the lake?"

"Yes. It's not too far."

"Our guests used to swim there," Derrick said. "But there's no swimming allowed now."

I paced the room a final time, as if some clue might have escaped detection for over seventy years. "So, Fitzgerald's stay wasn't productive."

"Not in a literary sense," Derrick said. "In 1935 he came here for his health because he thought he'd contracted tuberculosis. The next year he returned when Zelda was admitted to Highland Hospital. I don't think he seriously resumed his writing until he went to Hollywood."

"Nothing was written here?" Nakayla asked.

"I'm not a Fitzgerald scholar. Maybe a few short stories. Like I said, he was in pretty bad shape."

He headed for the door, but I side-stepped in front of him. "Do you know if he had anything to do with William Dudley Pelley?"

"Who?"

"A guy who lived in Asheville during the 1930s. He founded The Silver Shirts."

"Sounds vaguely familiar, but I've never heard the name in connection with Fitzgerald."

"We know they were interested in him. The Silver Shirts was an organization of fascists and Nazi sympathizers."

Derrick shook his head. "Are you sure about the year?"

"Yes," Nakayla said. "I found the date from several sources in the Pack Library."

"Sorry. I don't know of any Nazis that were here. Not at that time."

"Not at that time" caught my ear. "Were there Nazis here earlier?"

"No. But in the early forties, the government used the Grove Park Inn as a holding spot for Nazi diplomats. Just till they could be deported. There were guards on the grounds, but no barbed wire. To put it politely, they were unwanted guests."

I cut my eyes to Nakayla and saw her nod. In the 1940s, Ethel Barkley and her husband had lived only a few blocks away from the American-based brain trust of Hitler's Nazi patry.

Chapter Fourteen

Hewitt Donaldson stepped onto the terrace. He squinted against the setting sun and scanned the tables. I rose from my chair and gave enough of a wave to attract his attention.

He nodded without smiling and headed toward me. His suit had collected a day's worth of wrinkles. The ponytail was gone and his gray hair now fell around his shoulders in disheveled strands. To judge by appearances, Asheville's most flamboyant defense attorney had not had a good day in court. But then since I'd last seen him, his aunt had been murdered.

"Thanks for meeting me." He pulled out the opposite chair and glanced around as if to make sure no one he knew was sitting within earshot. "Where's your partner?"

"In the lobby. She thought you might want to see just me."

After our meeting with Derrick Swing, Nakayla had convinced me she'd be more valuable watching for who might be following us.

"No, she's welcome to sit in." He swiveled and looked back into the Great Hall.

"She ran into a friend," I lied. "Maybe we'll see her later."

Donaldson summoned a waiter and we both ordered Sam Adams. As soon as we were alone, he scooted closer to the table. "What the hell happened to my aunt?"

"She was killed by someone posing as a flower deliveryman."

"Why?"

"We don't know."

"Don't give me we don't know," he snapped. "What do you think?"

I was getting a taste of what Donaldson's cross-examinations must be like.

"I regret to say she might have been murdered because I tried to help her."

He stared at me, letting his silence push for further explanation.

"She was my client. I went to her apartment twice and I retrieved her lockbox."

"Lockbox?"

His question told me the police hadn't shared that information. I gave him the summary of my experience at the bank and the lockbox's disappearance from our office.

"You think that's why they broke in?"

"Maybe. But they bugged our phones. I think that's what they were doing when the guard discovered them. The lockbox might have been their reason, as well, or just something that looked valuable. Once they saw the contents, they must have figured your aunt either knew something that they wanted kept quiet or they thought she had more information. The problem is neither the police nor I have a handle on the motive."

Donaldson thought for a moment. Then he took a long sip of beer and set the glass on the table with a thud. He smiled, and that made me more nervous than when he was badgering me. "All right. I expect I'll be summoned to police headquarters for questioning as to any enemies a ninety-year-old woman might have made. I spoke with Aunt Ethel's son Terry. He's driving up from Charlotte and may wish to see you."

"Fine." I used the break in his questions to interject my own. "Is your cousin the sole heir?"

Donaldson laughed. "Right to the point. You're a man after my own heart."

"I'm not after your heart, but someone might be after your aunt's five million dollars."

He flushed. I wondered if the bank manager had told me a closely guarded family secret.

His voice dropped to a low growl. "I want no part of Aunt Ethel's estate or anything in the lockbox."

"Wouldn't it go to her son? I thought he was her only surviving child."

"Terry will get her personal assets—except for certain funds stipulated to be split between us. So the police will have to consider that I had nearly two-and-a-half million reasons to kill her."

"But I take it you're a successful attorney. Why kill her now?"

He shrugged. "Maybe I've got a terminal illness and I'm afraid she'll outlive me. Maybe I got nervous when she hired you to get the lockbox. I can read your face. You're already thinking through those possibilities, aren't you?"

Hewitt Donaldson wasn't a man to bluff against in a poker game.

"Why don't you want your share of the money?"

"I don't like what it represents."

"Money's money," I said. "It's what you do with it that's important."

He twisted in his chair and crossed his legs. A light evening breeze set his long hair dancing against his collar. "Sometimes money brings its past with it. I may be a lawyer, but I have a few shreds of decency that our so-called justice system hasn't stripped away."

I decided to stop playing games. "Where'd it come from? A Nazi payoff?"

Donaldson raised his half-empty glass and toasted me. "You are the right man for the job."

I kept my beer on the table. "Not me. The right man for the job is a woman. Nakayla did the research that led to the Silver Shirts. That's the money's source, isn't it?"

He left his glass in the air and the smile on his lips, but his voice rang cold. "Be careful what you say. Asheville may have dark secrets that some people want to keep buried."

I stared back at him. "Is that why I'm here? So you can tell me to stop digging?"

Donaldson leaned across the table so far he came out of his chair. "No. I want to hire you, Sam. I don't like surprises, and it's time I stopped denying the past and faced the truth."

"Is that because your aunt's dead?"

"Partly. I could never get beyond her mumbo-jumbo and the fantasy world she lived in."

"You could have hired a private detective years ago."

"Let's say maybe I never wanted to ask a question to which I didn't already know the answer. Being a lawyer isn't a vocation, it's a curse." He stopped and the façade on his face cracked. His eyes welled. "And that young guard might have died because of something I let go unchallenged."

"Sorry. I already have a client on this case."

"Who?"

"Your aunt."

He relaxed into his chair. "I visited her last Sunday and mentioned we had a detective moving next to our office. She likes to read mysteries. You could say I'm the reason she hired you. And she's not exactly in a position to pay you."

So Ethel's having Captain contact me hadn't been coincidence, and I now had an explanation for why her nephew happened to be beside us. But she hadn't told Donaldson she was hiring me. Why?

"She made an arrangement," I said. "I, too, have a few shreds of decency left. I won't double-bill a case."

"Then whom will you report your findings to?"

I wanted to say my conscience, but I'd just told Donaldson I was working for a fee under a contract that went beyond the client's death, assuming Fitzgerald's gift was still in the lockbox. "I guess the proper procedure will be to file a report with the executor of her estate."

His smile returned. "Precisely. And as the executor, I'm requesting that you say nothing to my cousin about your investigation. And that you clear everything with me before sharing information with the police."

I slid back the chair and got to my feet, my artificial leg buckling slightly with the rapid rise. "Then I'm resigning. Consider our conversation your final report."

"Hold on." He licked his lips and laid his palms flat on the table. "You're still going to investigate, aren't you?"

"You said you could read my face."

He nodded. "Sit down, please. Let me rephrase my concerns, and I hope you'll excuse my erratic behavior. I'm upset about what happened to my aunt and the young woman."

"And your own safety," I added.

"I suppose. You see I don't know what's going on. I don't like it. That's when I make mistakes, like trying to control you. Stay on the case and work however you want. If your fees go beyond what my aunt authorized, I'll make up the difference. All I ask is that you do your best to keep me informed. I'd appreciate not being blindsided, especially where it regards my father."

I eased into the chair. "All right. What about your cousin?"

"My cousin will have no qualms about the money. He resents that I'm due an equal share and he'll try to stop you from doing anything that might delay or negate the settlement."

"What could I do? I assume the will is straightforward, if you drew it up."

Donaldson lifted his hands and clasped them together so tightly his knuckles turned white. "But I didn't. My father drew up the will on file, the only one she's ever had."

"When?"

"In 1935. Ten years ago she had another attorney amend it naming me as the executor. Her son went ballistic, but I think for all of our differences, my aunt trusted me to carry out her wishes."

He stopped as our waiter approached the table.

"Would you gentlemen care for another round?"

"Not me," I said.

Donaldson also declined and asked for the check. The waiter cleared the empty glasses and left.

I began to understand what was troubling him. "Why are you in her will? In 1935, neither you nor your cousin had been born."

"That's right, and when my father died, my mother received my father's estate except for these same funds that were earmarked for his sister, with the stipulation that half of them would come back to his progeny upon her death, provided they hadn't been used."

"Your father went to a lot of effort to keep them intact, and your aunt must have never touched them." The obvious point came to me. "Wouldn't the probate of his estate have shown the source of the money?"

"Normally." Donaldson sighed. "Man, I've got to hand it to him. My uncle too. I'm sure they both put the scheme together."

"What scheme?"

Donaldson smiled with what might have been pride. "The funds came from a life insurance policy. Life insurance proceeds go directly to the beneficiary. There's no court filing, no income taxes, just a check. And no one goes back to look at the source of the premium."

"Have you seen the policy?"

"No. It would have been surrendered with the claim. But it had to be taken out before 1935, because my aunt's will references the policy. That'll come to light during her probate."

"Is there a policy number?"

"No. Just the company name. The Pollosco Life Assurance Society. I've checked on them. They were gobbled up years ago."

"What about old check records? Somebody paid the premiums."

Donaldson shook his head. "Maybe there's some record in the lockbox, but I suspect there was only one premium paid. He probably made a large enough prepayment that the policy was instantly in force and would never lapse. It would grow in cash value without any income tax liability, could be surrendered for cash or borrowed against, and paid out a death benefit that grew over the years, particularly if dividends were used to buy additional insurance."

"Maybe your father just wanted some life insurance."

"Then why didn't my mother get the money? Even if he took out the policy before he married, it's common practice for a new husband to change the beneficiary of his insurance."

Donaldson's suspicions were contagious. I couldn't come up with a plausible explanation.

"But there's another consideration I can't dismiss." He shifted in his seat, and I sensed he moved from prosecutor to defense attorney.

"What?"

He wagged his finger. "Remember we're talking 1934 and '35. The Great Depression. Thirty-eight percent of the banks failed. But only 14 percent of the life insurance companies went under. Limits had been put on how much of a policy's cash you could pull out or how much you could borrow. If you didn't need your money for a while, that regulation provided comforting stability."

My financial expertise bordered on zero. Only within the previous three months had I dealt with circumstances more complicated than depositing an Army paycheck. "But wouldn't that make your father's actions prudent even if the money had been earned legitimately?"

"That's my point. And maybe Aunt Ethel's husband was uninsurable, so my father was making certain she'd be cared for. In return, his offspring would share in the payout."

"What you're telling me is that you don't know."

Donaldson held out his hands palm up like they were a pair of scales. "I'd like to believe my father was very clever with his funds at a time of financial turbulence." He let his left hand drop lower as the right rose. "That the payout arrangement took care of his sister and both their heirs. On the other hand, why has my aunt been so secretive in preserving those funds for over sixty years?"

"Maybe she read more into your father's will than he intended."

"And maybe I'm reading more into the fact that he was a key member of the defense team when William Dudley Pelley went on trial for fraud in 1934 and again for sedition in 1942." He quickly reversed his hand motion till the left was above his head and the right smacked the top of the table. "My father represented a man who idolized Adolph Hitler, who wanted to confine the Jews to one city in each state, and who wanted to be the transitional dictator as he turned our country into a Christian bastion against what he called the International Jewish-Communist Conspiracy headed by Franklin Delano Roosevelt, whom he called the Russocrat." He brought his hands together and twiddled his thumbs, mocking the seriousness of his charge. "You're the jury. What do you think?"

"I think you need more evidence before you take a pass on two and a half million dollars."

The smile returned. "That's why I want to hire you."

"I'm working for your aunt," I repeated. "But I'll keep your questions in mind."

"Sam, the most important question in my mind is one I haven't asked yet. You said you were afraid my aunt was murdered because you tried to help her. What you didn't say was whether that was because you're a private detective or because you're Sam Blackman."

A shadow came over the table. Our waiter returned, but not from inside the inn. Donaldson looked up and reached for his wallet, expecting to receive the bill. Instead, the waiter handed me a slip of paper. "A gentleman at the edge of the terrace asked me to give you this."

Unfolding a torn scrap of a brochure, I saw a note written in the white margin. "Chief, he's here." I glanced back in the direction the waiter had come. Calvin leaned against a stone column at the edge of the terrace. The distant buildings of Asheville lay behind him, reflecting gold from the setting sun. He gave a quick jerk of his head toward the lobby and walked away. I crumpled the note and dropped it in my coat pocket.

"Sorry, something's come up," I whispered. "Would you mind waiting five minutes before leaving? I want it to look like I'm coming back."

Donaldson arched his eyebrows. "You didn't answer my question."

"That's because I don't know the answer." I stood, shifting my weight to make sure my stump was snugly fitted in my prosthesis. "But I expect that's about to change."

I caught the departing waiter. "Excuse me. Where's the restroom?" I asked the question loud enough for adjoining tables to hear.

He pointed through the terrace doors to the Great Hall. "Turn right at the registration desk and it's in the Sammons Wing on your right."

As I crossed between the giant fireplaces, I saw Nakayla sitting in a chair and thumbing through a magazine with her eyes subtly scanning the room. She froze when I motioned her to stay seated. Calvin's tall silhouette stood just inside the entrance from the parking lot. He waited beside the valet station where he could watch the doors to either side. The expression on his face was obscured by shadows, but his location told me our quarry was still inside.

I glanced back at Nakayla. She closed the magazine and stood. As she walked by, she whispered, "Behind information."

The information desk was less than twenty feet away, near the elevator we'd taken to Fitzgerald's room. A young couple had a map spread out in front of the attendant. I doubted our adversaries had a male/female team tailing me. Beyond them, a fair-haired man stood at a brochure rack. He looked up and for a split-second our eyes locked. Then he dropped his gaze back to the pamphlets and eased to his left, moving behind a column. He sported a neatly trimmed beard, and something about him seemed familiar. I couldn't swear to it, but clean-shaven he might have been Evan Lucas, one of the ex-Blackwater men whom our Ali Baba investigation had targeted.

I waited a few seconds for him to emerge. During that time, I took in the surroundings. A woman who looked like the grandmother was photographing an older man and child in front of the fireplace. Two businessmen exited from the elevator and walked toward me, momentarily obscuring my view of the column. I looked over my shoulder. Calvin took a step closer, his right hand reaching behind his back. He wasn't looking at the column but to the far end of the fireplace beside the entrance to the Vanderbilt Wing. Another blond man in a windbreaker was reading the quotations that had been written on the various stones. Even though the Great Hall was warm, he'd zipped his jacket to his neck.

"That's him," Calvin said. "He's been following you since the library."

"Stay with the exits," I said to Calvin. "I'll try to lead him where it's not so crowded."

Nakayla stepped beside me. "If he makes a break, there are too many exits to cover."

"He's armed. I want you out of the line of fire."

Nakayla's eyes blazed. "I'll be where I need to be to bring him in."

"Then call the cops and cover the parking lot in case he gets to his vehicle." I looked at the suspect. He'd turned from the fireplace and was watching us. With a single motion, he pivoted and walked into the Vanderbilt Wing. "Damn. We've spooked him." I hurried in pursuit, cursing myself for wearing the wrong leg.

What must have been a busload of senior tourists flowed along the Vanderbilt Wing's hallway toward me. Canes, walkers, and wheelchairs set a moving obstacle course impeding my progress. But above the gray heads, I could see Blondie also dodging his way. He looked back, saw me, and doubled his speed. Then I lost sight of him.

A glass door leading to the Vanderbilt Atrium blocked the end of the hall. I didn't see it open, which meant Blondie had turned left into an area of shops. Another split and I faced the choice of entering a restaurant or taking a second hall into the atrium. I gambled that the restaurant wouldn't have as many exits, which meant Blondie would avoid it.

I heard a commotion and saw a bellman's cart topple. People dispersed, revealing Blondie entangled with potted plants that must have en route to another location. I sprinted forward as fast as my leg allowed.

Blondie scrambled to his feet just out of my grasp. I pursued him into the atrium, a spacious room several stories high with a maze of open staircases surrounding a central elevator. The architect had peppered the stairs with landings where patrons could enjoy the internal view.

Seeing me, Blondie unzipped his jacket. I followed as fast as I could, snatching my pistol from its holster and flipping off the safety. I was no more than a few yards behind him, but I knew he'd beat me in a foot race. He veered right onto a landing that displayed an antique pool table. He turned down another short flight to a second landing. It dead-ended on the left at a staff entrance.

Straight across and more than ten feet away lay a separate landing below the glass door we had bypassed. That was the way to the ground floor. To reach it, Blondie would have to hurdle the railing, sail through the air, and safely clear the second railing. Not an impossible task for Jack Bauer or James Bond, but his challenge was more than Olympic athleticism. Nakayla crouched on the opposite stairway, her twenty-five-caliber pistol rock-steady and trained on Blondie's chest. Calvin eased down the stairs behind her, his gun pointed at the ceiling.

"Stop!" Nakayla shouted. "Hands in the air."

For a second, Blondie hesitated. Then he dropped and rolled. He came up on one knee, a coal-black pistol in his hand. He swung the barrel toward me.

I squeezed off three rounds. The Kimber jumped and the loud reports reverberated through the atrium like sonic booms. The silver-tipped .45s knocked Blondie backwards. I saw a muzzle flash from his pistol but heard no sound. My ears were already deafened.

He bounced off a rock wall and fell face down on the green carpet. Red splotches began soaking through the ripped fabric of the back of his windbreaker.

I don't know how long I stood there, my finger on the trigger and my eyes searching for any movement. The ringing in my head faded and I could hear Nakayla calling me. I risked a glance and saw her and Calvin with their weapons still drawn. Hewitt Donaldson stood on the stairs above them, his ashen face dwarfed by his wide eyes.

"Are you all right?" Nakayla asked.

"Yes. I think he fired once but the shot went wild. Keep him covered." I turned around, worried that the stray bullet might have injured someone in the atrium. People had come to the edge of the balconies all the way to the top floor. Most turned away when they realized they were looking down on a dead body. I approached the man with caution and kicked his pistol beyond his reach. Then I knelt and checked his neck for a pulse.

"Hewitt," Nakayla said. "Get Grove Park security and tell them to keep everybody clear."

"Is he history?" Calvin asked.

I nodded. History. But what history did this son of a bitch take with him? What history had he known that could keep us alive?

Chapter Fifteen

"That's the man I saw at the restaurant." Nathan Armitage made the positive ID as he knelt over the upturned face of the dead gunman.

"And you two say he's Evan Lucas?" Detective Newland asked Calvin and me.

Calvin nodded. "I was covering Chief's back and noticed this guy eyeing him. I sent Chief a note on the terrace, and when he saw us together he took off. I never got that close to Lucas in Iraq, but that's the ugly face I saw on surveillance photos."

The dead man wasn't so much ugly as plain. Straight straw hair, a broad nose that looked like it had been broken at least once, and skin both freckled and pockmarked. He hadn't carried any identification or room key. A set of Hyundai car keys on a Hertz chain and three hundred dollars in cash were the only items on his body.

"What about you?" Newland prompted.

"I agree with Calvin. I'm 90 percent sure he's Lucas."

Newland turned to the EMTs. "Then bag him and get him out of here. We'll lift his prints and run a check against those Nathan got this afternoon." He stepped away from the body and went up to the landing with the antique pool table. Calvin, Nakayla, Donaldson, Nathan, and I followed.

"Was Sam's the only weapon discharged?" Newland asked.

"Lucas fired at least once," Nakayla said. "He rolled where the corner of the rock wall blocked our line of sight, but I heard four shots."

Calvin walked over to the pool table. "I saw wood fly off." He bent over the corner. "There's a slug beside the pocket. If he wanted to play eight-ball, he should have called it."

I wondered if the man who fixed the bullet hole in Fitzgerald's ceiling was still alive.

Newland frowned. "I'll have the crime lab dig it out. We found only three brass. All from Sam's Kimber."

"His gun might have ejected the casing over the edge and it's below somewhere," I said. "He was whipping it around pretty fast."

"Thank God he wasn't fast enough," Nathan said.

"Do you need the Kimber?" I asked Newland.

"I'm satisfied he pulled a gun and fired. We don't know who else is out there gunning for you. Keep it, but drop by tomorrow and check with Efird. You and Nakayla can give your statements. I'll bring him up to speed, and he can have you fire a round for a ballistics match—just for the record."

"Anything else?" I asked.

"Yeah." Newland looked at Calvin. "You come with them. I want Efird to get your statement and a little more background on what's happened on your case since Sam was wounded."

Calvin gave him a thumbs-up. "You got it, man."

"Where are you going to be?" I asked.

Newland grimaced. "Close to a bathroom." He shifted his weight, obviously uncomfortable with further explanation. "I've got a colonoscopy scheduled. I've postponed it five times and my wife made me swear nothing short of a nuclear attack on Asheville would interfere."

Nathan shook his head in sympathy. "Been there, done that. But it's not tomorrow, is it?"

"No. Early Friday morning. Tomorrow's prep day."

Calvin laughed. "Riding the porcelain bus. Man, I'd rather be in another shootout than swallow Phospho-soda."

Newland didn't appreciate the ribbing. "You're kinda young to know what you're talking about. Wait till you've been through it."

Calvin's jaw tightened, and I knew he resented the putdown, slight as it was.

"Well, you've got my condolences," Donaldson said. "And that's coming from someone I know you consider one of the biggest asses in Asheville."

We all laughed, not so much at Donaldson's remark but to relieve the tension of what we'd just been through. The zip of the body bag punctuated the moment, and I knew the case was far from closed.

"How'd you get here so fast?" Newland asked Nathan.

"I still had someone on Sam and Nakayla. He called me when he spotted Lucas. Things went down so fast he wasn't able to help."

"Where is he?" Newland asked.

"I told him to lay low in case there's a second tail. He's still in the Great Hall."

"Blond hair and beard?" I thought Nathan's operative had to be the man Nakayla and I mistook for Lucas.

"No. Black hair and clean-shaven. He's very good. Half the shoplifters convicted in Asheville were nailed by Stu."

I glanced at Nakayla and could tell she was as upset as I was that we'd pegged the wrong suspect.

"I'd like to talk to him," Newland said. "We've got Ethel Barkley's killer on the loose, and I'd like to know if he saw anyone who might match the Hispanic description we got from Golden Oaks."

"Now?" Nathan asked.

"Sure. Might as well cram in as much as I can before I catch the porcelain bus." He winked at Calvin.

Calvin accepted the cue that Newland had gotten over his joke. "What can we do?"

"You and Sam put your heads together and come up with some way we can flush these guys out. How many do you think we're dealing with? What's the connection between your case and the missing lockbox? You know the drill. Bring me something we can work with. Together." He emphasized the last word and there was no doubt he was running the show, even if it might be from the john.

As we broke up, I heard Newland yell to his nephews to check the dead man's car keys against the vehicles in the parking lot and wire his description to the rental agencies.

It was nearly seven and I realized I hadn't eaten all day. "Where are you parked?" I asked Calvin.

"At the edge of the main lot."

"You want to grab a bite?"

"Is there someplace we can talk in private?"

I looked to Nakayla for a suggestion, but she stared straight ahead, her teeth clenched. My superior detective skills told me she was mad as hell. "Why don't Nakayla and I get some takeout? We can meet at the apartment, say eight?"

"Sounds like a plan." He clapped me on the back. "You did good, Chief. Ed and Charlie would be proud." He turned to Nakayla. "Nice working with you, pretty lady."

"The name's Nakayla." The words came out as brittle as ice.

"Well, nice working with you, Nakayla. You've got guts. You can cover my back anytime."

She shot him a glance as cold as her words. "I believe I was the one in front." She hurried her pace, pulling away from both of us. "See you at eight," she called over her shoulder.

"Spirited," Calvin said. "I like that in a woman."

"I like it in a partner." I hurried down the hill after her, figuring the chill of the September night would be a heat wave compared to the temperature inside my CR-V.

As soon as I was within range, I used my keyless remote to unlock the Honda. Nakayla got in the passenger's seat without waiting for me.

I slid behind the steering wheel. "What's the problem?"

Nakayla took a deep breath, held it a few seconds, and then spoke in a voice so tight a crowbar couldn't loosen her words. "The first problem is that you even have to ask the question."

"What? Are you mad because I was giving you orders? The Grove Park turned into a combat zone."

"I can take orders. What I can't take is you pushing me into the background. 'Stay out of the line of fire, Nakayla. Watch the parking lot, Nakayla.'"

"The parking lot needed watching."

"No. The suspect needed to be apprehended. I'm your partner, not your secretary or your research assistant. Either we're in this together or I'm out."

"Look, you're a terrific partner. That's what I told Calvin. But your experience in insurance fraud isn't preparation for confronting armed assailants. You were lucky tonight."

"Lucky?" Her sarcastic tone could have drenched Sunset Mountain.

I cringed at my word choice, but I was too far down the road to turn back. "We're partners. We've got to be honest with each other."

I took her silence for a yes. "You pegged the wrong man. If Calvin hadn't been there, we would have missed Lucas."

"The guy was watching me."

"A lot of guys watch you. Believe me, I notice."

"And I saw him walk close enough to the terrace to check on you and Donaldson."

"There's also a spectacular view."

"All right. I pegged the wrong man. But I knew the layout of the Grove Park and figured you'd chase him to that landing. If I'd been out in the parking lot, Lucas would have made it into the employee offices. No telling who could have been hurt."

I flashed on the image of Nakayla on the stairs, her gun level and her face set in fearless determination. No question her bravery had stopped him. But the man had been good. In a split-second, he'd seen the opportunity to roll out of her line of fire and take me out. I guess he hadn't counted on my being armed.

Nakayla's voice grew angrier. "But I can tell I'm not part of your boys' club. Newland wants you and Calvin to put your heads together. Forget me. And then Ed and Charlie, whoever they are, are going to be proud of your kill, like you'd bagged some twelve-point buck."

"Ed and Charlie aren't ever going to be proud of anything." I turned the key in the ignition and raced the engine for a second. Then as I put the gear in reverse, I said, "They were our two buddies killed when my leg was blown off. The man I shot was one of those responsible." I backed the car out of the parking space and started down the mountain. "Call it a boys' club if you want, but Calvin and I feel an obligation to see justice done."

She turned in her seat and looked at me for the first time since we left the inn. "Seeing justice done is one thing, seeking revenge is something else. I'm one who knows the difference."

She spoke the truth. Her sister had been brutally murdered and Nakayla's appeal for my help had been grounded in her desire for justice. I had to remember that revenge worked more on the innocent than the guilty. If that became my motivation, then I'd be in danger of shutting out Nakayla and anyone else who cared for me.

"Okay. I apologize. You're right, and you made a hell of a partner tonight. I promise I won't close you out. That'd be crazy because you're smarter than Calvin and me put together. I guess I'm not over my fear."

"Fear? Fear of Lucas?"

"Fear that they'd taken you. Maybe killed you. After Ethel Barkley was murdered, we didn't know who'd be next." I risked taking my right hand off the wheel and held it out between us. "I felt so helpless."

She pressed my palm between both of hers. "Apology accepted. And, for the record, I'm sorry I picked the wrong man in the Great Hall."

We headed into a series of curves and I reluctantly pulled my hand free to grip the wheel. "To be honest, I thought you were right about the guy. I guess it proves there's a blurry line between being suspicious and being paranoid."

"I understand where you and Calvin are coming from. You do have an obligation."

"Ed and Charlie were good men. They died serving their country. We all have an obligation to them."

Nakayla put her hand on my right leg, the leg that was still all me. "And justice should come from all of us. I'm not sure Calvin sees things the same way you do."

"What do you mean?"

"He strikes me as a hotdog."

"That's just Calvin. And I think he's got survivor's guilt. I've seen it in a lot of guys."

"Maybe," Nakayla said. "But I don't want his survivor's guilt to get you killed."

We rode in silence for a few miles. I mulled over everything she had said, especially the difference between justice and revenge. Calvin's obsession with the Blackwater swill could bite me. We were expected to cooperate with the Asheville police. But, as sure as I sat behind the wheel, I knew Calvin wouldn't hesitate to pursue his own leads, regardless of what Detective Newland or I said.

Nakayla broke into my thoughts. "Since we're being honest, I have to confess part of me is glad you shot that guy."

"Really? Self-defense isn't justice."

"And it's not revenge. But in that split-second after I yelled for him to stop, I saw something that still chills me."

"What?"

"He smiled at me. If that wasn't the face of a cold-blooded killer, then I never hope to see one."

Chapter Sixteen

"I think Chinese is what I miss the most." Calvin scooped the last of the beef and broccoli out of the cardboard container and onto his plate. "Something about Baghdad and hot and sour soup doesn't work for me."

We sat around my small dining table. Nakayla and I had eaten modest portions of the three dishes: beef, chicken, and shrimp prepared in classical Asian traditions. Calvin made sure nothing would be left to refrigerate.

I'd done most of the talking, filling them in on the murder scene at Golden Oaks and reviewing my conversations with Ethel Barkley for Calvin's benefit. While returning from the Grove Park Inn, Nakayla and I had discussed Hewitt Donaldson's request for help, and she pushed me to keep that information confidential. She said sharing details of what might be Donaldson's dirty laundry wasn't a good way to build a reputation for Blackman and Robertson. I had to agree.

"I have no doubt the police will match Lucas' prints to the guy who followed Nakayla this afternoon." Calvin jabbed his fork at me. "Your friend's description matched him, and we suspect Hernandez was killing the old lady at that same time."

"What do you think, Nakayla?" I got up from the table, carrying the dishes to the counter. Calvin's macho attitude wouldn't get any reinforcement from me.

"I think we're floundering. We have suspects, one less, thank God, but we're looking at motives that are miles and years apart."

"How's that?" Calvin asked.

"Something happened back in Iraq that brought these killers to Asheville." She turned to Calvin. "First they tried for you in Paterson, New Jersey, but you gave them the slip. Then they came for Sam. But the murders involved a lockbox with no ties to Iraq, and Ethel Barkley was tortured. Why? Maybe to give up some facts they wanted to know, or maybe to find out what she'd told Sam. We're floundering because the motives don't connect. What would a theft and smuggling operation in Iraq have to do with a ninety-year-old woman and her ties to F. Scott Fitzgerald? Or a fascist movement that collapsed in the 1940s?"

Calvin leaned back in the chair and crossed his arms. "Honey, I can tell you the motive. Greed. That's what I told Sam. It cuts through time and distance."

"That's what Sam told me. And he said we should turn their motive against them." She looked at me, and I could tell she was hesitant to go on.

"I doubt if Ethel told them anything they could use," I said. "She didn't know about my Cayman account, if that's what they were after."

Calvin rose and started pacing. "I think you're right, Chief. The old lady and the lockbox were a side opportunity. They bug your office, they hear about her money, and something in the lockbox arouses their curiosity. I don't have a clue as to what. Money or negotiable securities wouldn't mean they'd whack the old lady. But what if it was something they didn't understand."

"You mean like a code," Nakayla said.

"Yeah. Could be something like that."

"*The Great Gatsby*," I muttered.

"What?" Calvin broke into a grin. A green speck of broccoli clung to one of his white teeth. "You've figured it out, haven't you?"

"No. But you could be onto something. Ethel Barkley might have been a little loony, but she was also cagey. The password *The Great Gatsby* showed how she thought. I'm sure the Silver Shirts had their share of codes, secret handshakes, and mystic symbols."

I remembered the poem: "The Silver Shirts Are Marching!" "They fancied themselves at war with the U.S. government, an agent of God and doing his will."

Calvin snorted. "Sounds damn familiar, doesn't it? So much for time and distance."

"Yeah. And if Ali Baba had a political agenda, then I'd say we might be oversimplifying the greed motive. But that doesn't matter, because what we need to do to end this is the same whatever the motive."

I had their attention: Calvin looked eager and Nakayla worried, sensing what I was about to propose.

"They murdered two innocent women," I said.

Calvin slapped the table with his broad palm. "Hell, we're all innocent."

"Right. Which means any of us, or anyone close to us could be targeted."

The phone rang in the bedroom, the fourth call in twenty minutes. I suspected the press was scrambling to cover the Grove Park shooting. Detective Newland would keep them off me as best he could, but they'd be anxious to interview the man who pulled the trigger. The ringing ceased and a voice spoke on the answering machine. The closed bedroom door muffled the words to unintelligible sounds.

I continued. "I don't want to wait to find out who or when they strike next."

"Hernandez might be the only one left," Calvin said. "He knows he's going against both of us. And now he's got the police and your friend Nathan's surveillance people to deal with."

Nakayla sat stiffly in the chair. "And me."

Calvin pointed his index finger at her and moved his thumb like the hammer of a revolver. "Right, sister. Like you. That goes without saying."

Nakayla glared at him. "No, we're going to say it because I don't want you to forget it, like you've forgotten something else."

Calvin's dark face grew darker. "What's that?"

"Odds are that Hernandez is not the only one left. I've been thinking how they put a tail on me. If the fingerprints from Lucas match those on the glass, then he was following me. Someone, probably Hernandez, killed Ethel Barkley. But Sam is the bigger fish. Why wouldn't Lucas have dropped me, either to take care of Ethel or to tail Sam? I can't believe they would let Sam go unobserved. There has to be a third man."

Calvin pursed his lips. Then he slowly nodded in agreement. "And this guy you saw, the one with the blond hair and beard, he might be our third man?"

"We have to work that possibility. Sam saw him and got the same feeling I did. He was watching us."

"I trust Nakayla's instincts," I said. "That's why we've got to draw them out."

"How?" Calvin asked.

"Make them think we've got what Ethel Barkley wouldn't give them. We have to assemble the pieces we have into a story they'll believe. We have to set a trap, and I'm the only one who can do it."

"I don't know, Chief. I agree with Nakayla that we're dealing with more than Hernandez. You don't want to be bait for these jokers."

For the first time, Nakayla smiled at Calvin. "That's what I've been telling him."

I pressed ahead. "But we want them to think they still have the upper hand. And there's a difference between setting a trap and being the bait."

Calvin returned to his chair. "So, what's the plan?"

I looked out the window behind Nakayla. The sun had set about forty minutes earlier and constellations formed as stars broke through the darkening sky. My idea came as an illumination from points of light, needing only imagination to connect them.

"If Ethel Barkley's lockbox does contain something they don't understand, maybe a coded account book or map, then knowing how to decipher the code is what they want most."

Calvin held up his hand to stop me. "How about nailing our asses to the wall because they think we robbed their cache? And the fact they think your Grand Cayman account holds their money."

"That too. But you suggested that something about the lockbox intrigues them. I think it holds papers written in code, because I think I know the key to breaking it."

"You do?" Calvin and Nakayla exclaimed together.

"Yes. But knowing the information could be dangerous. If all you can give them is my name, then odds are they'll keep you alive till they get to me."

Nakayla scowled. "So you're going to be bait."

"No. I'm talking about a worst-case scenario using the code as a backup bargaining chip in case one of you is taken. We can't dangle that carrot because we don't know how to reach them. I'm planning something much simpler."

"What?" Calvin asked.

"We create a ruse. We find another lockbox. One that I dig up from a spot that might fit in with the information they have. I'll work that out tomorrow and keep as close to known facts as I can."

"What happens after you dig up this lockbox?" Nakayla asked.

"I leave it in the trunk of the car and then stake it out."

Calvin pushed away from the table and my proposal. "They'll smell it ten miles away."

"Not when they think the police aren't looking for them. If Newland agrees, then we plant a story that Lucas is the prime suspect in the murders of both Amanda Whitfield and Ethel Barkley. Newland can say Lucas probably followed me from the bank, broke in for the lockbox, and then went to Ethel's apartment in search of more money."

Nakayla shook her head. "The suspect was described as Hispanic."

"By witnesses that the police will say were unreliable. Captain will change his story for us."

She still looked unconvinced. "Who's protecting you while you're digging up bogus treasure?"

"I'll have Nathan handle that. You two need to be doing something else, something that will keep two of them occupied and make it look like I'm going behind your backs. Like you said, Calvin, a thief is going to project his own behavior on the situation."

Nakayla and Calvin exchanged a quick glance.

"Makes me nervous," Nakayla said. "I don't like you digging out in the woods by yourself."

"I'll be sensible."

She rolled her eyes. "Yeah, right. Your name and sensible don't belong in the same sentence."

"I like it," Calvin said. "If the spot's right, you can dig it up in broad daylight. That'll make sure they see you and you'll be less vulnerable to attack. What's your timetable?"

"We'll lay it out to Efird when we give our statements tomorrow. If he and Newland go along, the planted story should hit TV in the evening and the newspapers Friday morning. We'll stake out the car Friday night." I winked at Nakayla. "If we nail them, then we'll have had a good first week in business."

We talked through more details, agreeing that Nathan Armitage should be brought into the scheme. His men could handle burying the lockbox and provide the protective surveillance when I dug it up. Efird and his police team would stake out the car, and Nakayla, Calvin, and I would be elsewhere.

Calvin agreed to meet us at police headquarters at nine, where we'd give our statements and propose the plan to Efird. I figured Newland would approve, even if he had to do so by cell phone from the commode in his bathroom.

Nakayla and I took the elevator with Calvin to the lobby. Behind the locked doors, we watched him walk to his car and drive away. No one appeared to be following him.

I deadbolted the apartment door and slid the sofa in front of it. When Nakayla and I undressed for bed, I set the Kimber on the nightstand, a round loaded in its chamber.

As I'd thought, the messages on the answering machine were from reporters, one from the Asheville Citizen-Times and three from the network-affiliated TV stations in the area. All of them wanted to talk to me before deadline. I saved their phone numbers. Tomorrow I would use them to tell the story I wanted made public.

As I crawled into bed beside Nakayla, I did something I'd never done before. I left my prosthesis attached to my stump. Then I checked that my pistol was within easy reach. The gallows humor hit me. If the showdown came tonight, at least I'd be fully armed and legged.

Chapter Seventeen

I slept fitfully, a combination of discomfort with my leg and excitement that we were going on the offensive. In Iraq, the adrenaline rush came as we moved in for an arrest or when a sting operation reached the climactic moment. But this time the surge of energy arrived early and the anticipation of action accelerated my pulse. This time the confrontation would be personal, and I knew for all my talk about justice, I shared Calvin's desire for revenge.

At six, I rose, trying in vain not to disturb Nakayla. She bolted upright, throwing off the sheet. She'd slept fully dressed except for her shoes. "What's wrong?"

"Nothing. I just can't sleep. I'm going to run out for a while."

"Not by yourself."

"I'll be fine. It's early enough that anyone following me will stick out like a cat at a dog show." I slipped off my pants and released my prosthesis.

"Where are you going so early? And why are you removing your leg?"

I hopped to the closet and retrieved my second prosthesis, the one designed for more physical exertion. "I want to look for a place to bury the dummy lockbox. I don't want to approach Efird with missing details."

Nakayla grabbed her shoes from under the bed. "If you're going out in the woods, you're definitely not going by yourself."

I leaned against the wall, clutching my leg and realizing how vulnerable I must look to her. "There's a greater risk if you go with me."

She raised her head, one shoe dangling from her toes. "What? You think I'll be in your way?"

"No. But you'll ruin the story we want them to create. I'm supposed to be doing this behind everyone's back. If you're with me, then it looks like I've brought in an accomplice. That won't make sense."

She frowned. "Okay. But call in every ten minutes. Where do you think you'll go?"

"I'd like to check out Beaver Lake, the place where Fitzgerald injured his shoulder and where Grove Park guests could go swimming."

"It wasn't just for the guests. At one time, it was a public beach, but as long as I can remember, there's been no swimming. You could only use small boats or canoes. Once I saw an old postcard that showed diving boards and bathhouses. Those facilities were torn down long ago."

I grabbed a clean stump sleeve and sock from my dresser and sat on the bed to attach the leg. "Is the lake shore built up?"

"There are houses around it. Most are set back across the road. Merrimon Avenue runs along one side. You have to get a permit if you want to use a boat, and one end is still heavily wooded. There are walking trails, but at that end the path's more overgrown."

"Sounds promising."

Nakayla stared at me a few seconds and her eyes glistened in the dawn light spilling over the ridges. "You be careful, Sam. I mean it."

"I will. And I'll call in."

She followed me to the lobby, insisting that she watch until I reached my car.

I kissed her. "I'll see you at police headquarters."

"Oh, yeah? Well, I hope you're better with the details of your trap than your logistics for transportation."

"What?"

"We left my car at the library yesterday. Did you want me to take a cab?"

I kissed her again, longer this time. "I'll be back for you."

Beaver Lake lay several miles north of downtown. It was more a large pond than a lake, but as I turned left into the adjacent community, I looked down the length of water to the wall of mountains behind it. The tranquility of the scene suggested why the spot would have been so popular. The far end of the lake appeared as Nakayla had said, wooded with an overgrown shoreline, and I suspected I was at the spot where the diving boards and bathhouses once stood. Now there was just a boating area with a small hut that must be the source of permits or rentals.

I turned left again onto another residential street running along the west side of the lake. Looking across the glass-smooth surface, I saw no cars heading my way. Within a hundred yards, a barricade of trees shielded me from view, and I felt more confident that my scouting mission would go undetected. I made my second phone call to Nakayla and assured her everything was fine.

The road dipped closer to the water and what looked like little more than a logging road branched off. The CR-V bounced over the ruts until I braked at a chain stretched between two rusted metal posts. A white rectangular sign on a pole stood to the left, warning that Lake View Park was privately owned by the residents and forbidding swimming, skating, and use after dark. On the other side of the chain was a small clearing. Beyond, a wide path continued into the woods.

The paved road lay about twenty feet above me, but my Honda was still visible. As daylight intensified and traffic increased, someone would notice it. To the right of the chain, the gap between the post and the nearest tree looked wide enough for my small vehicle to slip through. I pulled closer, positioning the Honda to maneuver the space at the widest angle. Then I got out to make sure my clandestine action wouldn't end in the embarrassing feat of wedging my CR-V between tree and post.

My best calculation indicated the width had about a six-inch margin. I folded the passenger side mirror snug against the door, rolled down my window, and drove as close to the post as I dared. A squeal sounded as the mirror and bark rubbed each other. Nothing fell off, and I made it into the clearing without mishap. I was out of sight of the paved road but a sitting duck if another car pulled in and blocked my escape. The path veered to the left and stayed wide enough to let me drive into the trees where someone would have to come on foot to discover me.

The leafy canopy reduced visibility to predawn gloom. I locked the doors and walked deeper along the path. Too far and I'd risk losing any escape route if things went badly. I was searching for a location that wouldn't be that changed from the 1930s or 1940s.

A canoe lay on its side next to an old picnic table. Mold grew on the table's surface and spider webs paralleled the chain of a bicycle lock that wrapped around the upper section of the table's legs and looped the forward seat of the canoe. Had anyone wanted to steal it, simply chopping the wooden leg or removing the seat would have done the trick. Ahead, the path narrowed, and heavier ground growth indicated it was rarely traveled. I turned to the lake, figuring the canoe must be close to some water access.

Saplings and ragged shrubs hung over the shore. I retraced my steps a few yards and saw a narrow break not much larger than the width of the canoe. Stepping carefully and with the surer footing of my second prosthesis, I came to the edge of the lake. An old concrete piling jutted from the soil where the lapping of the water kept it clear of silt. At some point it must have been the foundation of a dock or maybe part of a broader launch site.

I snatched my phone from my belt and took a photo. Then I turned around and shot another of the picnic table and canoe. Here was the spot where I'd unearth a mysterious lockbox, and whether our enemies thought F. Scott Fitzgerald or Nazi sympathizers had buried it, I didn't care as long as the bait proved too tempting to resist.

I dialed Nakayla. "I'm done. I'm coming back."

"Good. Call me when you turn on Caledonia. I want to be in the lobby when you park. No sense—"

My mind shut out her voice as leaves crackled behind me. My gun hand held the phone; my back was an inviting target.

Leaves rustled again, softer this time. I slowly turned, keeping the phone to my ear and straining my peripheral vision for a glimpse of the intruder.

Out of the shadows stepped a white-tailed doe, her nose sniffing the air furiously and her long ears swiveling like radar antennae.

"Sam, can you hear me?" Nakayla shouted.

"Yes, dear."

I laughed as the doe bounded down the path, her beautiful white flag disappearing into a thicket of laurel.

"I don't know. Sounds too crazy to me." Detective Efird looked at the picture on my phone for a third time. "You want them to see you, but you don't want them to come after you. How are you going to guarantee that?"

"I'm counting on you. Just a couple men in camo on the perimeter. Hernandez and his people don't know the terrain. I think they'll watch me as best they can, but not risk a move. The area's not that isolated."

Calvin, Nakayla, and I sat with Efird in an interview room. We'd completed and signed our statements on the Grove Park shooting, and Calvin had briefed Efird on the Ali Baba case. His report had been concise and discouraging. After the ambush that killed Ed and Charlie and cost me my leg, the investigation had floundered. Because the primary suspects were civilians, the military lowered the priority. Calvin said he'd pressed for action, especially since he thought we'd been the victims of an assassination team, not a random insurgent attack.

Efird flipped through the folder in front of him. "We have a positive ID on Lucas. Blackwater matched the prints faster than the FBI."

Calvin tensed. "You got Blackwater involved?"

"Sam told us they were ex-employees. Newland sent the prints from the restaurant glass and they faxed us a positive first thing this morning. We'd already matched the body to the glass."

"What about Hernandez?" I asked.

Efird slid a photo across the table. The man before us had a bullet-shaped head and thick, muscular neck. Dark eyebrows formed a single line across his brow and he stared into the camera with undisguised arrogance. I wondered if he was the man who'd pressed a gun to my head behind my apartment building.

Nakayla passed the picture to Calvin. "A face only a mother could love," she said.

Calvin took a quick glance and tossed it back to Efird. "No. A grandmother who had bad eyesight."

Efird placed it on the folder. "I'll buy your theory that at least one other person is working with him. But I don't like Sam being exposed, and I don't like telling the media we think Lucas is good for both murders."

"We want them to relax," I argued. "They'll also think I'm making my moves because the police are off the case."

Efird tapped the picture of Hernandez. "But you're telling me this is the guy. Why shouldn't I have his mug on every TV in the county?"

"All I'm asking is twenty-four hours. We play the ruse and if it fails, you announce you're searching for this man."

Efird gnawed on his lower lip as he thought things over. "And if Hernandez kills someone else in the meantime, how do I live with that?"

"Who else? There's no one left but Nakayla, Calvin, and me."

"Hewitt Donaldson," Nakayla said. "And Ethel's son Terry. If this is some family secret, then that's who's left."

She caught me off guard. I hadn't thought beyond our immediate circle. Efird nodded, and I sensed my proposal heading
for rejection.

"But you could put them under police protection for a day,"
Nakayla suggested.

"We're not the FBI," Efird said.

"What about Nathan Armitage's men?" I asked. "I'll pay for
security. Nathan will need to be involved anyway because he can
take care of getting the box buried."

Efird shook his head. "You don't run a sting by getting a lot
of people involved."

"I agree. The people guarding Donaldson and his cousin
only know they're providing protective services. Nathan gets one
trusted employee to bury the box by the concrete piling tonight.
That's it. You'll have a few men shadowing me tomorrow when
I retrieve it, and then we stake out my car."

"For how long?" Efird asked.

"Through Friday night. If they don't show, then Saturday morning you release the photo of Hernandez and start the manhunt.
But you don't have any hard evidence against him. Just a few senior
citizens from Golden Oaks who'll say they saw a Hispanic-looking
deliveryman. Other than Captain, how do you think they'd hold
up under cross by someone like Hewitt Donaldson?"

Efird rubbed his hand across his mouth and sighed. "Okay.
You've made your point."

I may have made my point but he hadn't conceded. "What
about Lucas? Did you find his car?"

The detective pulled another sheet from his folder. "The key
fit a white Hyundai Sonata parked near the Grove Park athletic
facilities. A Hertz rental with a contract in the name of Greg
Franklin was in the glove box."

"He would've had to show a driver's license and credit card,"
Calvin said. "But these guys have access to fake passports,
whatever."

Efird looked at his report. "We called all the motels and hotels
in the area and found our boy at the Appalachian Mountaineer.

Front desk had a Greg Franklin registered and a white Sonata listed under vehicle. The room was clean and no one showed all night."

"Did you dust?" I asked.

"Yeah. And that's the odd part. The room had been wiped. The motel might have good housekeeping, but I doubt even the Grove Park staff would do that good a job."

Nakayla pointed a finger at Efird's file. "Why would Lucas have keys but no identification?"

"Maybe he was there for a hit," Calvin said. "In New Jersey, the gangs always make a hit between five and six o'clock. You know why?"

"Enlighten me," Efird said.

"Shift change at the police station. Our man's got a gun, cash, and a getaway car. It wasn't locked, was it?"

Efird checked his notes. "Good guess. Even though it was a keyless remote, the doors were unlocked."

Calvin grinned with satisfaction. "No guess. If he's there to take somebody out, then every second counts for getting away. And he probably had an accomplice holding his ID in case he was taken. He stays mum and buys his partners a little more time to blow town."

"Makes sense," I said. "Then somebody cleaned down the motel room because they knew Lucas had been killed and the police would find it sooner or later."

Efird smiled. "And to follow your logic, if he was there for a hit, then who was the likely target?"

Nakayla, Calvin, and I didn't say anything. The target had to be Calvin or me, and Efird wasn't going to take responsibility for a trap if the primary goal of our quarry was to kill me.

Efird closed the file. "Sorry. Your plan's too risky. We're sending the photo of Hernandez to the media and all law enforcement agencies. Don't worry. We'll get him."

I made one final pitch. "At least run it by Detective Newland."

Efird stood. "Newland's got his hands full this morning. So to speak. If I talk to him, I'll mention your idea. Maybe if our way doesn't net results, we'll reconsider."

The judgment had come down. I knew there would be no reconsideration.

"Have you got your Kimber?" Efird asked.

I patted the pistol under my jacket. "You want that ballistic check?"

"Yes." He turned to Nakayla. "And I called in a sketch artist. I want you to work with him on the man with the beard. Maybe someone will recognize him."

Calvin took a step forward. "What about me?"

"When we've got the sketch, you run it through your military channels. I'll also send it to Blackwater. If he's part of your Ali Baba gang, then he must have crossed paths with Lucas and Hernandez."

Calvin nodded, but he didn't look happy. I knew he was disappointed that Efird had squelched our plan. If Detective Newland had been there, the outcome might have been different.

"There's a restaurant a couple blocks down Biltmore Avenue," I told him. "City Bakery Café. I'll be there as soon as we fire the Kimber."

Calvin smiled. "Right, Chief." He read my mind.

To hell with the Asheville Police Department. We didn't need them. We'd set our plan in motion without them.

Chapter Eighteen

"It's you and me, Chief. That's the way this started and that's the way we'll end it." Calvin made the pronouncement hunched over the small café table, his large black hands wrapped around a cup of steaming coffee and his eyes darting between the door and me. "We're the last of the team."

I held a glass of fresh orange juice. My circuitry didn't need a jolt of caffeine. "It's more than us. Ethel Barkley and Amanda Whitfield deserve justice as well. We'll need help watching all the loose ends."

Calvin took a sip of coffee and grimaced. "I don't know. Efird's right about keeping the number of players as small as possible, especially since we're bucking the police."

"I'm not bucking the police, I'm looking for the lockbox stolen from our office. That's a legitimate case Nakayla and I are working. I'm free to hire Nathan and his company, and I'm asking you to help me as a friend."

"So we do everything as planned, except no police?"

"Yes. Including putting security on Hewitt Donaldson and Ethel Barkley's son."

"You really think they're in danger?"

I finished my juice and ran my finger around the rim of the glass. A low hum vibrated through the air. "I've been thinking about something Nakayla said."

"Yeah, she mentioned to Efird she thought Donaldson was a possible target."

"This was earlier, just to me."

Calvin's eyes narrowed and he leaned closer. "What?"

"She said when she yelled for Lucas to stop, he looked up and smiled."

"Maybe because he thought she wouldn't shoot."

"Maybe. But it could have been one of those fateful moments when he saw his target and knew he couldn't do anything. It could have struck him as funny."

"He'd already seen Nakayla and me in the lobby."

"I'm talking about Hewitt Donaldson. He was on the steps right behind you."

Calvin looked past me, staring back to those seconds in the Vanderbilt Atrium right before the shooting began.

"Interesting," he murmured. "He might not have known Donaldson by sight till he saw him drinking a beer with you."

"How would he have known we were meeting?"

"Did you talk to Donaldson on the phone?"

"Damn. I left a message from my cell."

Calvin opened his broad palms. "There you go. They've probably got an intercept on your cell. I just don't understand why they care about the lawyer."

"Here's something I haven't told anybody, not even Nakayla. And I don't want you saying a word in case it's a chip we have to play."

Calvin nodded quickly. "Hey, man, it ain't never getting past these lips."

I lowered my voice. "After we fired the ballistic test, I asked Efird to take me to the evidence room. He wouldn't let me remove anything, but I wanted to re-examine Ethel Barkley's copy of *The Great Gatsby*. There's an underlined passage she showed me when she explained why a swastika was on her lockbox."

"We've been through that," Calvin said.

"Yes, but this time I noticed more. In addition to being circled, the first letter of the underlined section had a faint number one penciled over it."

"What had you told Efird?"

"Just that I wanted to look at the book. I checked the inscription in the front and flipped through the pages searching for more underlined passages."

"Did you find any?"

"No. But on the page after the swastika paragraph I found an equation lightly written in the margin: $Z=Z$."

"I almost didn't get my high school diploma because of math, but even I can see that's nuts. Of course, Z equals itself."

"Unless it doesn't." I moved my glass to the side and traced a Z on the table in front of me. "What if Z being Z was unusual because other letters didn't equal themselves?"

I saw understanding flicker in Calvin's eyes.

"A key to a code," he said. "For some reason one of the letters remained the same."

"Yes. I didn't have time to work it out with Efird watching me."

"You couldn't talk him into loaning you the book?"

I shook my head. "And break his chain of custody? Hardly. But I don't need it. Any bookstore should have a copy."

"Do you want me to get it?"

"That's down the priority list. I'll pick it up before tomorrow. It's only a prop till we recover the lockbox."

"A prop?" Then Calvin grinned. "I get it. You have it with you when you're digging at Beaver Lake, like the location is hidden in the book."

"We know it was published in 1925, way before the events in question, but I doubt Hernandez is a connoisseur of the Jazz Age."

"A mug like his fits better in the Stone Age." Calvin laughed. "So, what next?"

I glanced at my watch. A few minutes after ten. "I need to brief Hewitt Donaldson and his cousin on why I want them in protective custody, and I need to bring in Nathan Armitage to go over the plan."

"You want me there?"

"No. It looks better if we part ways. Remember I'm supposed to be doing this behind your back. You should go to police headquarters and check on the artist's sketch Nakayla's compiling. I agree with Efird. You should run it through Baghdad."

"Okay." He checked the café's entry door for the umpteenth time. "But I hate just waiting."

"That's about all I'm going to do until I dig up the decoy box tomorrow. I'll return some calls to the press and stress that I think the man I shot killed Amanda Whitfield and Ethel Barkley. It goes against the official police theory, but it sets me up as thinking I'm out of danger."

"How are we going to stay in touch?"

"You may as well reactivate your cell phone. They know you're here. I'll text okay when everything's in place. You do the same when you're at the back of my apartment building, and I'll let you in. Those simple words won't give anything away. We'll wait together for Nathan's signal that something's going down."

Calvin looked unhappy. "Man, this Nathan friend of yours, what's he got? A bunch of fat ex-cops walking through office buildings or driving through shopping center parking lots? Blackwater swill are first-rate mercenaries. They'd give Special Forces a run for their money."

"Nathan's an ex-Marine who served in the First Gulf War. He'll be straight with what he can provide. If he doesn't have the resources, then we'll think of something else."

Calvin's hands balled into fists. "The something else should be you and me within striking distance. It's payback time and I don't want some rent-a-cop screwing it up."

Calvin and I split at the corner of Pack Square. He walked down the block to the police station, and I crossed Biltmore Avenue to my office. I regretted not calling Hewitt Donaldson earlier in the morning, because he was probably now in court for the day. Maybe Cory, his paralegal, or Shirley from *Night of the Living*

Dead could get a message to him. He'd said his cousin Terry wanted to talk to me, so there was a chance he'd call.

When I got off the elevator, I walked past our office, relieved that no reporters stood poised to pounce. I opened Donaldson's door without knocking and discovered Shirley sitting behind her desk with her head tilted back parallel to the floor. She held a bottle of eye drops in one hand and pressed a tissue to her cheek with the other. My sudden entry startled her and she squeezed the soft plastic container, shooting a stream of its contents into her right eye.

She snapped straight up, dabbing furiously as the overflow cut furrows in her chalk-white makeup. "You scared me to death."

"Sorry. You okay?"

At the sound of my voice, both eyes opened and, as the old song goes, her face turned a whiter shade of pale. "Mr. Blackman. Someone tried to kill you."

"No kidding." I looked myself over. "Seems like they failed."

"Mr. Donaldson said it was like a Wild West shootout."

"More like western North Carolina. Is the lord of the manor in?"

Before Shirley could answer, a voice bellowed from somewhere around the corner. "God damn it! He's got no right to go through my mother's things. I don't care what she told him to do."

"Family reunion?" I whispered. "I thought your boss would be in court."

"Cory's there. He came back after the judge instructed the jury. A verdict won't come till after lunch. Jurors never pass up a free meal."

"You dumb ass!" Donaldson's voice rose even louder. "Someone's willing to kill for what's in the lockbox and you want to stop Blackman from finding out who?"

"I love client testimonials," I said.

Somewhere behind Shirley a door opened. "And I heard he's a one-legged hotdog trying to prove how tough he is. I want

Blackman out of it, and if I have to get my own lawyer to remove you as executor, I will."

The speaker barreled into the reception area, his head still turned as he shouted his final words. Shirley looked at me. A blush rose in her cheeks, the first sign she had blood in her veins.

The man wore a dark blue suit, and his gray hair had been plastered into a comb-over with the part below his right ear. A strong wind would have raised it like a kite. When he saw me, he froze.

Donaldson rounded the corner and stopped behind his cousin. He winced.

"That's all right, Hewitt. We can't choose our relatives." I stepped up to Terry Barkley. He had to be in his late sixties, and he stood a few inches taller with a good fifty pounds on me. "You know, in the land of the no-legged hotdogs, the one-legged hotdog is king."

The big man turned so red I thought he'd go incandescent. "We'll see about that." He brushed past me and headed for the door.

"You'd better take my gun," I said. "Then maybe you'll make it to your car."

He hesitated.

"Come on, Terry," Donaldson said. "Let's go back to the conference room. You should at least hear what Sam has to say."

Barkley pivoted and took a deep breath. "He can talk all he wants, but there's nothing wrong with that money."

"I don't care about the money," I said. "But if you're dead, what I care about doesn't really matter, does it?"

Donaldson's conference room contained a single round table surrounded by six chairs equidistant from each other. Shelves of law books and framed degrees were conspicuously absent from the walls. Instead, classic album covers hung mounted behind Plexiglas panels. Bob Dylan, The Stones, The Beatles, Deep Purple, Iron Butterfly, and others whose names I didn't recognize provided Hewitt Donaldson's credentials as a 1960s throwback.

The three of us took chairs leaving empty ones between us. Donaldson didn't whip out a legal pad. He leaned back and asked, "What's the latest?"

I kept my eyes on Barkley. He folded his arms across his chest and glared.

"The dead man's been identified as Evan Lucas, although he was using a fake name. He's a former Blackwater employee, fired for reasons the company has kept secret, and a leading suspect in a case I was investigating that involved smuggling gold, ancient artifacts, and other booty out of Iraq. We believe he's part of a team of at least three who came to Asheville in search of me, believing that I'd been a thief of thieves who absconded with one of their richest caches."

"Who's we?" Barkley asked.

"A military colleague of mine who tipped me off to their mission. He's suggested that an ambush that killed two of our buddies and turned me into your one-legged hotdog was masterminded by this group we dubbed Ali Baba."

This time my reference to Barkley's demeaning characterization of my injury forced him to look away.

"Your mother hired me to retrieve her lockbox and return something to the heirs of F. Scott Fitzgerald. A very odd request that has led to my learning about William Dudley Pelley and The Silver Shirts."

Barkley leaned closer to his cousin. "What did you tell him?"

"Nothing. He learned it himself. He's a detective, you idiot."

Barkley turned to me. "So who killed my mother?"

"One of Lucas' partners, a man named Manny Hernandez."

"And they stole my mother's safe-deposit box?"

"Yes. I think that happened because they saw me take it out of the bank. After they had the lockbox, they followed me to your mother's apartment. Something had sparked their interest."

Barkley looked astonished. "You're saying this is a coincidence?"

"Not exactly. Your mother hired me because I'd solved a case with high publicity. I wasn't a random choice, and I had to pass her palm test."

"My mother wasn't mentally stable."

I shook my head. "But she was sharp in her own way. Very clever and very determined. The only coincidence I see is the timing of your mother's request, that it came when I was being stalked. But then timing's not a coincidence when the same event generates two courses of action."

Donaldson held up his hand. "I don't get what you mean."

"I mean I don't like coincidences. In detective work, a coincidence leads you nowhere. But I think the common event that led to the intersection of your mother and Manny Hernandez goes back to the earlier case this summer. My name and face were in the national news. I'm sure the story played over the Internet and in the *International Herald Tribune*, which would be read by Americans in Iraq. They found where I was and came after me."

"Did you steal from them?" Barkley asked.

"No. But the important thing is they think I did. So everything I do is viewed as confirmation of my guilt. My job is helping people learn or find things without police involvement. My actions involve snooping, spying, research, interrogating, all the things that make me look like I'm sneaking around. Hell, I am sneaking around. Toss in the fact that your mother's lockbox has a shadowy past of its own—"

"Wait," objected Barkley.

"Shut up," Donaldson said. "Our family history's made to order for Sam's theory." He signaled me to continue.

"At first I wasn't sure if I was dealing with two separate groups—someone after me and someone after the lockbox. But that would be a real coincidence, having two cases involving two murders. And after yesterday, I think the people after me have targeted Hewitt."

"Me?" Donaldson's voice squeaked with surprise.

"This is just conjecture, but Nakayla said Lucas smiled when he saw you on the stairs, as if he'd been looking for you."

"I have no idea what these people would want from me." He pointed at his cousin. "What are you into?"

Barkley threw up his hands. "Nothing. I just think our family's business is nobody else's business."

"Somebody's made it their business," I said. "And I can't guarantee they'll back off just because I killed one of them. I think both of you need protection, at least for a day or two while the police follow their leads."

"What kind of protection?" Barkley eyed me with suspicion, but the bluster behind his words had disappeared.

"I want Armitage Security Services to give you bodyguards."

"Bodyguards!" Barkley shot a glance at Donaldson. "This is absurd. I'm not going to waste my money when I've got a double-barrel Marlin 12-gauge in the truck."

"I'm paying," I said. "These are very bad people. Two of my buddies came home in body bags, and I walk on the reminder of their ruthlessness every day."

"How long?" Donaldson asked.

"Like I said, a couple days. A week at most. Things are coming to a head."

I could tell Barkley was shaken. He mulled his options for a few seconds. "How soon?"

"I'm phoning Nathan Armitage as soon as we finish here."

The older man nodded. "Then make the call."

"When we're finished here," I repeated. "What's in that lockbox, Terry? I know the code. I want to know what it translates."

Incredulity replaced the anxiety on his face. "She told you? She wouldn't even tell me."

"No. But I'm pretty sure I've figured it out. Now tell me what you know or you can fend for yourself. The other option is I tell the police you're holding out on them."

"How will this information help you?" Donaldson asked.

"Our enemies know what's in the lockbox. I'm in the dark. I'm trying to lure them out, and I've got to make them think I know something they don't." I shut up. That was all I was going to tell them.

"Well, I'll talk," Donaldson said. "And, Terry, as executor of your mother's estate, I advise you to cooperate. I trust Sam to watch out for our interests more than I trust the police."

Barkley didn't answer. He stared straight ahead, his thoughts hidden behind an unreadable mask.

"Hold up a second," I said. "If you're going to help me, then I'll call Nathan right now and set things in motion. Can I use your phone? They've bugged my office once already, and my cell might not be secure."

"Sure," Donaldson said. "Use the one in my office. Next door on the left farther down the hall."

At first I couldn't find the phone because Donaldson had so many papers and folders piled on his desk. I explored the biggest lump and found the receiver under a thick folder labeled "Selected Minutes: House Committee on Un-American Activities." I was tempted to thumb through it, but Donaldson had trusted me alone in his office. I dialed Nathan's cell from memory and he answered after only a few rings.

"I was hoping I'd hear from you," he said.

"It's been a little crazy, but I need your help big time."

"Just ask, pal."

"Can you come to my office right away. I'm creating a story for our friends, and I need you to be in it."

"What should I wear?"

"Come ready for any occasion. And I need a supporting cast."

His voice turned serious. "What's happening, Sam?"

"Not for the phone. But Hewitt Donaldson and his cousin Terry Barkley need experienced guards. Plain clothes but I want anyone to see they're carrying."

"Okay. Where should they report?"

"Donaldson's office, or if he's gone back to court, have your man meet him there. I'll tell his cousin to stay put."

"That it?"

"No. To finish this story, I need good men. No disrespect, but closer to combat training than jiggling locks."

"Whoa," Nathan said. "Where are the police in this?"

"They didn't like the plot so Calvin and I are writing them out. I wanted to give you a heads-up in case you need some prep time."

He was silent a moment. "How soon?"

"Twenty-four hours. And with six players to be safe."

"Counting you, me, and Calvin?"

"No. In addition. And as for you, my friend, you're under doctor's orders to take it easy. I've already gotten you shot once."

"You want my help or not?"

Without Nathan's help, there was no show. "I want your help as long as it doesn't endanger our chance for success."

He got what I was saying. "Fair enough. I'll make sure no one's life depends on me. But I'll want to be close by."

"There's plenty for you to do. What about the men?"

Again, he hesitated. "I can get them. I'm afraid I'll need freelancers, but I can vouch for them."

"That's good enough for me."

"Where's Nakayla in all this?" he asked.

His question caught me short. I was putting my team together and I'd left her off the roster. "We haven't had a chance to talk. Do me a favor, Nathan. If she's with me when you get here, follow my lead. Don't mention the number of men you've enlisted unless I bring it up."

Nathan chuckled. "Sam, I'm warning you. If you try to keep that woman out of the action, then the fight with Ali Baba will seem like a picnic on the Blue Ridge Parkway."

Chapter Nineteen

When I returned to the conference room, Donaldson and Barkley were speaking in hushed tones.

I rapped on the doorjamb. "Nathan is sending two men. Hewitt, if you've been called back to court, look for one of them when you leave. He'll be just outside the courtroom. Terry, your man's going to meet you here." I sat. "Okay. I'm all ears."

Donaldson rested his forearms on the table and took a deep breath. "Let me say right up front that you're going to hear two different stories. The truth might be somewhere in-between, or one of us could be completely off-base."

I saw anger simmering in Barkley's eyes, but he said nothing.

"The reason, and I think Terry will agree with me, is that our mothers saw things very differently. What my mother proclaimed an embarrassment, Terry's mother embraced as a virtue."

"Because in her mind she was standing firm for her Christian beliefs," Terry snapped.

"I'm not here to make judgments," I said. "I just want the facts of what happened."

"But that difference is a fact," Donaldson said. "Probably the central fact through which everything else is colored. If Terry and I can agree to disagree, then you need to accept you'll hear different truths from each of us. We're cooperating as best we can, but you can't consider conflicting testimony to be perjury."

I understood Donaldson's precaution to keep me from sounding like a prosecutor. Barkley would erupt if he felt I was attacking him or his mother.

"Don't worry," I said. "I've conducted enough interviews to know even eyewitness testimony usually conflicts. We all have the same goal here, justice for Ethel Barkley and for your families."

Barkley relaxed his clenched jaw. "Then I'll tell you what I know. After Hewitt."

Donaldson smiled. "All right, cuz. I'll give you the last word as long as you don't interrupt." He paused to collect his thoughts and then began his story.

"My father, Hugh Donaldson, was born in 1900, November third to be exact. One month to the day after Thomas Wolfe. They knew each other as kids, though my grandmother discouraged their playing together."

"Why?" I asked.

"Because she thought W. O. Wolfe was a nut. Tom's father was bad to drink. My father grew up on Woodfin a few blocks away, and my grandmother told me Mr. Wolfe would often lurch along the street late at night, screaming verses of Shakespeare at the stars.

"Tom's mother Julia was a real piece of work. A shrewd businesswoman but paranoid that people were taking advantage of her." He gave a polite nod to Terry. "Aunt Ethel told me F. Scott Fitzgerald went to the Wolfe house when he was in Asheville, and Mrs. Wolfe threw him out, saying she didn't rent to drunks."

"That's true," Terry confirmed.

"My father and Tom both went to Chapel Hill. Tom a year earlier because he was such a bright kid, and a few times he and my father rode home on the train together. Tom went on to Harvard, my father got his law degree from UNC and returned to Asheville."

"You never knew your father?"

"No. He died six months before I was born. Most of what I know came from my mother, aunt, and paternal grandmother. Mother was quite a bit younger. Her mother had died in childbirth, and she was reared by her father, a strict Methodist circuit-riding preacher, and later by a stepmother whose affections shifted to her own natural children as the marriage produced them."

"Were your mother and your aunt close in age?" I asked.

Donaldson nodded. "A perceptive guess. My father was seventeen years older than both of them. My mother and Aunt Ethel met working at the Sears-Roebuck back in the 1930s, after Ethel left the Grove Park Inn. My mother told me she knew she wasn't the great love of his life, but she'd made peace with being in third standing."

"Third?" I glanced at Terry and he looked surprised.

"Yes," Donaldson said. "His first girlfriend, Ina Tribble, was also his first fiancée. She died in the flu epidemic of 1919. He threw himself into his law practice and didn't date for fifteen years. Mother said she could never replace Ina in his heart and she could never be a greater priority than his work. What really hurt was knowing he put the Silver Legion of America and William Dudley Pelley ahead of her. Fascism over family."

Terry rapped his knuckles on the table. "No. Your father and my mother were doing what they thought was best for the country they loved."

Both men's voices had begun to rise to the levels I'd heard when entering the office. I made a "T" symbol with my hands. "Time out. You'll get the last word, Terry, so let him finish."

Barkley settled back in his chair, a scowl on his face.

Donaldson continued. "When William Pelley came to Asheville with his claims of traveling into the afterlife, he hired my father for legal work in setting up Galahad Press and the other propaganda organs he developed. Pelley saw the rise of Hitler as the great hope for ushering in a new age. He formed the Silver Legion of America the day Hitler assumed the chancellorship of Germany, but he put as much emphasis on religion as politics. A theocracy disguised as a democracy.

"Pelley's efforts to undermine the basic principles of the U.S. Constitution gained momentum in those early desperate days of the Depression. My father helped guide their expansion. As the Silver Shirts' membership grew, my father and Terry's father, the accountant for the operations, moved into the inner circle.

"At the height of their national influence, the movement became unglued as charges of stock fraud were leveled at Pelley by the state of North Carolina."

I remembered seeing Pelley's face on the wanted poster issued by the sheriff of Buncombe County.

"And as the violence and atrocities of Hitler's reign became known, the movement fizzled. But my father and my Uncle Terrence stuck by Pelley, even after he was convicted of fraud in Asheville and later charged with sedition by federal prosecutors in 1942.

"My mother told me she was appalled that my father, so decent and kind in so many ways, would have held such outrageous and unpopular beliefs."

"Was your father ever charged with anything?"

"No. And neither was Terry's father."

Barkley's tight lips softened into a smile. "That's because they never did anything wrong."

"They were on a list drawn up by the House Committee on Un-American Activities," Donaldson said.

Barkley shrugged. "Who wasn't? The country was paranoid. Hell, it still is."

"Did your father have to testify?" I asked Donaldson.

"No. And after Pelley went to jail, the spotlight moved elsewhere. But my father still kept his network together, writing letters and dispensing legal advice. They would visit the German POWs in Hendersonville and other areas of the state."

"Were they passing information?"

Donaldson cocked his head and eyed me cynically. "What do you think?"

Barkley swiveled to face him. "There's no proof they did anything but offer humanitarian assistance. They made sure the prisoners were well treated. I'd hope someone like my father and Uncle Hugh would have been doing the same for our soldiers."

"Yes," Donaldson snapped. "Fixing them strudel while the cattle cars carried women and children to their deaths." He leaned over the table, trapping me with a hard stare. "I have some sympathy for the German people. They'd been sold a bill of goods. After my father died, over a thousand German prisoners burned their uniforms when they saw the newsreels of the liberated concentration camps. But my father had a choice, and he backed a fascist megalomaniac who saw himself general of a righteous army, marked by big scarlet Ls on silver shirts glittering in the sunlight as they marched over everything in their path."

I thought about the poem I'd found in Ethel's book. Donaldson's verbal picture came close to that imagery, and I suspected he'd searched for clues as to why his father chose to work for such reprehensible ideals.

"You can bet it wouldn't have been long till these Silver Shirts would have been herding those they didn't like into their own concentration camps," Donaldson said. "My mother had hoped that with my birth our family would have moved up his chart. Part of her clung to that belief after he died. But he left his insurance to his sister who claimed she held it for others who would come for it."

"Who was that?" I asked.

He glanced at Barkley. "I think she expected Pelley to return. My father's instructions had been to use the money as a last resource. And as far as I know, she never touched any of the policy's proceeds. Pelley was released from prison in 1950 on the condition he stay clear of politics and make no attempt to reactivate his Silver Legion of America. He went to Indiana where he died in 1965. And my mother died in 1990, a woman whose marriage was haunted by what might have been. But Aunt Ethel never stopped waiting." He looked away and spoke to the wall of 1960s music. "Imagine placing your hope in such a despicable cause."

Barkley twitched with nervous energy. "She wasn't right in the head, but she loved you and she loved me. That counts for something."

"Was she active in the Silver Shirts?" I asked him.

"No. Look, Hewitt is obsessed with this nonsense."

"The facts speak for themselves," Donaldson said.

"You've had your say, now I'll have mine." Barkley turned in his chair so that Donaldson wasn't in his peripheral vision. "My father had a job. That's all it was. I don't remember him very well, as I was only four when he was killed. But when he came home, he left his office behind. Mom and I were the priorities of his life."

"Did he work for other clients?" I asked.

"Of course. Pelley had several businesses and his political organization, but my father served many other small businesses and industries. Why he kept the books for one of Asheville's Jewish furniture stores."

"And Hitler loved little children," Donaldson said.

"He's telling his story," I warned.

"The Silver Legion of America wasn't about Hitler," Barkley insisted. "It was created because our country was in real danger of becoming a socialist state. Pelley might not have had the right solution, but 15,000 voices of the middle class got Washington's attention, and limits were put on Roosevelt's efforts to take over the government. Look how he tried to pack the Supreme Court."

I didn't want to get into a historical debate that would degenerate into a shouting match. "Was your father a member of the Silver Shirts?"

"Yes," Barkley admitted. "Just like Hewitt's father."

"And unlike Hewitt's mother, your mother was proud of your father's actions?"

"Yes. And her brother's actions. My mother idolized Hugh Donaldson."

"Is that why you think the insurance money went to her?"

Barkley paused a second. "Probably."

"Why not to your father?"

"They were killed in the same wreck."

"You're saying they planned to die together?"

Barkley's head jerked back like I'd slapped him. "No!"

"There was the need for an insurable interest," Donaldson said. "Otherwise, the company wouldn't have issued the policy. It keeps people from taking out insurance policies on total strangers and making themselves the beneficiaries. It eliminates an incentive for murder. My father could make his sister the beneficiary without any trouble."

"Thank you, counselor," I said with exaggerated gratitude, "but I wanted to hear Terry's answer."

Donaldson reddened. He realized he'd butted in when I already knew the answer. I was probing for Terry's opinion of the relationship between his father and his uncle.

Barkley shrugged. "I guess what Hewitt said. My mother was blood-kin."

"And would she have been more likely to carry out Hugh Donaldson's wishes?"

"Yes. Like I said, she idolized him."

I smiled with reassurance. "What did your mother tell you about the money from that insurance policy?"

"That we were to keep it ready. A time would come when we would be asked for it. She told me that Hewitt and I might be called forth. That's the way she phrased it."

"But you did nothing all these years?"

Barkley threw up his hands. "It was her money. Maybe if she'd spent some of it I wouldn't have had to work three jobs to get through college. She only took out enough to pay each year's taxes on the interest earned."

He was expanding on his answers and I knew if he were going to tell me anything significant, he would say it in the next few minutes.

"Where do you think the money came from—the money to buy the insurance?"

"I don't know." He looked over at Donaldson. "But it wasn't foreign money. Mother said it was Americans standing up for America. Christians standing up for God."

I kept my eyes steady on his. "Grim men. Christ's men."

Barkley looked at me blankly, but Donaldson nodded with recognition of the line of poetry.

"And there wasn't any money in the lockbox?" I asked.

"Not that I know of," Barkley said. "I only saw inside it one time."

Donaldson's head jerked around. "When?"

"I guess I was ten. Mother had taken my toy soldier maker and I wanted to know why."

"What's a toy soldier maker?" I asked.

"A kit for casting lead figures. I had molds for an infantryman, cavalryman, and cannon. You melted the lead in a little cooker, poured it in the mold, and then painted the finished piece after it cooled. If it broke, you just re-melted and cast it again. God knows how much lead I absorbed."

"And your mother had taken it?"

Barkley looked at his cousin. "You remember that old butcher's block table she had in our kitchen?"

Donaldson nodded.

"Mother had the burner going under my ladle and she was melting down my soldiers. I told her to stop but she said she'd buy me more fishing weights. That's where I got my supply of lead. Beside her on the floor sat an old chest. It contained papers and the kind of books my father used to write in. Ledger books I guess."

"Anything else?" I prompted.

"No cash or jewels. I saw something wrapped in pretty paper. I asked her if it was a birthday present and she said it was for someone who would never have another birthday."

"The gift for Fitzgerald," Donaldson said. "The one Aunt Ethel wanted you to have if she couldn't pay you."

"What?" Barkley eyed me warily. "Whatever's in there is my property."

"No. That was the arrangement," I said. "And that's why I have a contract that goes beyond her death."

"I want to see it in writing," Barkley said.

Donaldson clucked his tongue with disapproval. "You're piss-ing on a friend, Terry. A verbal agreement is binding where it can be proven to have occurred. I didn't know about that wrapped gift until Sam told me what your mother told him."

Barkley grumbled under his breath, and then continued his story. "Well, she melted down my toy soldiers and poured the lead in a pool over the top of the chest. Then she took half a potato and pressed it into the cooling surface."

"A potato?" I asked.

"Yes. She made me stand back because the potato's moisture sizzled and splattered the lead. She wore an insulated oven mitten. She waited a few minutes and then cut the potato away. I saw a swastika raised on the seal."

"She'd carved the mold into the potato," I said. "Clever. What year was this?"

"I'm not sure. Probably 1950. I was old enough to know we'd beaten the Germans in the war. Mother said we should be kind to them."

"1950," I repeated.

"The year Pelley was released from prison," Donaldson said. "The news would have made the papers back here."

"And she got things ready for him with a decorative flourish. Did you ever see the chest again?" I asked Barkley.

"No. I knew she had a safe-deposit box, but she kept its contents a secret. I suspected it held the chest."

Donaldson gave a barely perceptible nod signaling he thought his cousin was telling the truth. "As far as I know, Pelley never came back to Asheville. If money was involved, I can't believe he wouldn't have worked out some method for getting it."

"Unless he worried he was under constant surveillance," I said.

"Yes," Donaldson agreed. "In the 1950s, our government saw spies and saboteurs on every street corner. Although I suspect Senator Joseph McCarthy would have given Adolph Hitler a plea bargain if he could have turned in a couple of mom and pop Communists in Peoria, Illinois."

Barkley abruptly stood and walked away from the table, his movements stiff and agitated. "You two refuse to look at the obvious explanation. Pelley had no reason to contact my mother because there was no money that belonged to him. End of story."

"You could be right," I said. "Or Pelley didn't know there was anything left in the Silver Legion of America's coffers. It doesn't matter. You've confirmed that ledger books and possible account numbers were in a box sealed with a swastika. That's blood in the water and these sharks aren't going to go away until we give them what they want."

"We don't have anything to give them," Donaldson said.

"Yes, we do."

"What?" Donaldson and Barkley asked together.

In an instant I recalled the end of one of my favorite movies, *The Maltese Falcon*, and Sam Spade answering the police detective's question, "What's this?" as the officer lifted the heavy bird. I was counting on my thieves to be as obsessed as the villains Sam Spade took down.

"What do we give them?" I held out my open, empty palm. "The, uh, stuff that dreams are made of."

Chapter Twenty

We were in our customary seats, Nakayla on the sofa and Nathan and I in the armchairs. They'd listened without interruption as I briefed them on my meeting with Donaldson and Barkley. Then I'd laid out the plan for Nathan burying the decoy.

"I'll take care of getting the box and stressing it to look old," he said. "The lead and potato-mold trick should work as well for creating a similar seal."

"What about me?" Nakayla asked.

"You need to carry on with business as usual," I said.

She crossed her arms over her chest. "You've got to be kidding. After three days of being in business, three people are dead. We're averaging a body a day. I'd prefer we try business not as usual."

We were heading toward the argument I dreaded. No matter how equal our partnership, I wanted her out of harm's way. "You and I'll stay in the office today. I'll return phone calls to the media and say I think Evan Lucas' death solves the two murders."

"And what was the motive?" she asked.

A good question and one that any good reporter would ask. "Money," I said, and looked to Nathan for support.

He nodded. "They'll believe it because we believe it. Sam's just giving them a simplified version. With a little digging, reporters will learn Ethel Barkley had a sizable bank account and they'll conclude that Lucas mistook Sam's access to her safe-deposit box to be a withdrawal of cash."

"I'll tell them I think Lucas killed Amanda Whitfield while searching our office, and then he went to Ethel Barkley's apartment the next day. My story doesn't need to pass a thorough examination, it just needs to generate headlines in the morning that make Hernandez and his pals think I'm letting down my guard."

Nakayla considered my argument. "And then what do I do tomorrow?"

"I'm going to call in sick. You'll be here and tell that to anyone who asks. I'll say the same thing to Calvin in case they're monitoring his cell phone. Then when I'm sneaking around Beaver Lake, they'll be more suspicious."

Nakayla slid off the sofa and paced behind it. "No. You're too vulnerable. What's to keep them from jumping you as soon as you dig up Nathan's box?"

"I'll have men in place," Nathan said. "But I think Hernandez will wait to see what Sam does before making a move."

"We'll stay together tomorrow night," I told Nakayla. "Let's pick up some steaks and wine to make it look like an evening in. Nathan, have your men select a spot at the apartment where they'd prefer I park the CR-V. I'd like it as isolated as possible in case these guys put up a fight. We'll have the manpower to overwhelm them, and I don't want any shots fired if we can avoid it. The police will be more forgiving of our vigilante action if things go down quietly."

"You gave Efird the chance to be alpha dog," Nathan said.

Nakayla leaned over the sofa and stared down at us. "He can still bite you. That's the second thing I don't like about the plan, cutting out the police."

"I'll call Efird as soon as we see that they're making a move."

"With what?" she asked. "You think your cell phone's compromised, and I wouldn't trust the apartment's landline."

"I'll get a prepaid cell."

Nathan shook his head. "If someone's tailing you, it looks like you're not in this alone. I'll drop two secure cells off later today. I agree with Nakayla that we need the police as soon as we know

Hernandez and his men are hooked. I also don't like us not being able to talk. Something goes wrong with every plan."

"Should you get a phone for Calvin?" Nakayla asked.

"We won't see him till tomorrow night," I said. "He needs to stay clear."

Nakayla circled around us and stared out the window. "Where are your men coming from, Nathan? This operation's quite a few notches up from routine security."

"I have contacts from the service. These guys are first-rate. They've all seen action and are used to working together. They'll be in town later this afternoon."

"Please tell me they're not coming from Moyock," she said.

Moyock. The headquarters of Blackwater.

Nathan's lips tightened, and then he said softly. "These people killed my employee. I'll use whoever and whatever it takes."

Justice and revenge. I'd debated Nakayla on those motives for Calvin and me, and had completely forgotten that Nathan Armitage carried his own personal anger. The vision of Amanda Whitfield's twisted body had to be burned in his mind. I hoped it hadn't clouded his judgment. If our enemies still had allies in Blackwater, they might know every detail of our plan.

"Oh, my God," Nakayla whispered.

"I trust them with my life," Nathan said.

She didn't hear his assurance, but stepped closer to the window. "It's him. The third guy. The one from the Grove Park."

Nathan's two good legs got him to the window a few seconds ahead of me. "Where?"

"By the reproduction of Thomas Wolfe's angel."

I stepped beside her as she pointed to the nearest corner of Pack Square in front of Pack Place, the building housing the Asheville Art Museum, a theatrical stage, and other cultural organizations.

A man wearing khaki pants, an open-necked shirt, and a blue blazer waited by the sculpture's base. Our third-story window wasn't so high that I couldn't make out the light beard cropped close to his angular chin, and I had no doubt that he'd been watching us at the Grove Park the day before. Now he was scoping out our office.

He glanced up. The three of us stepped back into the shadows.

My heart raced. "If Hernandez shows, we'll call Efird. The guy's right outside the police station."

Nathan pulled out his cell. "They'll need a few minutes to organize. I'd better get downstairs where I can follow him if he leaves." He started for the door.

Two men crossed the street. I saw a gray ponytail bobbing against a dark suit. "Wait. Donaldson and Barkley are down there. They must be going to the courthouse. Damn. I wish I'd shown them the sketch."

Nakayla had brought us several copies of the composite the police artist had created. She held one in her hand and said, "A good likeness."

To my amazement, the bearded man stepped forward as Donaldson and Barkley approached. They exchanged a few words. Our suspect looked up at our office window, and then he and Barkley walked down Biltmore Avenue. Donaldson continued in the direction of the courthouse.

Nathan still held his phone halfway to his ear. "What the hell was that about?"

Nakayla turned to me. "Has Donaldson played us for suckers?"

My stomach flipped. Not only had Nathan brought Black-water into our ruse, I'd taken Donaldson for an ally. Somewhere I'd missed a step. "I don't know, but we're going to have to watch our backs."

"You need to tell Efird," Nakayla said.

"But we don't want to spook our mystery man if he'll lead us to Hernandez. And we don't know how Barkley and Donaldson fit in."

Nathan picked up a copy of the artist's sketch. "It's definitely him. I didn't see him at the Grove Park but this is the man. I agree with Nakayla. We can't shut Efird out. If the police get him to talk, then we can break the case without using you or the decoy box as bait."

They were right. "Okay. But I don't want to be involved. Remember, I'm supposed to think that Lucas was working solo. Tell Efird you saw him on the street walking with another man and then describe Barkley."

"What about Donaldson?" Nathan asked.

"Let's leave him out of it. He knows you and might wonder why he didn't see you." I looked out the window. "If you were walking on the other side of Biltmore Avenue, you wouldn't have seen Donaldson because he was around the corner."

Nathan nodded. "All right. I'll call Efird from the street. Will you stay here?"

I glanced at my watch. Eleven-forty-five. "No. Our story is that Nakayla and I left for lunch at eleven-thirty, right after we gave you a copy of the artist's sketch. You didn't call us because you wanted to get to Efird right away. That ought to put you in his good graces."

"We'd better hustle," Nakayla said. "Not that Efird would have reason to check, but we'll want to be in a restaurant if he calls."

"I have a better idea. Let's go to Malaprop's. I need to pick up a copy of *The Great Gatsby*. We could've been browsing for thirty minutes before ordering something to eat."

Malaprop's Bookstore & Café was only a few blocks away, but the opposite direction from where Nathan would phone Detective Efird. Nakayla and I slipped out the back door of our building without encountering other tenants, and in less than ten minutes I was scanning the fiction bookshelves for F. Scott Fitzgerald.

I found a paperback edition of *The Great Gatsby* published in 2004. Although the page count seemed different from the first edition in Ethel's apartment, I remembered that the sentence I suspected to contain the code appeared near the end. Flipping from the back, I'd turned only ten pages when I saw "The Swastika Holding Company" at the top of 170. Whether my deduction bore any connection to the truth didn't matter.

The word swastika in the sentence and the swastika seal on the lockbox provided enough of a link to fit my purpose. In fact, if somehow Donaldson was tied into the conspiracy, I might drop that tidbit of information in his presence to further enhance the bait.

I paid for the book and joined Nakayla in the café section of the store, where she waited in front of the bakery display.

"See something you like?"

"No. A little late for a muffin. Why don't we walk down to Old Europe? You've got your receipt that shows we were here."

Old Europe Bistro had a great selection of soups, salads, and sandwiches, but the killer items I couldn't resist were their gourmet cookies. Usually several had my name on them.

We'd gone about half a block toward the restaurant when my phone vibrated on my belt. The ID read Nathan's cell. I caught Nakayla's arm and pulled her into a side alley.

"Sam. Have you finished your lunch?" Nathan's voiced sounded odd—more formal than usual.

"Yes. What's up?"

"I'm at the police station. You need to get over here. Efird wants to talk to you."

I wondered why Efird hadn't called me himself. Had the detective learned we were working behind his back? Was Nathan trying to warn me? "All right. Nakayla and I'll come straight there. Has anything changed?"

He hesitated a few seconds. "Not really. I'm sure you'll be free to go about your business as planned. Just an unexpected twist. We'll be in interview room three." He hung up.

I clipped the phone to my belt. "Well, that was interesting."

"Did they catch the guy?"

"I don't know. Nathan said he was calling for Efird and someone must have been within earshot. But our plans haven't changed, so the guy must still be at large." I curled *The Great Gatsby*. "Hide this in your purse and let's see what Nathan means by an unexpected twist."

By the time we reached Pack Square, my stump had started to ache. The sky had grown overcast and the rising humidity coupled with my physical exertion had increased the moisture in my prosthetic's sleeve to where I needed a dry one. As soon as I finished with Efird, I'd make the change in my office. Then I needed to return calls to the media before I missed their deadlines.

At the door to the station, I took a final glance overhead. Rain appeared imminent. Although the job would be messy, a heavy downpour would help insure the burial of the decoy by Nathan's men would go undetected. If the forecast held true, colder, clearer weather would follow, and my task of digging up the box would be easier. More importantly, I'd be easier to observe.

We were admitted through the reception area and went unescorted to the interview rooms. Nakayla and I'd spent many hours there during the investigation of her sister's murder and I knew the layout of the Asheville Police Department as well as I knew my apartment.

The door of interview room three was shut. I leaned close to Nakayla's ear. "Let's take our cue from Nathan. I have no idea what this is about."

"You mean play dumb. Well, you're the undisputed master." She rapped her knuckles on the door hard enough to wake the dead.

"Come in." Detective Efird's voice boomed.

Nakayla pushed open the door. Efird and Nathan sat on the near side of the table, half-turned in their wooden chairs to see us. Seated across from them, a man held the artist's sketch in front of his face like a mask. He whipped the drawing aside to reveal the flesh-and-blood original. A broad smile split the beard. "Congratulations, Ms. Robertson. A most impressive display of observation and detailed memory."

Nathan stood, sweeping his arm toward the stranger. "Let me introduce Craig Keith, special agent for the FBI and liaison with the Department of Homeland Security for Domestic Terrorism."

"Pleased to meet you," Agent Keith said. "You've made me a celebrity in the Bureau, a person of police interest whose likeness has been faxed to every law enforcement agency in the state of North Carolina. How many FBI agents can say they were a suspect in their own case?" He waved us to take a seat in the extra chairs cluttering the room. "But I guess it's only fair." His icy-blue eyes focused on me. "I had you pegged as a suspect in your case, ex-Chief Warrant Officer Sam Blackman. And for the record, I wouldn't have hesitated to bust your one-legged ass if the evidence substantiated an arrest."

I looked at the sketch he'd laid on the table. "Your cartoon face has a better personality. Maybe you should keep that drawing on your shoulders, since your real head seems to be located elsewhere on your anatomy."

The man's lips twitched and then an uncontrolled belly laugh erupted from his slender body. "By God, you live up to your billing. I'll say that. Have a seat, Sam. It's time we laid our cards on the table. I don't think any of us knows exactly what's going on, and it's my belief that ignorance can get you killed. It's also my belief that you're probably the guy in the crosshairs, and I'd like to keep you alive, if only to trade insults."

I wasn't ready to show my cards when I didn't know the game or the wager. "That's hardly a challenge if my opponent is an FBI agent who ran from a shootout."

Keith's smile froze for an instant. Then he shrugged. "I don't pull my trigger till I know the good guys from the bad guys. Maybe you do things differently, but one thing I do know about you, you're not stupid. So leave your attitude on the other side of the door and let's see how we can help each other."

From the corner of my eye, I saw Nakayla take a seat. In my head, I heard Donaldson's admonition to his cousin, "You're pissing on a friend, Terry." What did I have to lose? This FBI agent was right about one thing—I was in the crosshairs. And if he could keep me alive, why shouldn't I listen to what he had to say. So what if he made me mad. Better to be pissed off than pissed on.

Chapter Twenty-one

I gave Craig Keith a closer look as I eased into a chair at the end of the table. He had me by a couple years—probably in his mid- to late thirties—and his clipped accent pegged him north of the Mason-Dixon line.

"What did I do to come into your sights?" I asked. "Surely the FBI and Homeland Security have bigger fish to fry."

"You found a body next to my girlfriend's office. You know the statistics as well as I. How many times does the first person to report discovering a body turn out to be the murderer?"

"Then your girlfriend is Cory DeMille, Hewitt Donaldson's paralegal?"

"Correct. And when she picked me up at the airport Tuesday night—actually one o'clock Wednesday morning—and told me about the murder, I got interested. Hewitt said the only thing missing was his aunt's lockbox, and that piqued my curiosity further. Cory told me Hewitt was meeting you at the Grove Park so I showed up." He nodded to Nakayla. "I underestimated your abilities."

"And why were you at the Grove Park?" I asked.

"To size up a potential suspect. Like I said, the first person to find a body is often the murderer."

His story seemed a little too pat. "You just happen to be dating Cory DeMille, and you just happen to be an FBI agent?"

"According to Detective Efird and Mr. Armitage, you just happen to be a former Chief Warrant Officer being hunted by international thieves who just happened to steal a lockbox that you just happened to have in your office. Which is more preposterous?"

I turned to Nathan, seeking some clue as to how much he had told the agent.

He cleared his throat. "I saw Agent Keith eating lunch with a man in the window of the Kanpai restaurant half a block from your office. I called Detective Efird who brought him here."

"Before I finished my pad Thai," Keith interjected. "On the bright side, Terry Barkley got stuck with the bill."

Efird picked up the story. "When I learned he was FBI, I told him about your Ali Baba case and that your friend, Warrant Officer Calvin Stuart, had warned you Hernandez and Lucas thought you'd ripped them off and were coming after you."

While Efird spoke, I kept my eyes on Nathan. He gave a slight shake of his head and I knew he hadn't said anything about our plan. But now I had an even bigger worry. If Keith had set the resources of the FBI in motion to scrutinize me, how quickly would they turn up the offshore account and the gems and gold I was laundering for Nakayla? Her illegal inheritance was what had convinced Ali Baba I'd stolen their loot and would certainly fuel an FBI investigation.

I decided I needed to be on the offensive. "So you think my situation is preposterous? These guys cost me my leg and killed two of my buddies because I was closing in on them. Check the military case record. Earlier this summer, I broke a high profile murder that linked to Thomas Wolfe. That brought me to the attention of Ethel Barkley, who claimed to have an F. Scott Fitzgerald manuscript. She must have thought I was some literary expert. Check the police record. She came to me."

"And should I excuse the timing of all this as coincidence?" Keith asked.

"Ask Amanda Whitfield about timing," I snapped. "People can be in the wrong place at the wrong time. Ethel Barkley hired me at the wrong time, the first day Nakayla and I opened for business. For nearly six months of this year I was in a damn V.A.

hospital. Then my name gets plastered all over the news and Ali Baba comes after me as soon as they can. Both events coincide because of earlier, separate events. You, on the other hand, show up on the night of the murder and happen to take an interest it what is clearly a case for the Asheville Police Department. I find that preposterous."

Efird grinned, but I didn't know if it was because he enjoyed seeing me angry or because he'd witnessed the FBI take over cases before and he was rooting for me.

Keith kept his cool. If my barbs bothered him, he didn't show it. "I know you're aware of the Silver Legion of America."

"Yes. Ethel Barkley's husband and her brother, Hewitt Donaldson's father, were members."

"And you're right. I didn't just happen to be here." Agent Keith paused and then slid his chair closer to the table. "This isn't for public consumption, but I came to Asheville about six months ago as part of a small project jointly run by the Bureau and Homeland Security. We called it Resurrection Watch."

The rest of us exchanged glances. The name meant nothing.

"It was more of a to-do list than a full-scale operation," Keith explained. "Since so many things had been missed in the buildup to 9-11, we wanted to make sure we weren't repeating mistakes. Like assuming we know who our enemies are. So, somebody got the bright idea to check on all known antigovernment groups, present and past, not only abroad but of domestic origin: the Klan, the neo-Nazis, and the Christian militias, to name a few. These organizations go through cycles, and charismatic leaders can appear who resurrect and reinterpret old doctrine and demagoguery to build their own powerbase. Sometimes they simmer below our radar until they break out with some act of violence designed to gain notoriety and recruits."

"You went all the way back to The Silver Shirts?" I asked.

"We went back as far as we had information to follow. A thick file had been built on Pelley and the Silver Shirts in the early 1930s, and though they'd supposedly dissolved in the 1940s, we eventually got around to them. The only current activity, other than the occasional scholarly paper, had been a series of petitions from an attorney in Asheville, North Carolina, named Hewitt Donaldson. He requested any information on Hugh Donaldson."

"A son trying to understand his father," I said.

Keith rolled his eyes. "I'm not a shrink. But since he was linked in our database with the Silver Legion of America, I decided he'd be a good starting place."

"And then you could check them off your list if he proved harmless."

He pointed a finger at me. "Hey, you wouldn't believe how many nutcases out there have formed so-called citizen action groups, and the Internet is like a primordial soup breeding these vermin."

"I think it's called free speech," I said. "And you're still here. Was Hewitt Donaldson not harmless, or did Cory DeMille turn out to be the one you wanted to more thoroughly investigate?"

For the first time, Agent Keith's composure faltered and even beneath the beard I could see his cheeks redden.

"That's okay," I said. "Nice to know you're human. So, in order to spend more time with Ms. DeMille you got Donaldson copies of the minutes from the House Committee on Un-American Activities and any other declassified information you could access, and he told you about his aunt's lockbox, which is why we're all sitting here."

Agent Keith looked like I'd trotted out his mother and revealed indisputable evidence she was Osama Bin Laden's concubine. His mouth and eyes popped open in amazement. "Hewitt told you that?"

I grinned at Nakayla. "We're detectives, Agent Keith. Like you said, I'm not stupid, and I'm good at my job." I had him off balance and pressed for more information. "Did you ask Hewitt Donaldson to get you access to the lockbox?"

"Sorry. That falls under an ongoing investigation."

Efird had tilted back on the rear legs of his chair during our exchange and came crashing forward. "Bullshit! You were chasing Sam, the wrong man, and you were present at a shooting where you didn't identify yourself as a federal agent."

"I'd left before it happened."

Efird looked at me with an invitation to jump in. I accepted. "Oh, so you followed the wrong man and then missed the right man. Maybe the Grove Park's video security cameras will back your story, maybe they won't."

His blue eyes appeared to near absolute zero as he glared at me. "What do you want?"

"Some cooperation," I said. "Detective Efird's working two murders and I have a vested interest in staying alive. Do you know if Donaldson pressed his aunt to give him the lockbox?"

"Yes."

"Which explains this timing issue, doesn't it? Ethel Barkley got spooked when she thought the FBI was coming for her sacred trust, and she got me to get it out of the bank and handle anything that would be personally embarrassing. She'd learned about me through Donaldson but thought it better to approach me through someone else."

"I don't know what was going through the old lady's head. Hewitt said she was crazy as a loon."

"And there you're both wrong. She took prudent steps to complete what she saw as her mission. What's so important to the Bureau about the lockbox?"

Keith shrugged. "It's a loose end. That's all."

I shook my head. "I'm not buying it. My experience with the politics of the military is probably not that different from the politics of the Bureau. Nobody wants to be embarrassed, and when something's a loose end, the translation means it's an uncontrollable unknown that might come back to bite somebody. You've learned something in helping Donaldson that's raised your interest in that lockbox. It can't be a secret to bring down the Third Reich or demolish the Silver Shirts. What is it?"

The room grew quiet. We stared at the FBI agent: four against one waiting for an answer that might show our government placed a priority on truth and justice.

Keith focused on Detective Efird, one lawman to another. "Hugh Donaldson was an FBI informant. He was recruited when William Dudley Pelley moved to Asheville and he was instructed to keep tabs on him. When Pelley founded the Silver Legion of America, Hugh Donaldson became a very valuable asset, not only for his inside information on an organization that wanted to subvert and rewrite the U.S. Constitution, but for the close association Pelley sought to establish with the Nazi regime. Donaldson moved to the inner circle, at the expense of his reputation and his relationship with his family. No one knew, and his sister and her husband were true believers in Pelley's vision."

"This information would have been too sensitive to be in the reports of the House Committee on Un-American Activities," I said. "Does Hewitt Donaldson know?"

"No. I just read the confidential file last week. When I got here, the guard had been murdered and the lockbox stolen. I was still getting my bearings."

Efird stood and leaned against the back of his chair. "If Hugh Donaldson was one of the good guys, then what's the Bureau afraid of?"

Keith looked at me. He and Efird may have shared the bonds of law enforcement, but he knew I understood the fickle currents of political intrigue and public opinion.

"The Bureau's concerned about what Hugh Donaldson did," I said. "We're in the midst of heated debates on water-boarding, prisoner humiliation, due process for enemy combatants, and the uneven implementation of questionable policies that could be viewed as undermining our Constitution as severely as William Dudley Pelley sought to do in 1935. Hugh Donaldson was an attorney whose client was the person the FBI targeted for undercover surveillance. How do you accomplish that and maintain the attorney-client privilege that's at the heart of our judicial system?"

Nathan gave a low whistle. "A seventy-year-old black eye is still a black eye, and it couldn't come at a worse time."

"We don't know the particulars," Keith said. "Maybe Hugh Donaldson did his absolute best for Pelley."

"And maybe he had his sister steal a manuscript from F. Scott Fitzgerald for Pelley and not the FBI, an agency that hasn't exactly had a stellar relationship with the artists and writers of our country."

Keith's eyes swept the room, making sure he had our undivided attention. "Let's cut to the chase. Anything in that lockbox that's a record of Hugh Donaldson's undercover work is the property of the FBI. I'll cooperate with the local investigation as much as I'm able, and given your suspects hatched their scheme in Iraq, then traveled to New Jersey where they threatened your friend Calvin before coming to Asheville, I think a case can be made for full Bureau assistance. You'll get your murderers, Detective Efird, but I'll get my documents."

Efird stood still for a few seconds. Then he said, "You're free to go. Give me one of those fancy FBI business cards and I'll be in touch. I'm not making any promises till I talk to my partner and our Chief."

Keith reached in his coat pocket and flipped a white card on the table. He left without shaking a hand. No one offered one.

After his footsteps died down the hall, I asked, "What do you think?"

Efird wrinkled his nose. "He's the kind of guy who'd ask you to turn around so he could stab you in the back. I believe most of his story and we'll have to work with him. Chief Buchanan won't want to antagonize the Feds when the payoff's a double murder conviction. I'd like the Bureau to run Lucas and Hernandez through both foreign and domestic databases for any known associates. You and Calvin think there's a third man involved, and now that Agent Keith's been cleared we have no clue what the guy looks like."

"How soon can you request that?" I asked.

"As soon as I talk to Newland."

"Isn't today his colonoscopy prep?"

Efird grinned. "He's got his cell phone with him in the bathroom. Talk about multitasking." He headed for the door. "You know the way out. Stay safe."

I went to the open door and closed it.

"What do you think?" Nathan asked.

"As far as I'm concerned, we press ahead. It'll take the Bureau a day or more to get engaged, and in the meantime Efird's got limited resources." I turned to Nakayla. "You okay with that?"

"No. But I don't have a better suggestion. I hate to say it, but I trust Nathan's Blackwater operatives more than I do the FBI."

"Then we're committed. Nathan will bring us the secure phones by the end of the day, and I'll talk to the press as soon as we get back to the office."

Nakayla caught my arm. "There's one other thing I want to do. Agent Keith grilled you about the coincidence of timing. I want to check on his flight schedule. He said he was delayed and didn't arrive till after Amanda Whitfield was murdered. Convenient, wasn't it?"

Nathan wrapped his arms around us in an impromptu group hug. "You really are detectives. Well, as the Master said to Watson, 'The game's afoot.'"

Chapter Twenty-two

"The door that I pushed open, on the advice of an elevator boy, was marked 'The Swastika Holding Company,' and at first there didn't seem to be anyone inside."

I sat at my new desk and studied the sentence from *The Great Gatsby*, remembering Ethel Barkley's copy with the numeral one penciled over the first T and the Z=Z equation on the following page. A computer would have cracked the code in a few seconds, but I had neither a software program nor an encrypted message to use as a target. If my deductions were correct, a simple letter substitution would give me the alphabet I needed. Despite Agent Keith's warning, I wanted to be prepared to decode any documents before the FBI forever confiscated them.

I realized my efforts could be little more than busy work while Nathan executed the details of our plan. Calvin's supposition that the lockbox contained something requiring interpretation or deciphering was a plausible theory, but only a theory.

If T was identified as one, then it made sense that T would equal A. The next letter, H, would be B, and E would be C. I scribbled the letters down in two columns: the left held the letters from the sentence and the right ran in alphabetical order from A to Z. I skipped letters when they appeared again like the second O in door. The sentence contained twenty-two letters of the alphabet, and my sequence ended with the G in "Holding" equaling V. Four letters remained without a coded equivalent: W,

X, Y, Z. I looked back through the letters of the sentence. Four hadn't been included in Fitzgerald's sentence: J, Q, X, and Z. I assigned them to the missing letters of the alphabet and wound up with Z=Z, the equation written in the margin. I clapped my hands with satisfaction.

"What is it?" Nakayla called from her office.

"That sentence in *The Great Gatsby* generated an alphabet that fits the Z=Z equation. I'm pretty sure I've broken the code."

"How do you hope to use it?" She'd walked to my doorway and leaned against the jamb. "Keith will grab the lockbox at his first opportunity."

I held up my worksheet with the two columns of letters. "I've got this. Hernandez and his people might have Ethel's lockbox with them, or once we bring Efird in the picture, he'll probably find it where they've been staying. He'll want the contents decoded if only to help build his murder case."

"And our payment is in there," Nakayla said, emphasizing "our."

"Right, partner."

She circled behind me and gently massaged my shoulders. "You're tense. Are you sure you want to do it this way? Why not dig up Nathan's decoy and simply rebury it. The area's more isolated and you know they'll check out what you were doing."

"Too many ways for them to slip away on foot. My apartment's atop a mountain and the parking lot can be easily sealed. I want them to think I'm making a break. We need to force their hand."

She gave the back of my neck an extra squeeze.

"Then let Nathan and his Blackwater buddies do the dirty work. We can spend our time dancing in front of the window."

"Really? That'll draw a crowd in the parking lot."

Nakayla cupped her hand around my chin, closing my mouth. She kissed my ear and said in a sultry whisper, "At least no one can accuse you of having two left feet. Or even one."

I grabbed her wrist and ran my forefinger across her open palm. "That's what I love about you. You're all heart line."

She kissed me again. "Your Napoleon needs to meet my Josephine."

"That's a dance I could get into—but not in front of the window."

The office phone rang, saving me from falling into a bad impersonation of Humphrey Bogart. I snagged the receiver. "Blackman and Robertson."

"Chief?" Calvin's voice sounded strained. "You okay?"

"Yeah. How about you? Everything cleared up?" I didn't think our office lines had been re-bugged, and Calvin must have agreed. But I wanted both of us to be cautious.

"I think so, but I heard you spent some time at the police station, and before I left town I wanted an update."

"The police picked up another suspect. Turned out to be a false alarm." In case Calvin's line was tapped, I didn't want to mention the FBI and scare off our friends.

"So you think we're done?" he asked.

"Yes. The police got a positive ID on Lucas. He'd been following us, and the so-called witnesses at that old folks home aren't sure what they saw. I think Lucas is good for both murders."

"Well, I'll pick up the trail in Baghdad. Sure you don't want to come with me?"

"That's one trail I never want to walk down. Watch your back. I plan to see you again."

Calvin laughed. "I will. You taught me well, Chief. And good luck with the detective business. Kiss that partner of yours for me and tell her you're a poor substitute for the real thing." He hung up.

"A problem?" Nakayla asked.

"No. Calvin probably witnessed the police pick up Agent Keith and wondered if our plans had changed. He'll be at the apartment tomorrow night. Everything's on go." I looked out the window at the steady drizzle. "The rain will shield Nathan's operation tonight, but I hope they don't leave muddy signs for tomorrow."

"I hope these guys keep their distance and determine you dug something up after you're safely away."

"If things go according to plan, they'll see me load the chest in the CR-V."

"Right." Nakayla headed for her office. "When have things ever gone according to plan?"

"What did you learn about the flights?"

She stopped and turned around. "The airport manager is supposed to call me back before the end of the day. I figured that would be faster than trying to contact each airline."

"And if we discover Agent Keith lied?"

She put her hands on her hips and feigned surprise. "You want my opinion?"

"No. I like to hear myself ask questions."

"If Keith lied, then we postpone this ruse of yours until we find out why. And that should be left to Detective Efird. I'm not ready to take on the FBI."

I shook my head. "If Keith lied, then I bet we aren't taking on the FBI but something more sinister. And that, dear partner, will be troubling indeed."

Ten minutes later, Nathan Armitage knocked on our door. Beads of water clung to his long raincoat, and he declined Nakayla's offer to help him out of it. "I can't stay, and I'd just shake water all over your floor. I'm meeting the team at my house in an hour. I didn't want to have to explain them to my office staff."

"How's the fake chest?" I asked.

Nathan grinned. "Looks terrific. I used an old rusty tackle box. And the trick with the potato created a perfect swastika. It took a couple tries but for future reference, put the carved half of the potato in the freezer. The lead will harden before the heat eats at the mold. By the way, you need to replenish all my fishing weights."

"I'll throw in a fish dinner if we pull this off."

"How are you feeling?" Nakayla asked him. Unlike me, she'd remembered his recent release from the hospital and his weeks of rehab.

"Good. I won't be doing any digging, and a little rain won't bother me. A small price to pay." He stuck his hands inside the pockets of his coat and pulled out two cell phones. "These will be safe. There's a push-to-talk feature, but avoid that. I've taped your names on the back so I'll know who has which number. I've written it under your name. Memorize them and destroy them." He handed us each a phone. "I don't program numbers into the directory in case it's ever lost or stolen."

"Thanks," I said. "Call me when the chest is buried, no matter what time."

"Given the weather, we might move a little earlier. I think Beaver Lake will be quiet after midnight."

Our business line rang and Nakayla stepped in her office to answer it.

Nathan backed toward the door. "See you tomorrow. We'll get them. I can feel it."

Before I could reply, Nakayla said, "Mr. Garrett, thank you for returning my call."

I held up my hand to Nathan. "Wait. That's the airport manager."

"Yes," Nakayla said. "The flight arrivals for last Tuesday evening."

Nathan and I moved into her office where she stood listening.

"So, not just the flights out of Charlotte? What did land on time?" After a few minutes of silence, she gave us a thumbs-up. "Thanks, Mr. Garrett. I hope the rest of your week is smoother." She dropped the receiver onto the cradle. "Well, Agent Keith's story checks out. Asheville and Charlotte weren't the only cities with severe weather problems. A wall of thunderstorms from North Carolina to New York played havoc with the schedule. Charlotte was under a tornado watch from six to eight, and wind sheers kept the runways closed for nearly an hour."

"Keith claimed to leave from D.C," I said.

"The evening flights come to Asheville from regional hubs. Charlotte is the primary feeder. Garrett said a few flights came from Atlanta. Even though Atlanta was spared the bad weather, the connecting routes from the Northeast were delayed. Garrett speculated passengers from the South or Midwest would have been more likely to make connections, but after the storms passed through Asheville, the backlog of arrivals slowed all landings. Keith's evening flight probably had problems in both D.C. and Charlotte."

Nathan breathed a sigh of relief. "So, unless he flew in earlier in the afternoon, his timing fits the conditions. I'm glad we're not dealing with some rogue FBI agent." He cinched the belt of his raincoat tighter. "I'll be in touch. I suggest you two stick together tonight. I'll have a man on watch at the apartment."

Nakayla looked at her watch. "It's after four now. I need to go by my house and pick up a change of clothes."

"Then I'm following you," I said. "We're too close to the end to take any chances."

Although Nakayla and I went to bed at ten, neither of us could sleep. We kept Nathan's phones within reach on the night-stands and talked about where we should be when the trap was sprung. The lower level of the Kenilworth had an outside door off the back wing that opened directly into the rear parking lot. Nathan and his team wanted my CR-V in the center where it would be the greatest distance from the two exit driveways. Nathan expected to surround Hernandez and his cohorts in less than ten seconds. Calvin, Nakayla, and I could emerge from the Kenilworth's rear door and block an escape route into the building.

During our pillow talk, I didn't argue against Nakayla's participation, but I insisted Calvin and I go first. We had combat training and carried weapons with greater stopping power. Nakayla agreed to the plan.

I was just drifting off when the secure cell rang. It was nearly one-thirty.

"No problems," Nathan said. "We buried the chest behind the concrete piling. It was raining like a son of a bitch, which will pat down the earth and wash the loose soil off the leaves."

"You think midmorning is good?"

"Yes. Right after the rain ends. It makes sense you'd be out there before things clear enough for any lake activity to begin. I realized you need a shovel. Give me your access code and I'll have one set inside the back door on the lower level for you to carry out in the morning. Also a fishing pole."

"Fishing pole?"

"They'll expect you to have devised some plausible cover for being at Beaver Lake."

Nathan made a good point, and I was embarrassed I hadn't thought of it. "And you'll have men in place all day?"

"Only at the lake until you make the retrieval. Then we'll be at the Kenilworth. I know Frank Howington, the owner of your building, and there's a vacant apartment on the second floor overlooking the parking lot. Frank made arrangements for me to have it for the next two days."

"What did you tell him?"

"That I had a client who thought she was being stalked."

I looked at Nakayla in bed beside me. She'd propped herself up on one elbow and watched me with anxious eyes. "I'm worried about that part of the plan too—Nakayla driving to the office alone."

Nathan picked up on my concern and understood that I was prompting him. Nakayla wouldn't be as argumentative if he were dictating the steps of the operation. "I get it. Tell her I'm sending a man for her in the morning. He'll be in a silver Audi and come to the porte-cochère. That way I won't have to waste a more experienced man tailing her. She can call for a ride from the office when she's finished for the day."

I repeated his instructions.

Nakayla frowned. "Won't that make them suspicious?"

Nathan must have heard her because he added, "I scanned your cars and found GPS transmitters planted on both. These guys came prepared."

"Or they have access to resources here."

Nathan said nothing, and I knew he was second-guessing his decision to involve his Blackwater friends.

"At least I won't have to worry about leading them to Beaver Lake," I said. "And it might be good if Nakayla's moving without their electronic surveillance."

Her eyes widened as she realized her car had been tagged.

"What time do you want Nathan's man to be here?" I asked her.

"Eight forty-five."

I confirmed that we'd look for a silver Audi to pull in front at eight forty-five. I'd be watching from the recesses of the lobby to make sure no one intervened, and Nakayla promised to call me as soon as she reached the office.

Somewhere around three I fell asleep.

Fog lay in the valleys like rivers of milk. I would descend into its thickness, visibility decreasing to a few car lengths, and then I'd climb a knoll to emerge like a swimmer breaking the surface into the morning sunlight. I knew a dense covering would hover over Beaver Lake and the surrounding shoreline. My enemies might have placed the tracking device on my CR-V, but I was turning it to our advantage. The challenge would be making sure they saw me carrying Nathan's doctored tackle box.

When I reached the backside of the lake, I decided not to squeeze the CR-V between the gatepost and tree, as I had on my scouting trip. Instead I pulled close to the taut chain blocking access to the narrow dirt road. My walk in would be farther, but the Honda would be visible to anyone looking for it.

I popped open the rear hatch and pulled out the fishing pole, shovel, and my new copy of *The Great Gatsby*. The casual observer would see an enthusiastic angler prepared to dig his own worms and then fish while reading a good book.

I heard a vehicle approaching on the paved road above. A white van materialized out of the fog and glided past. Moisture coated the driver's window, blurring a face into a shock of black hair and deeply tanned skin. A chill ran through me as the van disappeared in the mist. The driver had to be Hernandez, the man who had bludgeoned Ethel Barkley to death.

His curiosity would be aroused. I hoped he would delay any action until he thought he understood what I was doing. I counted on the Ali Baba gang being clever enough to create a story out of all the pieces they would have discovered: Ethel Barkley's fortune, William Dudley Pelley's Silver Shirts, and the contents of the swastika-sealed lockbox, including F. Scott Fitzgerald's papers, a gift from his paramour of 1935, and something else they'd found but didn't understand. My unearthing the buried chest should prove irresistible to conspirators who were convinced I had conspired against them. Where I had justice as a motive, they acted out of greed and revenge, a powerful combination that could be their downfall.

As the sound of the van's engine faded in the distance, a light breeze fanned the fog into wisps that danced across the ground. Grabbing the shovel and fishing pole in one hand and the book in the other, I headed down the narrowing trail, putting my life in the hands of Nathan Armitage and the unseen men who had once worked with my enemies.

The rotting picnic table and canoe appeared undisturbed, and the leaves near the water showed no sign that anything but rain had pressed them down. I leaned the fishing pole against the canoe and used the shovel as a cane to negotiate the uneven ground. I made a show of looking at my decoded page and pacing off steps from the path. I banged the blade of the shovel against the concrete piling as if that had been the marker I'd been seeking. Then I backed up a few feet and stabbed the spade into the earth.

Digging presented a potential problem. I had to shift all my weight onto my artificial leg to put my good foot on top of the shovel blade. Fortunately, the recently turned earth yielded easily and my handicap posed no hardship. Every few minutes, I'd pause and listen. Somewhere a squirrel chattered. I wasn't enough of a hunter to know if his noisy rant was a warning or a playful call to a mate.

After about ten minutes, the spade struck metal. Nathan and his men had taken the time to bury the chest a good three feet deep. I knelt down and pulled up the old tackle box by its top handle. Smeared with dirt and rusted at the corners, it looked like it could have been buried for a hundred years. I set it aside and began refilling the hole. If our plan were going to go wrong, now would be the moment. The chest had been uncovered, I was alone with my back to the path, and the lake blocked any hope for escape. Nathan's men had shown no sign of their presence, and even if they were watching, they had to be too far away to be of immediate assistance.

I tucked the Fitzgerald book inside my jacket and hurried back to the CR-V with the fishing pole, shovel, and muddy chest. The fog had lifted and the road above was clearly visible. I unlocked the hatch and threw the shovel and pole in first. Then I set the chest right above the license plate where anyone could see it. The swastika seal appeared to be a dead ringer for the one on Ethel Barkley's lockbox, and I wiped away the dirt to make it even clearer. I removed my jacket, not concerned that my Kimber and shoulder holster were exposed, wrapped the nylon windbreaker around the chest, and pushed everything farther into the cargo space. I closed the hatch, took a final look around, and then quickly backed onto the paved road and headed for the apartment.

Using Nathan's secure phone, I called Nakayla. She'd let me know when she'd arrived at the office and I'd promised to tell her when I was safely away from Beaver Lake.

"Look out your window in about five minutes. I'll be driving by."

She sighed. "Thank God. Everything okay?"

"I believe Hernandez made at least one pass. There could be another vehicle. Once the fog lifted, they might have been able to use binoculars to see me from across the lake. I think they're going to bite."

"This afternoon?" she asked.

"Maybe, but they'll probably wonder why I didn't take the chest into the apartment. They'll assume I'm either leaving soon or waiting till after dark to remove it. Since they've got a GPS track on the CR-V they probably won't come too close during daylight. Or they could swing in, smash the rear window with a crowbar, and try to snatch it. It could happen so fast we don't have a chance to be involved."

"I'll probably call Nathan's man for a ride around four. Since I'm supposed to think you're sick, I should leave early to check on you."

Her suggestion made sense, and as soon as I was back in the apartment I'd like to have her safely with me. I looked at my watch. Ten-thirty. "Anything shaking at the office?"

"Agent Keith came looking for you. I told him you were sick. He wanted to know why you told the press you thought the case was wrapped up. Efird telephoned with the same question."

"What did you tell them?"

"That you didn't like the press and you'd say anything to stop them from pestering you."

I laughed. "Good answer."

"Keith asked me to join Cory and him for lunch. I said okay as long as we went someplace close."

Being with an FBI agent was probably a good idea during these final few hours. I certainly didn't want Nakayla going to lunch alone. "Sounds fine. Don't let him pump you for too much information."

"I'll hold the martinis to two," she said. "Call me if something breaks before I get there."

"You got it, partner." I hung up, but the sound of her voice stayed with me. The woman was something special. I glanced up at our office window as I drove by Pack Square. She had the good sense not to come to the glass and wave.

As I headed down Biltmore Avenue toward the turn for the Kenilworth, I dialed Nathan.

"You near?" he asked.

"About two miles out. The chest is wrapped in my jacket."

"Good. I heard the white van circled a few times."

"I never saw your guys."

He laughed. "You weren't supposed to. Although one said he buried himself in leaves where a squirrel was hoarding nuts and the critter's squawking liked to wake the dead. Report is you played your part well."

"We'll know in the final act, won't we?"

"Come in slow," he said. "I've got a man in a green Subaru Forester who'll back out of a parking spot when he sees you. Take that place, go up to your apartment, and wait for me to phone when we have activity."

"Nakayla's going to call your man around four," I said. "Calvin will come after dark."

"Fine. Suits me if it's all over before then and we can tell them about it over a round of drinks."

I swung into the rear parking lot and a Subaru in the center row immediately backed up. I didn't want to go into the building with my shoulder holster visible so I tucked the Kimber in my belt, folded the holster rig, and slid it under the seat. I locked the doors and looked around. The only life I saw was a gray-haired man being pulled by a Schnauzer of matching color to what the residents called the poop zone. More than half the Kenilworth's tenants had dogs, and the management provided poles with plastic bags and depository cans conveniently placed to encourage pet owners to scoop up their animals' excrement. I hoped the turds we'd be scooping up would be dumped in a can forever.

Morning slowly stretched into afternoon with no call from Nathan. Odds were nothing would happen till after dark, but the waiting was still tough. I had the loaded Kimber on the kitchen counter closest to the door; I changed the sleeve on my athletic prosthesis. Finally, I resorted to the most desperate of all measures, watching afternoon TV. When four o'clock came, I sat in the chair by the window staring out at the parking lot. My apartment was on the front of the building, and I would see Nakayla ride to the entrance.

When the bells at All Souls Episcopal Church in neighboring Biltmore Village rang four-thirty, I opened the secure cell and dialed Nakayla.

"Chief Warrant Officer Blackman?" The cold, heavy voice of a man rumbled in my ear.

My breath caught in my throat. "Who is this?"

"The man you screwed over. The man you're trying to play for a fool with your little box and parking lot charade. The man you're going to have to deal with if you ever hope to see your lovely partner and Warrant Officer Stuart alive again."

Chapter Twenty-three

"What do you want, Hernandez?" My question came out terse and hard. No pleading for compassion would dent this killer's conscience.

"Like I asked you before, I want the account numbers and the passwords. You're a smart guy, Blackman. Give me what you took and I'll let them go."

"Not till I know they're okay."

Muffled, unintelligible words sounded for a few seconds, and then Nakayla spoke in a hoarse whisper. "Sam, I'm okay."

"How many are there?"

"He has the two of us. Calvin's in a bad way. He tried to resist and they beat him unconscious. He's alive, but timing is critical. Like Tuesday, his timing makes all the difference. It won't fit unless you do what they tell you." Her voice faded as someone snatched the phone from her mouth.

"Satisfied?" His sarcasm held a cruel edge.

"How do you want to play the exchange? I can text you the information as I see them being released."

Hernandez laughed. "I bet you could. No, you're coming to me. I've got a satellite hook-up and we'll move the funds together. I understand you've done a little code-breaking. I want that as well. Consider it a surcharge for the inconvenience you've caused."

Meeting Hernandez face-to-face would be suicidal. But I had no other option. "I don't have a car. Mine's under surveillance."

"Then that's your problem. Your girlfriend's car's still at your apartment. I had her call your friend to say she didn't need a ride. I'm confident you'll be able to get to it unobserved. But I'll be watching. Any sign of police or my old Blackwater friends and you'll be attending a double funeral. And you'll be looking over your shoulder for the rest of your short, miserable life."

I wanted to reach through the phone and strangle the bastard. How had he gotten the jump on both Nakayla and Calvin? But she'd clued me that there were two of them when she'd answered my question "How many are there?" with "He has the two of us." What else had she told me in those brief sentences?

"Blackman. What's it going to be?"

"Okay. But I need a little time. My copy of *The Great Gatsby* has the code and it's still in my car, where you know I can't get it. I'll have to recreate the key sentence from memory." The code sheet was tucked safely in my wallet, but Hernandez had no reason to doubt my lie. I was playing for time. "And I'll have better success of slipping away if it's after dark."

"You have ninety minutes. If you haven't left by six, I'm moving to Plan B. Trust me. You won't like Plan B."

"Where are we meeting?"

"The one spot no one will look in this hick county. Beaver Lake. The scene of your little performance this morning. Come unarmed and alone."

The connection terminated.

Hernandez had caught me in my own trap. All of our resources were focused on the wrong place. I had no doubt he'd be watching for any sudden change at the apartment building. Hidden men would have to expose themselves if they were redeployed. He would probably come to the Beaver Lake site after me, and he'd be ready to act. No doubt his computer would be programmed to handle a wire transfer, and he'd match my Fitzgerald code against whatever documents he'd found in Ethel Barkley's lockbox. The location was not that isolated, but in five minutes, he'd have everything he needed, and either let us go or kill us. I didn't like the odds.

Hernandez had acquired every critical piece of our plan. He knew the box I dug up was a decoy and that Nathan had brought in outside help. Someone had fed him key information, and that someone was close to us. Had Nakayla or Calvin been forced to talk? Nakayla had lunch with Agent Keith and Cory. What if she'd never returned? What did we know about Cory? She could have left Donaldson alone the night Amanda Whitfield was killed. Told him she needed to use the restroom and broken into our office. Maybe she and Keith were both dirty and she'd picked him up earlier in the afternoon. The weather delay was an added bonus for his alibi.

But Nakayla said there were two of them. If Cory were in on it, Nakayla should have given me a clue for three. Unless Cory wasn't with them. She could be the one watching my apartment. Now I was forcing connections that lacked evidence. Nakayla hadn't mentioned Keith directly, only that timing didn't fit for Calvin. What an odd way to phrase it, if time was running out for my injured comrade. Nathan had said Keith's timing fit the conditions when Nakayla checked the FBI agent's alibi. And she referenced Tuesday—"his timing makes all the difference." What did she mean by "It won't fit?"

Then it hit me. Timing. I'd been looking at the whole case from the wrong perspective. Nakayla's message had been brilliant. Pieces tumbled into place as the jigsaw puzzle formed itself, and the picture sent a wave of anger rushing to the core of my bones. I knew they'd never let us leave the exchange alive.

I also knew if I varied from their plan they would cut their losses and run. I couldn't bluff them. Hernandez was convinced I'd sold his loot and put the cash in my offshore account. As wrong as he was, I'd have to give him my number and password. Once a thief always a thief. I counted on that giving me a sliver of hope. And I might face them alone, but somehow I'd be armed.

Although sunset wouldn't occur for a few more hours, shadows already began to deepen as the sun dropped behind the high western ridges. I had another hour before Hernandez expected me to leave. My life depended on how I used it.

◇◇◇

As I steered Nakayla's Hyundai off the pavement and onto the dirt side-road, I could see ripples spreading over the dark lake water. An early fall chill had moved in behind the rain, and the dropping temperature and rising wind had sent Friday afternoon shore walkers and canoeists home for the evening. For a location in a populated community, the backside of the lake quickly became desolate, much like I imagined parts of Central Park became isolated, dangerous pockets at night, cut off from the hundreds of thousands of people living within a quarter mile radius.

I turned on the headlights as I neared the chain stretched across the road. Although Nakayla's car could slip around the barricade easier than my CR-V, I saw no point in pulling the vehicle deeper into the woods. Instead, I turned around so I was facing out and parked the car halfway up the bank where I hoped the incline would be too steep for Hernandez' van. If we managed to break free, I didn't want my escape to be totally blocked.

Nakayla had given me a spare key to her car several weeks ago, and I left it in the ignition where a quick turn would start the engine. Sneaking out of the Kenilworth hadn't been a problem. I'd waited in the lobby till a family happened to come down the elevator, a single mom and two kids. We'd chatted a few times in the hall so I walked with them out to the front parking lot. With a ball cap pulled low on my forehead, I hoped we'd passed for a family headed for pizza or burgers. The entire front expanse of the old grand hotel had hidden me from anyone watching the rear lot. Then I'd zipped down the mountain by a circuitous route that should have confused even Daniel Boone.

I opened the car door, reached up, and switched the courtesy light to the off position. One less opportunity for me to be a target.

I stepped carefully onto the weed-covered bank. My stump ached at the uneven pressure and I leaned against the hood as I gingerly made my way to level ground. I rested against one of the gateposts, waiting for whatever approached. I was strangely calm, becoming the hunter and not the hunted, all thoughts of justice driven from my mind.

The low rumble of a slowly moving vehicle came from around the bend. Then a white van without headlights coasted down the side-road and braked a few yards from me. The driver had pulled adjacent to the Hyundai, giving me a narrow but passable escape route.

The engine coughed into silence. Only a featureless shape was visible behind the wheel.

"Hands out to your side and walk toward the rear of the van. I'll tell you when to stop." Hernandez barked the orders with military precision.

I moved as naturally as I could with my arms outstretched like a tightrope walker working without a safety net. I passed the driver's door and saw a swarthy face grinning at me through the open window. Although I'd never seen Manny Hernandez in person, I recognized the face of someone who would as soon kill you as look at you.

"That's far enough." He hopped out of the van and pointed a Glock automatic at my chest.

I stopped beside the cargo section. "Who's going to open the door? You, me, or Calvin?"

A click sounded from inside and the sheet metal vibrated as someone yanked down a handle. Then a gap widened to reveal the interior. Calvin wore dark jeans and a black wool shirt. A few strands of thread hung where the top button should have been. He wore a shoulder holster with an ugly M1911 forty-five at the ready. He crouched in the doorway, eyes wary, the surprise he'd intended for me bouncing back on him.

"How'd you know?" he demanded.

I'd knocked some of the cockiness out of him, and I needed to take full advantage of the moment. I paused only long enough to see Nakayla lying on a remnant of green carpet, her hands and feet bound with duct tape and a single strip stretched across her mouth. Her eyes fixed on me. Between her and Calvin, a laptop sat open with its screen filled with numbers and a satellite phone plugged in its side.

I took a deep breath. There'd be one chance to tell my story. Truth and lies had to weave together perfectly. My audience wasn't Calvin; I was betting our lives on Hernandez.

"Tuesday night," I said. "When you and your buddy here staged that little scene outside my apartment, you gave yourself away. That was just the first time."

"How?" Calvin asked.

"Christ, get him in the van," Hernandez ordered. "What difference does it make?"

"The same difference it made to Lucas," I snapped. "Or aren't you interested in staying alive?"

Hernandez shot a glance at Calvin and I saw a flash of hesitation.

"Did you pat him down?" Calvin asked. "He carries a Kimber forty-five."

Hernandez stepped closer. "Turn around." He ran his left hand under one arm and then the other.

"He fingered Lucas at the Grove Park," I whispered. "I didn't know him from Adam. Why? Because he didn't care which one of us was killed."

"Shut up," Calvin said.

"I thought you wanted to hear how you botched your plan, Cal. You're not going to get away with killing the three of us and then staging the scene to look like you overpowered Hernandez too late to save your friends." I turned my head and spoke over my shoulder. "He'll shoot you with his gun, and then kill us with yours."

I felt Hernandez' hands stop on the inside of my left thigh before moving down the hard surface of my prosthesis feeling for a calf holster. Then he repeated the motion on the right.

"He's clean," he said. "Get in, peg leg."

I stood still. "You screwed up, Cal. You told me you flew in Tuesday night, but none of the flights could land in time for you to be at the Kenilworth. The guy you saw at the police station today is an FBI agent connected to Homeland Security. He gave the police the security tapes from the Asheville airport. They want to know why you lied to them. They know you came in earlier, and you saw me retrieve the lockbox. The police have that button missing from your shirt. They found it under the body of the girl you murdered in our office. They planned to pick you up tonight as soon as you showed at my apartment."

"Yeah. Well, I ain't gonna show at your apartment."

Hernandez poked me in the back with his gun barrel. "Move."

"Whose idea was it to kill Ed, Charlie, and me in Iraq? I'm betting you came up with that bright idea too, Cal. You told Hernandez and Lucas we were getting too close, and when the hit had been arranged, you took a colonoscopy prep to insure you'd be in the infirmary with the runs. You spelled that out loud and clear to Detective Newland, smart boy."

Calvin's jaw tightened and his hand moved toward his shoulder holster. Hernandez poked me again, but not as hard.

"So, now you've managed to alert both the FBI and Homeland Security. Nice work, asshole. Good luck getting out of the country."

"Get him in here," Calvin ordered.

"Better do what he says," I taunted.

Hernandez shoved me and I stumbled a few steps.

"Sorry. I've got to crawl in backwards." I sat on the lip of the door facing Hernandez. "You guys took my leg from me so you're going to have to let me get in my way." I looked along the inside wall and saw Ethel Barkley's open lockbox near the rear. "How appropriate. The Nazis would feel right at home."

I stared Hernandez in the eyes. "You know I didn't take anything from you. My offshore account has funds I got from my parents' death. I'd say Calvin bribed some villagers to tell you I'd taken your cache when he did it himself. With me dead, why would you think otherwise? But I didn't die, and the medics whisked me away so fast I was beyond his reach. Until I had the misfortune to make the national news and you picked up my trail. Then Calvin had to act."

Hernandez' thick lips started working in and out. He was either thinking things over or getting ready to hit me.

"You want my account number and password? Fine. It's in my shirt pocket along with the code for whatever you found in that chest." I pulled out a folded sheet of paper and handed it to Hernandez. "But it's not going to do you any good. Like I said, my money's legit, so when the FBI asked this afternoon if they could put a flag on the account, I said sure. Now every transaction is monitored and intercepted."

Hernandez' face darkened. He looked up at Calvin. "You stupid, arrogant bastard."

"He's bluffing. He's making it up, just like he made up his Fitzgerald ruse."

"Right. I'm bluffing." I scooted backwards and swung my legs in the van, lifting my prosthesis with both hands and pushing the release button while Hernandez and Calvin glared at each other. "You know your account number, Hernandez." I pointed at the laptop screen. "Bet you double or nothing Calvin's got the wire transfer already programmed for a different account."

Hernandez started to climb past me, his attention focused on the computer.

"That's enough out of you," Calvin growled. His hand whipped to his shoulder holster.

With my left hand, I yanked my prosthesis free of my stump and with my right grabbed the Kimber that had been digging into my flesh.

But Calvin's eyes were on Hernandez. The big man crawled up in the van with his gloved gun hand grasping the door. Too late he saw Calvin's pistol level with his head.

The gunshot roared like a concussion grenade. Hernandez flew backwards into the open air. As Calvin swung his automatic toward me, I fired three shots as fast as I could—one for Ed, one for Charlie, and by God one for me.

I crawled to Nakayla. "Are you all right?"

She nodded, and tears of relief spilled over her cheeks. I took a corner of the duct tape and peeled it off her lips as gently as I could. She started to speak, but I silenced her with a kiss.

After a second, she yanked her head back. "You idiot. Check that they're dead."

"Okay, and then we've got to move fast." In the spill light from the van, I could see that half of Hernandez' head was blown away. Calvin's eyes stared at the roof of the van and blood seeped from underneath him. Gravity pulled it from his body as at least one of my shots had stopped his heart.

I returned to Nakayla. She was struggling to free her hands, but the duct tape had been wound many times around her wrist. I went through Calvin's pockets and found a buck knife. The keen blade quickly severed the tape.

"You know more about computers than I do," I said. "Look at that screen. It should be ready for a routing and account number to transfer the funds."

She bent over the keyboard. "Yes. There's a To and a From prompt."

"Good. Copy the To account information onto the From blank.

She stared at me in disbelief. "You're not serious?"

"Damn right I am. Whose money is it? A corrupt Iraqi government's? The FBI's? If we could return the stolen artifacts and gold that would be one thing, but we can't. So let's make sure something good comes of it."

I slid out the van door, balancing on one leg. The sheet of paper lay under Hernandez' arm. I hobbled like a three-legged dog to the dead man's side and grabbed it. Nakayla took it and then pulled me up next to her.

"Enter our account information and then if you don't see an exact amount in Calvin's, try for total balance. We don't have much time. Surely neighbors heard the shots and must have called the police. If you're successful, try to delete a record of the transaction."

She typed in the numbers as fast as she could. A pull-down menu gave a "Balance" option, and she clicked the "Transfer" prompt and reclicked the "Confirm Transaction" safety. A green line grew across the bottom of the screen as from some unknown location money flowed as electronic bytes of information. A chime sounded and a window popped up. "Transfer Complete. 2,345,750 USD."

Nakayla turned to me. "Holy shit."

Sirens sounded in the distance.

"I've got to call Efird. Otherwise we'll raise suspicions. Is this transfer program resident on the computer?"

Nakayla studied the screen. "No. I think it's linked to some server that they logged into."

"Then log out and clear the browser records."

For the next thirty seconds, Nakayla went through a series of keystrokes until the normal desktop screen appeared. "Done," she said.

I slid back from the computer and picked up my forty-five. "Get behind me."

When she was flat against my back, I aimed the Kimber at the center of the keyboard and fired.

Chapter Twenty-four

"For the record, let me get this straight." Detective Newland smiled amiably, but his eyes held an intense curiosity. "You really didn't suspect Calvin Stuart until Nakayla spoke to you on the phone?"

He sat across the table from me in interview room three. His nephew Al stood in uniform at the door. In another room, Detective Efird and Al's twin brother Ted held a similar conversation with Nakayla. I wasn't worried about our stories matching. Nakayla had been cool enough to warn me while Calvin pressed a gun to her temple. She could handle Efird.

I glanced at the wall clock. Nine-thirty. Newland had arrived about twenty minutes earlier. He'd looked tired but excited, eager to close two homicides in a day that started with a colonoscopy, a fair bargain for any cop.

"That's right," I said. "When Hernandez put her on, I thought Calvin had been taken with her. But she emphasized timing, that it didn't fit. They probably thought she was urging me to hurry. After Hernandez gave me his ultimatum and hung up, I realized what Nakayla meant by the emphasis on her words. 'They have the two of us'—there were two captors. 'He's in a bad way'—linking Calvin and bad. 'Timing is critical. Like Tuesday'—the phrase most likely to catch their attention but she pulled it off right under their noses. I understood the timing had fit for Agent Keith's Tuesday night alibi. He couldn't have been in Asheville. Yet Calvin was in Asheville when he shouldn't have been. He'd told me he'd flown in that night and come straight to my apartment, but no flights could land."

I took a second to rub my forehead and recreate my mental processes. "I started thinking about other timing, how Calvin was sick the day we were hit by what we thought was a random insurgency attack, and how he knew exactly what you'd take to purge your colon, the very symptoms that got him in the infirmary. Timing coincidences started to add up."

Newland nodded. "He was the third guy. You were right that they hadn't pulled someone off you when Hernandez killed Ethel Barkley. Calvin tailed you under the guise of protecting you."

"I'm convinced Calvin betrayed everyone." I paused, remembering Ethel Barkley's lament that there was no crime worse than betrayal because a betrayal has to involve trust, even love. I don't know how you define love among soldiers who wear the same uniform and risk their lives for the same flag, but I'd trusted Calvin. So had Ed and Charlie, and he'd sent them to their graves.

Newland jumped in. "He was in a position to play both sides against each other."

"More than that. He'd come from prison administration, the perfect place to work favors for Iraqis who could bribe their way out with offers of stolen valuables. I figure he hooked up with Hernandez and Lucas, who worked outside the military and answered to no one. But when Calvin betrayed them, he needed a fall guy. You're looking at him—only I'm not supposed to be alive."

Newland leaned forward. "Did he come to Asheville to kill you?"

That question had been gnawing at me. Calvin had tried to kill me in Iraq on the day Ed and Charlie died. And he wouldn't have wanted his partners to have the chance to interrogate me. Why hadn't he just shot me?

"Yes," I said. "But Calvin had to go through the motions of trying to get back what he'd told Lucas and Hernandez I'd stolen.

I think he placed that first call to me to rattle my cage and see what I'd do. He was probably already in Asheville. Unfortunately, I got Ethel Barkley's lockbox out of the bank and that set a chain of events in motion."

Newland seemed satisfied, but then he scowled. "How'd he get into your office?"

"Using a skeleton key or picking the door lock would have been no problem. He had the tools. You saw the sophisticated listening devices. When he bugged our office, he learned about Ethel Barkley's five million dollars, and he thought he held a lockbox that was a key to a treasure. Once a thief always a thief."

I shifted on the hard chair. My stumped throbbed where I'd bruised it on the Kimber wedged in the socket of my prosthesis. I couldn't tell Newland the real reason Calvin kept me alive. He'd learned about my offshore account and assumed it held the three million dollars from by parents' wrongful death suit. Once a thief always a thief.

"He and Hernandez staged that attack Tuesday night so Calvin could rescue me. He hoped to gain my confidence. It was a plan he could sell to Hernandez and Lucas, because they thought he'd learn where I'd stashed their money." Another thought occurred to me.

Newland looked up from the legal pad where he'd jotted a few notes. "What?"

"When we were chasing Lucas in the Grove Park Inn, Nakayla said he looked up and smiled at her."

"He saw Calvin."

"Coming down the stairs behind Nakayla. So Lucas went for me because he thought Calvin would take her out."

Newland sighed. "Talk about being in the catbird seat. If you killed Lucas, that was one less partner to deal with. If Lucas killed you, well, maybe Calvin lost the way to your money, but Hernandez and Lucas then had no way of knowing he ripped them off."

I yawned and stretched my legs under the table. A knock sounded at the door, and Efird entered.

"You two still jawing away?"

"About done," Newland said. "Just a couple things I don't understand."

I felt my stomach turn but kept my face frozen in what I hoped passed for idle curiosity. "What?"

"The computer we found. What were they going to do with it?"

I shrugged. "They didn't say. Probably wire money out of my Wachovia account. Hernandez demanded I bring the number and Calvin knew about the lawsuit settlement."

"And you shot it?"

"I guess so. Things happened fast. I knew I had to goad Hernandez into thinking Calvin would kill him too. When they went at each other, I grabbed my pistol and started firing. The first shot went wide because the gun got hung up on my prosthesis." I looked at Efird. "Nakayla probably has a better idea of what happened."

Efird and Newland exchanged glances and the younger detective sat on the edge of the table. "That's basically what she said. Too bad. There was a lot we could have learned from that computer."

I shook my head in sympathy. "Maybe Keith can get the FBI techs on it."

Again Efird and Newland looked at each other. Newland folded his arms across his chest. "We haven't called Keith in yet. I'll leave that overture to Chief Buchanan, and I wouldn't want to disturb the Chief till in the morning."

The detectives didn't want to lose control of their case. Given the international and military connections, Keith would swoop in like an avenging angel snatching up everything he could lay his hands on.

"I see. Well, I think Calvin's missing button ties him to Amanda Whitfield's murder. But we don't have to build a prosecutorial case, and I'm convinced the description of Ethel Barkley's attacker and the white van make Hernandez good for her death."

"Except for one thing." Newland uncrossed his arms and drummed the fingers of his right hand on the table for a few seconds. "Where's the lockbox? That would nail both murders to your Ali Baba conspirators."

"If you could keep it away from the FBI." I met Newland eye to eye. "Things have a way of turning up. Maybe they left it in a motel room. I assume you're searching for where they stayed. Or you'll find it in Calvin's rental car."

"Calvin said there was something that needed deciphering," Efird said.

"And Calvin said a lot of things to keep me hooked. I think he was baiting me to confide in him as to what else Ethel had of value. He'd heard about her five million dollars through the office bug and assumed the lockbox was a key to more."

Newland nodded slowly. I couldn't tell if he was buying my line or confirming to himself that I was holding back.

"Why Nakayla's car?" he asked.

I hadn't told Newland about Nathan and our ruse that went so wrong. A quick call from the van had alerted him to clear out and play dumb, because I didn't want Efird and Newland to know we'd gone around them. So, why Nakayla's car? It was a good question.

I gently massaged the flesh above my prosthesis. "Damn leg. Her car's easier to get in and out of. It's lower. Once I figured out a way to stash the Kimber in the socket I knew walking would be painful."

"Lucky she left it," Efird said. "You were sick, huh?"

"Yeah." I smiled at Newland. "Sympathy pains. I decided to stay in and rest in case something broke later in the day."

"And Nathan Armitage sent a driver since you and Nakayla wouldn't be riding together," Newland said.

"She objected, but I didn't want to take a chance. Guess I screwed up because when Calvin came to the office this afternoon and said I'd called him to bring her home, she went willingly."

Newland flipped his legal pad closed. "Okay. I guess that's almost everything for now." Another quick glance at Efird. "You know, Sam, how cops are always being second-guessed by their superiors?"

"Yeah."

"Since Nakayla's car is technically part of the shooting scene, we really should go over it. Do we need a search warrant?"

"It's not my car."

"But you were the last driver. I'm just asking."

I looked up at Efird. "If it's fine with Nakayla, it's fine with me." I turned back to Newland. "You're not hinting I should get a lawyer, are you?"

"Oh, God, no. I wouldn't wish a lawyer on my worst enemy. Especially a lawyer like Hewitt Donaldson. Imagine having a confidential relationship with that asshole."

I got the feeling I hadn't fooled the old fox for a second.

Chapter Twenty-five

Hewitt Donaldson came to his back door wearing a pair of cutoff jeans and a purple Hawaiian shirt. I was surprised not to hear Jimmy Buffett wailing "Cheeseburger in Paradise" in the background. For three o'clock in the morning, Donaldson's eyes shone bright with fire. He waved Nakayla and me into his kitchen, but I stopped at the threshold and held out a dollar.

"I want you to represent Blackman & Robertson as well as Nakayla and me individually. We may have broken the law and need to have the protection of the attorney-client privilege."

He snatched the bill from my hand. "Don't expect any change."

I went back to my CR-V parked in his driveway and unloaded the lockbox. In the spill-light from his house, I could see his expression transform from curiosity to amazement.

"But how?" he sputtered. "The news showed the shot-up van and Nakayla's car surrounded by police. I thought they would have confiscated everything."

I set the lockbox on his granite kitchen counter with a loud thud. "And I couldn't tell you any differently when I called. I don't trust cell phones. Sorry it was so late, but we couldn't retrieve it until the vehicles and bodies were removed."

"You had time to hide this?" He ran his hand over the chest's surface and picked at a severed piece of a swastika arm where the lid had been jimmied open.

232 Mark de Castrique

"I didn't." I nodded to Nakayla. "She ran down the path to a canoe I'd seen by an old picnic table and slid it underneath. She got back to the van just as the first patrol car pulled in."

"You were hiding evidence," he said.

"Of a burglary. And who's going to be charged for the crime? Nakayla and I'd been hired to deliver this to your Aunt Ethel, but I'm afraid we're a little late."

Donaldson wrapped an arm around my shoulder. "Well, let's see if we've got anything to be worried about." He reached forward to lift the lid.

"Wait. There are some things I need to tell you. First, Detective Newland suspects I have it."

"What?" Donaldson pivoted so fast his bare feet squeaked on the floor. "And he let you leave with it?"

"He didn't know where it was, but he figured out I'd taken it. He even hinted I should hire you."

"You're kidding."

"No, but for God's sake don't tell him I said so."

Donaldson shook his head in disbelief. "Maybe I've underestimated my old nemesis. Why would he do that?"

"I think because the eager beaver boyfriend of your paralegal would love to get his hands on it, and then none of us would see it again. Newland's betting I'll come clean if there really is evidence he should see."

Donaldson bit his lip as he thought the situation over. "And I have a feeling that's one of your conditions for this little present."

I didn't answer yes or no. "Have you talked to Agent Keith?"

"No. We were supposed to get together this week, but with my aunt's death, the funeral arrangements, and the shooting at the Grove Park, I've put him off."

"Detective Efird pulled him in for questioning because I thought he was following us. He was. To save himself the embarrassment of having his superiors learn he'd been busted by the local police, he told us he'd been doing you a favor."

Donaldson turned cagey. "Favor?"

The Fitzgerald Ruse 233

"Yes. When I used the phone in your office, I saw the file on the Selected Minutes from the House Committee on Un-American Activities."

The color rose in Donaldson's cheeks.

"You have my word I didn't look in it, but I may have led Keith to believe I knew more that I actually did."

"What did he tell you?"

"That you wanted information on the government's investigation of the Silver Shirts. More specifically, anything about your father."

Donaldson's blood pressure lowered. "So. Why are you telling me this before I open the box?"

"Context—because I haven't looked in it. What Keith wants to tell you is that he's found evidence that your father was working for the FBI. He'd been recruited as soon as Pelley hit Asheville."

Donaldson trembled so violently I thought he might be going into cardiac arrest. He tried to speak but the sound stuck in his throat. Nakayla took his arm and her touch calmed him.

After a few seconds, he said, "He wasn't a fascist?"

"No," I said.

"Why didn't we ever know?"

"I imagine Congress in the 1930s was the same leaky sieve it is today. They consider secrets as only currency to be spent. Keith said it took a lot of digging in the FBI files because any documents about the true identity of your father were kept away from Capitol Hill. That could be why he was never called to testify."

"And Aunt Ethel and my Uncle Terrence?"

"I don't know. I suspect they were believers in Pelley's movement." I looked at the chest on the counter. "You said your aunt adored your father. She went to great lengths to protect something she mistakenly thought he valued. I just wanted you to know that however unflattering or even vile those contents might be, your father was one of the good guys."

Donaldson's eyes glistened. "A good guy who put his wife and son through hell."

"Who knows what might have been," I said. "By the end of 1944 the tide of the war had turned. Had your father lived he surely would have emerged from his double life. I think the son became the lawyer the father would have been."

Donaldson swallowed hard and patted the back of Nakayla's hand. "Then let's examine the evidence."

He stood between us. Dry hinges squealed as he lifted the lid. We saw my folded sheet of legal paper lying on top of a pile of items. Donaldson picked it up. "This looks new."

"I worked out a possible code based on what your aunt told me. Nakayla hid it in case the police searched me."

"Code to what?"

"I don't know, but Calvin suggested this box might contain something that needed deciphering. We now know he wasn't speculating."

He handed the sheet to me and then removed a roughly eighteen by nine inch rectangle half covered in ripped, yellow-tinged wrapping paper that was once white. He pulled free a picture frame whose back had been pried loose. A dust jacket for *The Great Gatsby* stuck out from the top as if someone had partially removed it. A woman's disembodied eyes and lips floated in a night sky over a brightly lit amusement park. The image was strangely haunting. Strangely modern.

"The gift," Nakayla said. "The one the summer lover gave Fitzgerald and he gave to Ethel."

In the lower right corner of the front flap were written the words: "To my darling Scott. No novel can capture my love for you. Beatrice."

Donaldson laughed. "If I remember your deal correctly, then here's your payment."

I took the framed book cover and set it aside.

A manila envelope with "Fitzgerald" penciled across the front was the next item. Donaldson pulled out a sheaf of papers covered in handwriting. There was no title or numbering to the pages. He flipped through them quickly and we saw blocks of words crossed out.

"Hmmm," Donaldson muttered. "I don't think this is a story. More like notes." He passed a few pages around.

I didn't know Fitzgerald's work enough to understand what I was reading.

"This section is like a true confession," Nakayla said. "He's going on about the sense of futility and the inevitability of failure."

"'The Crack-Up,'" Donaldson said. "That was the name of an essay he wrote for *Esquire* that came out in the spring of 1936. A mea culpa of his despair. The irony was that by lamenting his mental collapse, he proved he could still write."

"This is what your aunt felt guilty about taking?" Nakayla asked. "Some notes for an essay?"

"Ethel saw things differently," Donaldson said. "These rambling reflections must have destroyed Pelley's hope that Fitzgerald could be enlisted as a voice for his cause. Not exactly the fervent rallying cry equal to 'The Silver Shirts Are Marching.' But Ethel read the pain and anguish underneath. She would have thought it a betrayal to make this public. Even seventy years later. Yet I'm sure she couldn't bring herself to destroy a raw view into Fitzgerald's soul." Donaldson collected the pages, slid them in the envelope, and dropped it behind the chest.

Next he pulled out a thin file folder closed with a rusty paper clip. The tab read "Pelley vs. the State of North Carolina."

"That's the case where your father was one of the defense attorneys," I said.

"Yes. But this should be much thicker." Donaldson extracted only two sheets of paper. The first was an invoice from his father's law office for $10,500 of itemized charges and expenses for the case. The second was a receipt from The Pollosco Life Assurance Society for a single premium of $10,500 paid on a permanent life insurance policy with a term rider.

"There's the money trail," Donaldson exclaimed. "His legal fees. The rider probably bought term insurance with dividends to increase the face amount over time."

"So Ethel's money is clean," Nakayla said.

"No. It might not be a Nazi payoff, but it's dirty."

"Why?" Nakayla asked.

"Because my father was Pelley's attorney, and he was spying on him for the FBI. How could he take money from a man he was supposed to be representing while betraying him?"

"Does that mean your father didn't do the best job he could?" Nakayla asked. "The court records showed Pelley was charged with sixteen counts of stock fraud and related offenses. His defense team got thirteen dismissed, and of the three remaining that went to the jury, he was convicted of only two and received a suspended sentence. I'd say your father did his job well."

"The law is based on principle, not the circumstance of success."

"So he distanced himself from his earnings," I said. "And in uncertain economic times, he kept them as a last resource for his family. Would you rather he be a fascist?"

Donaldson studied the documents in the file. "No. But my share of the money will be a resource that I can feel good about. Amanda Whitfield's quadriplegic husband needs a lifetime of medical care. I'll guarantee he has at least two and a half million dollars worth."

I looked across Donaldson and saw Nakayla smile. We'd made nearly two and a half million dollars in our first week as a detective agency. With Donaldson's gift to Amanda's husband, we'd be splitting our take two ways instead of three, giving an equal share to the families of Ed Cuomo and Charlie Grigg, the men who'd come home in body bags because of Calvin's betrayal.

Donaldson set the file aside and pulled a ledger book from the bottom of the chest. On the cover, a scarlet capital L had been painted in the center of a silver oval.

"The insignia of the Silver Legion of America," Donaldson said. "And there's a matching book underneath this one." He set the first volume on the counter and opened it.

The pale green lined pages were filled with letters and numbers. None of the words made any sense. Donaldson flipped from page to page. Occasionally a heading would be sandwiched between two blank lines, but that too was unintelligible.

"This would have driven them nuts," Donaldson said. "I can see why they came after my aunt."

I unfolded the matrix of letters I'd created from the underlined sentence in Ethel Barkley's copy of *The Great Gatsby*. "Turn to the first page." Across the top line appeared LONNOX JD—EIPOR. "Have you got something to write with?"

Donaldson fished through a kitchen drawer for a pen. I ran down my columns, converting each letter to its equivalent.

PELLEY WD—CHIEF

Donaldson clapped his hands. "By God, you figured it out. Chief. That was the title Pelley's followers used for him."

"Sounds a lot like Führer," Nakayla said.

Chief. The nickname Calvin had chosen for me.

Donaldson looked at me with undisguised amazement. "How the hell could you do that without knowing what you were decoding?"

"The clues were in your aunt's book, her copy of *The Great Gatsby* that the police have."

"You mean your copy. I'll work it out with my cousin to make sure you get it." He pointed to a header in the middle of the next page. "See what this is."

TNTHTVT transcoded into ALABAMA. Under it, TSOYW YHM became AKERS RBT.

"I'll bet it's the name Robert Akers," Donaldson said. "The next lines are probably his address." He placed his index finger under the number 150000 written to the right of the name. "And this must be his contribution. I'd say it's $1,500.00 without any decimal point."

"Pelley's whole organization," Nakayla said. "Laid out state by state."

"Ethel kept it ready for him," I said. "And she thought the money was part of the deal. But Pelley's condition for a pardon was no political activity, and he never came back to Asheville."

"Are you going to give this to Agent Keith?" Nakayla asked.

Donaldson shut the ledger and dropped it back in the lockbox. "Hell no. What would the FBI do with it except create pain for families whose loved ones are either ancient or dead and buried. The past is hard enough to escape without the government throwing it in your face."

Can you ever escape your past? I thought. Mine had come back with a vengeance and left a string of bodies in its wake.

Donaldson turned to a cabinet behind us and pulled down a bottle of Glenfiddich single malt scotch. "I don't know about you, but I could use a shot."

"It's late," I said, and looked to Nakayla. She'd had the worst of the ordeal—kidnapped, bound, and gagged.

"Maybe a short one," she said. "I read somewhere a good detective never turns down a drink."

Chapter Twenty-six

Todd Creek Baptist Church had been erected on a hill a few miles west of Asheville. The brick building consisted of a sanctuary and an el-wing for offices and Sunday School classes. After getting only three hours of sleep, Nakayla and I arrived twenty minutes before the eleven o'clock service. The gravel parking lot was filling quickly as a community came together on a Saturday morning to remember someone they loved. Amanda Whitfield had obviously touched many during her brief life.

We found seats in a pew near the rear. Across the aisle I saw Detective Newland flanked by his twin nephews in their uniforms. He nodded a greeting and then cocked his head with a question in his eyes. I shook mine to tell him there would be no new revelations for his case file. His lips tightened and I knew he was disappointed. I could only hope he trusted my judgment.

I looked down at my bulletin. A single cross projecting rays of ascending light graced the cover. Beneath it were the words "Celebrating the Life of Amanda Whitfield—September 15, 2007."

The service was short and sad, although the minister and music focused on joy in the hereafter. I heard Nakayla sniffle a few times, and I took her hand. In some ways, the heritage of her African-American homegoing funerals like the one I'd attended for her sister let emotions break out with greater freedom and cathartic release.

At the end of the service, we were told that the family would greet people in the Fellowship Hall in the basement, and that the women of the church had prepared light food. Nakayla and I had expected a small country congregation would have a covered-dish reception, and we stopped by my car before joining the throng. Downstairs, I approached one of the ladies behind a long table and handed her the box of fresh-baked blueberry muffins we'd picked up from City Bakery Café.

At the head of the receiving line sat a good-looking young man in a wheelchair, his arms and legs useless appendages and his head cushioned into a fixed position on the backrest. The soreness in my stump seemed but a faint echo of the physical and mental pain that young widower endured. For all the courage required of me the previous night, I couldn't muster enough to speak to him.

"When can we catch up?"

I turned to find Nathan Armitage behind us. He shook my hand and hugged Nakayla.

"God, that was close," he said, and his voice choked.

"We're okay," I said. "Sorry to abandon you, but I had no choice."

He shrugged. "You two are a helluva team. My friends were very impressed."

"I assume the black water flowed back to its source. Let me know what I owe you."

"Nothing. They were glad to assist. No one likes to think they've trained criminals."

"Seems to be our national pastime," I said, and then regretted voicing something so petty as politics at Amanda Whitfield's funeral.

Nathan had more class and let my comment slide. "Maybe tomorrow afternoon you'd drop by the house. The Panthers are playing and we could sort through things."

"Sure," Nakayla said. "We'd like that."

◇◇◇

The residents of Golden Oaks entered the assembly hall in a parade interspersed with walkers and wheelchairs. Nakayla and I made sure all the seniors had seats before finding our own. The afternoon service came right after the dining hall closed and we'd had to hurry from Amanda's to be on time for Ethel's.

Here were the professional funeral attendees who'd lost so many friends and family that mixing solemnity with gregariousness had been perfected into a fine art. The chaplain of the retirement center led an informal ceremony. Hewitt Donaldson spoke on behalf of the family, thanking Ethel's friends and the Golden Oaks' staff for their kindness toward his aunt.

A number of the old timers stood at their seats as the chaplain brought a wireless mike for them to use for sharing memories. The P.A. system blared so that even the deaf could hear.

Harry Young got a round of applause for his story about Ethel reading his palm. That triggered a number of Ethel's palm reading stories, and I noticed how many of the fading generation looked down at their hands, seeming to marvel that such lined and wrinkled things were attached to their bodies.

Afterwards, I greeted Hewitt Donaldson and his cousin Terry Barkley. We said nothing of our early morning search through the lockbox, but Barkley shook my hand vigorously and thanked us for our help. I doubted Donaldson had told him much other than we'd safeguarded his inheritance. He didn't need or want to hear any more.

I left Nakayla with them and went to find Captain. He was speaking to the chaplain and when he saw me, he came as fast as he could push his walker. He stopped about a yard away.

"You got them, boy. You told me you would, and you got them."

I gave him our customary salute, but instead of returning it, he slung his walker aside and closed the distance between us on his frail legs, not stopping till he'd embraced me. I felt his tears on my cheek.

Old soldiers never die, but the good ones are man enough to cry.

◇◇◇

"There's plenty of beer and guacamole." Nathan Armitage handed each of us a bottle of Heineken and then set a plate of corn chips and dip on the coffee table. A widescreen TV on the wall tuned in the game between the Carolina Panthers and Houston Texans. "Now eat up, or Helen will think I was a bad host."

"She's not a football fan?" Nakayla asked.

Nathan popped the cap from his beer and sat in a leather lounge chair. "She gets into it when the Panthers make the play-offs. She's at some church committee meeting this afternoon. If I heard her correctly, it's a committee studying committees. I increase my pledge just to stay off the damn things."

"You want a rundown before she comes home?" I asked.

"If you're up to telling the story."

Nathan was well aware of our financial picture so Nakayla and I told him everything including our raid on Calvin's secret account.

When we'd finished, he sat quietly for a few minutes, twirling his empty bottle between his palms. He looked worried. "You sure there's no way anyone left in Ali Baba will discover what happened?"

"I can't be completely sure, but I think anyone else would be local Iraqis who wouldn't have been privy to anything other than their immediate tasks. And even Hernandez and Lucas didn't know Calvin had siphoned off their funds, so the account's untraceable."

"You got a way to get that money to the families of your buddies?"

"That might be trickier than I thought. It's one thing for Nakayla and me to keep money offshore and bring it in through the detective agency and another thing to get money into someone's personal U.S. bank account with a plausible explanation."

Nathan stood and held the empty bottle by his side. "I'd say you ought to learn more about the families and what they need. That could lead you to the best way to help them." He thought a second. "And you might feed Hewitt Donaldson enough information to get his take. He's a crafty bastard and he owes you more than a book."

Nakayla and I laughed.

"What?" he asked.

"The book's a first edition," I said.

"So, what's it worth? A couple grand?"

"Pretty close," I said. "Maybe even four."

"Not too shabby," he conceded.

"But the cover. Tell him, Nakayla."

Her face lit up. "I did a little Internet search this morning. Seems there are only about twenty known dust jackets for that first edition still in existence and most of them are in poor shape. At a recent auction, a copy of *The Great Gatsby* with its dust jacket went for near $50,000."

"And ours is signed to Fitzgerald by his lover," I added.

"What are you going to do?" Nathan asked me.

"I thought maybe I'd read it."

Acknowledgments

Although this book is a work of fiction, certain real events and locations provided inspiration for the story.

F. Scott Fitzgerald stayed in Asheville, North Carolina, during the summers of 1935 and 1936. His favorite room in The Grove Park Inn was 441, and I'm indebted to Derrick Swing, Bill Kelley, and the staff and management of The Grove Park Inn and Spa for their assistance and cooperation. Special thanks to Derrick for making an appearance in the novel.

Laura Guthrie Hearne was a palm reader and the part-time secretary of F. Scott Fitzgerald. Her account of that relationship appeared in the December 1964 issue of *Esquire* as an article entitled "A Summer with F. Scott Fitzgerald." Tony Buttitta's book, *The Lost Summer: A Personal Memoir of F. Scott Fitzgerald*, is a fascinating look at Fitzgerald in 1935. Fitzgerald introduced Buttitta to his "dollar woman," Laura Guthrie Hearne, and had her read his palm.

In 1933, William Dudley Pelley founded the Silver Legion of America, headquartered in Asheville, and at one point the fascist organization had more than fifteen thousand Silver Shirt members in chapters across twenty-two states. Pelley was indicted and convicted on two stock fraud charges in 1934 and on sedition charges in 1942. Fitzgerald and Pelley never met, although Buttitta describes Fitzgerald as being scornfully curious about the man.

The poem "The Silver Shirts Are Marching!" is from a 1936 bound and hand-typed manuscript, *The Door to Revelation: An Intimate Biography by William Dudley Pelley*. I'm grateful to the Pack Library of Asheville for research assistance with Pelley materials. The character of Hugh Donaldson was not Pelley's attorney and is my creation.

The Kenilworth Inn opened in 1891 as a grand hotel and for many years was a military hospital and mental health facility. Developer Frank Howington rescued the Kenilworth from demolition, and the renovated and restored building is now listed on the National Register of Historic Places. Thanks to Frank and Mikell Howington, Pete Parham, and Allie Broman-Fulks for making Sam Blackman and me feel at home.

Blackwater Worldwide is a security services corporation headquartered in Moyock, North Carolina. Its relationship with the U.S. government has generated controversy that led to an examination of contracts involving the outsourcing of paramilitary and security operations, particularly in Iraq. No Blackwater employees or former employees have any connection to the fictional events of this story. However, on September 16, 2007, seventeen Iraqi civilians died during an altercation in Nisour Square, Baghdad, involving Blackwater guards escorting a convoy of U.S. State Department vehicles. As of February 2009, five guards have been indicted on federal manslaughter and weapon charges and a sixth entered into a plea-bargain agreement. Defense attorneys say newly released Blackwater radio logs lend credence to claims that the convoy was under fire. One can only hope that justice will prevail for all involved, Iraqis and Americans.

Getting this novel to readers has been a collaborative effort. Keys to that process are my editor Barbara Peters who keeps the story focused; my wife Linda, daughters Lindsay and Melissa, and son-in-law Pete who review the manuscript and offer ample criticism; my brother Archie for his life insurance expertise; my agent Linda Allen; publisher Robert Rosenwald and his staff;

and the many librarians, booksellers, and mystery lovers whose kind response encourages me to continue thinking "what if?"

Mark de Castrique
The Kenilworth Inn
Asheville, North Carolina
February 7, 2009

To receive a free catalog of Poisoned Pen Press titles, please contact us in one of the following ways:

Phone: 1-800-421-3976
Facsimile: 1-480-949-1707
Email: info@poisonedpenpress.com
Website: www.poisonedpenpress.com

Poisoned Pen Press
6962 E. First Ave. Ste. 103
Scottsdale, AZ 85251